# Dangerous Season

*a novel*

I0538293

by

Jack Voller

{ Graveyard Revels  Press }

*for*

*those who have gone before*

*yet*

*linger in memory still*

Summer's indeed a very dangerous season.

- Byron, *Don Juan*

*Los Angeles, May, 1993*

## prologue

I guess I never really understood foreboding.

Perhaps that's because for me it was always linked to prophecy, to a clear vision of the yet-to-be, which in turn was never really more to me than some ancient superstition I turned into a personal game when I first read, in early adolescence, of the seers of ancient Rome finding auguries in the flights of birds and in the entrails of animals. I became fascinated by the possibility of such prognostication, tried it myself, tried to see if that flock of crows on my right as I rode to the nearby market for ice cream meant the store would be out of my favorite flavor. They weren't. OK, perhaps the right side is the auspicious side. A huge flock of starlings, an endless ribbon of birds flowing left to right across the cloudless pale blue of a spring Saturday, surely meant we were destined to win that regional playoff. We lost 8-2. Wrong species maybe. Try another: but that hawk on the roadside fencepost to my right as I drove to ask the girl of my crush to the prom did not ensure the "yes" I'd been aching to hear for weeks. Maybe that was supposed to be the left side, I thought driving home, or maybe I'm supposed to slit him open and read the coils of his intestines to see the future but I'm vegetarian by this time so that's not going to happen. Perhaps I just wasn't a seer, just didn't have the touch. No matter, it was just a game. But still: to catch glimpses of what's to come – what a gift that would be, I often thought. What a gift.

Somehow I simply never thought about the grim implications inherent in prophecy: to see something monstrous coming, some dark horror you can find no way to evade, no hope of action but only the unnerved awaiting of an inevitability, living in growing dread and crushing doubt and naked paralysis. That, yes, would be foreboding.

Foreboding. The concept is grim to the core but I have to confess I loved the very word, the heavy rounded vowels, the massy rolling syllables that spoken aloud were like a blow to the chest that could stop your heart. It was a word that came draped in black and announced itself like a death knell.

But it was just a word. We bandied it about in mythology class when we read of Oedipus. Seek to escape the prophecy and the black sense of foreboding it conjures by taking a hero's course of action: tear yourself from those you love so you can save them and yourself from the horror you see coming only to run straight to that horror and, failing to recognize it, embrace it.

And we read of Cassandra and how she'd been cursed by Apollo's dual gift: to see what was to come yet when she spoke that truth to be met only with disbelief. That, I understand now, was someone who would have known the darkest foreboding, known it with a terrifying and all-encompassing intimacy, in all its suffocating certainty and juggernaut implacability. Who, I wondered, could survive such knowing?

But now I wish I'd had some small share of her gift, of any such gift, something that would have allowed me to see that what I took to be a trivial omen, that day I arrived in LA, was the dark subtle harbinger of all the catastrophe that followed.


It seemed so inconsequential at the time, nothing more than the projection of my annoyance with traffic and the LA smog that had been dominating the horizon for miles. It was just a sign. No omen, this: an actual sign atop a towering metal pole. Surely I'd passed it before even though most of my visits to LA had been family trips taken by plane. Yet somehow I'd never remarked it. But on that day there it was, inescapable in its garish plastic simplicity, a looming intrusion that demanded recognition for a moment before it disappeared into the landscape that had been rolling interminably away behind me since I left San Francisco that morning. An amusement park sign that read, in part, "Magic Mountain."

At that instant it put me in mind of Thomas Mann's novel, which I'd read a few years ago, slogging my way through it despite its grim tediousness. It was the tuberculosis I remembered right then, breathing as I was the palpable contagion of LA that already enveloped me, an inversion layer of atmospheric corruption that draped the horizon in a pall of hazy glare. It was no great leap to the novel's mountaintop sanatorium, to its clustered invocations of lung disease, lingering illness, slow decay, a nineteenth-century death of rotting from the inside as dark stormclouds gather ominously in the world. Grim mortality's creeping shadow. And seeing that sign I told myself I had just become a self-admit for the summer.

      The word that came to mind, though, was not "foreboding" but merely "vexing," a word for small annoyances and minor inconveniences, at its greatest stretch applicable to readily surmountable challenges. I knew that after just a few months in LA's mountain-ringed basin of toxicity I'd be gone, not a lifetime's change so that sign's augury was merely "a vexing prognostication," as I muttered to myself – and I do confess to thinking in such terms, six years of higher education in English and creative writing having done their full meed of damage. But nothing more serious than that occurred to me.

      Certainly not the sense of black foreboding that would have been appropriate, that would if recognized have sent me to the nearest emergency turn-around and back north on I-5 with every bit of alacrity I could summon. Cassandra would have seen it coming: my cousin dying a death intended for me, before that my horrific and destabilizing discovery of dark places, utterly unsuspected and utterly foreign, within myself that no trick of grace or forgetting has yet allowed me to address or cover over – all of that Cassandra would have foreseen. I wish I too could have foreseen it, felt the companion foreboding it would have brought, for I would have fled in stupefied terror and prevented it all if I could, at whatever cost if I could.

      But there was no foreboding, there is no gift, so this story only makes sense as it unfolded, a gradual and at first imperceptible slide into a gathering darkness shaped by my uncertainty and confusion.

**story**

A phone call from my cousin Hayden began it all.

Hayden: at thirty-two he's five years older than I am and the most crooked branch in the extended family tree. He's worlds smarter than any of us, one of those odd-but-brilliant people you usually only read about — sometimes in clinical case studies, more often in *Forbes*. He has an over-130 IQ and a fistful of degrees, most of them in computer something or other. He's worked for aerospace and computer firms since high school, and had just moved back to LA from a stint in D. C. that apparently had something to do with the Pentagon or the CIA or both, though he was thoroughly evasive on the matter. He's not quite a run-of-the-mill computer geek, though he's a closely related species. He dresses expensively in an avant-garde, boutique-pretending-to-be-street kind of way, an elite cyberpunk hacker with money and taste if that's not an oxymoron. His pallor and lank slenderness are unmistakable evidence of an exclusively indoor existence: I suspect he'd blend in nowhere, but in Southern California he looks almost terminal, like an inmate of that other Magic Mountain. His hair is a mop of fine pale blond that reminds me of angel's hair or Andy Warhol, depending on my mood, or his; it gives him a vaguely Einsteinian halo at certain times. A hiply dressed young Einstein in need of a few good meals and a life. And then there's his memory, capacious and near-photographic: he astonished the hell out of me one night by quoting all of Eliot's "Prufrock" from memory. Accurately, too, as far as I could tell when I reread the poem the next day.

We'd never been all that close growing up, seeing each other every few years at some family event but for six or eight years now I hadn't seen him at all though we'd exchanged a few perfunctory emails. So I was surprised when he called one April evening, then astonished by his offer. He'd been back in LA for a new job only a few weeks, he explained, staying with his parents until he found a place of his own, and then came the "how can you possibly refuse this?" deal of a short lifetime.

"Nearly a mansion," he said with mock understatement. "Spanish style, back in the hills, five or six bedrooms – can't keep track – solarium, window walls everywhere, chalet fireplace, huge master suite, hot tub, pool, the whole list and then some. I told Mrs. Parkinson, bless her store-bought tan, that house-sitting a six-thousand square foot house would be a lonely ordeal and I'm at work on a major project that will have me out of town a lot, which is almost the truth. But the poor old dear, who's loved me ever since my mother had me help her dear departed husband figure out his computer, trusts me profoundly and wouldn't hear of my refusing her offer, so I took the opportunity to describe you in the most glowing terms — all of it lies, of course —"

"Thanks." I couldn't help but grin.

"— extolling your maturity beyond your years and your literary achievements —"

"Spare me," I said, chuckling but impatient to hear the outcome now that I guessed what he was going to ask.

And I was right: he wanted me to join him for the summer, till I headed off to grad school in September or till the house sold or till whenever; he was clearly in no hurry to find a place of his own. I really had nothing to keep me in northern California, just some planned hikes to say farewell to my favorite mountains, some writing I needed to do but that I could do anywhere. Sandy and I had already talked about our relationship, realized it may not survive my relocation but we'd just take it as it came. So I told Hayden I'd think about it. He'd made a remark about "a summer's worth of life lessons to turn into literary capital once you get to the uninterrupted dullness of the soybean fields" and I admit that resonated, struck some honest inner chord. Iowa's creative writing doctoral program is renowned, I was honored to be accepted, but hell, it was still Iowa.


And I did think about it, vacillating but unable finally to dismiss his remark about "literary capital." I've never lived anywhere but the Humboldt area in far northern California, and while I've traveled the West a bit I'd long harbored a nagging suspicion I needed to do more with and in my life if I were going to write the sort of stories I felt I could write.

It was a conversation with my thesis director that pushed me to accept Hayden's offer. A week or so before my Master's oral exam my director asked me about my summer plans. Almost disdainfully I mentioned Hayden's offer, at which point my director laughed his short bark of a laugh, rubbed his salt-and-pepper beard and explained that an old and still-close grad-school friend, a full professor at Cal State Covina, had lamented to him just last week that her graduate assistant had suddenly left for a Peace Corp opportunity, and now, at the end of the semester, she was in urgent need of help until the fall crop of grad students appeared on her commuter campus. My director offered to contact her, see if the job was still open; neither of us had much hope that, academic bureaucracies being what they are, I could be hired anyway, but thinking myself both safe and reckless, I gave him my permission to ask. Four days later he called me: the position was open and due to some arcane confluence of grant money and lucky timing and the sort of professorial clout that occasionally overcomes bureaucratic rigidity, I could be hired for the summer provided I applied and enrolled, as a visiting student, for an independent study course which would be tied to the job.

I'm not by nature anything close to being impulsive, so it was with a sense of strangeness — a strangeness that yet felt appropriate, maybe even comfortable —that I immediately agreed to take the job. I didn't care that the money was bad — this was the humanities, after all, the ghetto of American education — because I'd have no rent payment, nor did I even ask at the time what the job involved, finding out soon enough that it was glorified data entry for a research project on some obscure South Pacific language I'd never heard of and of which I came to understand not a single word. Not that it mattered, then or now, for from the moment I got that call I felt myself committed to the "adventure," as Hayden had called it, that was the real point of all this. And I was ready. The feeling was akin to that you have when you're just about to begin a *glissade*, that instant when you've seated yourself at the top of an icy slope, poised your ice axe for the control you hope to maintain and just eased your body loose, freeing yourself from that almost magically maintained friction that's kept you perched above hundreds of yards of ice. And suddenly you're off, liberated into gravity, sliding at what feels like eighty miles an hour to certain death below until the initial adrenaline rush of anarchic panic subsides and you suddenly find the tip of your axe in the snow to be a crude but effective brake. Time resumes its normal dimensions and the certain death below is forgotten as the slope's pitch decreases and you roll to your side, digging the point of your axe deeper into the snow, bringing yourself to a calm and graceful halt under the jubilant white sun of high altitudes. And you exult in your mastery of gravity, ice, danger.

Right.

The *glissade* metaphor occurred to me at the time, but so did the recognition (a thin mask over my uncertainties, I suppose) that a High Sierra ice slope is a long way from the Byzantine concrete-and-drywall maze/madness of LA — a distance measured in more than miles.

Very much more.

But I did it. Despite my fear, or maybe because of it — and I suppose I'll have to look into that some day — I did it. I wrote the letters and filled out the forms and made the arrangements and on a beautiful Friday morning in mid-May loaded the last few boxes into my Toyota pickup, bid farewell to my parents and the cat, and set out for LA. The old Taoist aphorism had been running through my mind for days: "A thousand-mile journey begins with a single step." Indeed it does. But what about those journeys we measure in something other than miles? How do we know when they end? Or even if?


What was I doing here?

*Where* is here? was perhaps the more urgent question. I confess my metro-incompetence: I got lost twice between that decidedly un-magic mountain and the Glendora Hills house that was my destined abode for the months ahead. So lost that to this day I have no clue as to where I went astray: countless automobiles, a numbing blur of freeway lanes and numbers, a vast sea of Hispanic and black and white and Asian faces, the sunbleached and oppressive clutter of buildings too new to be as worn and time-ravaged as they appear. I've pored over maps, to no avail, and find my confusion strangely appropriate, even satisfying.

Not that it matters: being lost in LA is a relative piece of business, like being unable to find your way around a ship that's been adrift for the better part of a century. But this isn't an LA story – I leave that to those who can know this place, unknowable for me.

And that it forever will be, for it's a place, now, to which I can never return. In the aftermath of this summer's events I've thought about LA and what happened to me almost obsessively, but prior this summer, despite multiple visits, I'd never really given it a lot of thought. I had always seemed to me, perhaps unfairly, of a complexity than no cartographic or demographic  principles could ever truly map, that no anthropological investigations could ever meaningfully illuminate.  It's the monster in the room, certainly, a chicken-wire-and-plaster Mont Blanc looming over the cultural horizon of our time like the Disneyland Matterhorn over Anaheim, but it never felt graspable to me even before that day I drove down to find myself, finally, standing on the porch of a mansion looking for the doorbell button.

Maybe not "mansion," but close enough: a sprawling pseudo-Spanish-style construction that seemed to promise exactly the sort of excess Hayden had described.  My first thought, though, as I hesitated for a moment on that front porch, was the hope my genius-but-sometimes-distracted cousin hadn't inadvertently misdirected me to the house of some old rich crone who will take alarm at my stammered explanations and bloodshot eyes and have me arrested.  But I push the button because I'm six hundred miles from home with the better part of my possessions in the back of my truck and there's nothing much else to do.  After the solemn tones of the doorbell fade I hear footsteps, the faint beeping of five rather postmodern tones, a deadbolt being thrown and sure enough just as I suspected —

— there stands Hayden, all six-feet-two scrawny inches of him, his trademark lopsided grin that I've hated for years and his hair wildly out of control.  I haven't seen him in the flesh for years but he looks more or less just as I remember him.

"Son of an undeleted bitch you finally found me," he said, his voice ringing with mock surprise.  Before I could respond in kind he handed me a bottle of very cold St. Pauli Girl and added, with mock formality and a sweeping gesture, "Welcome to L.A., cousin.  What was it the old *boyar* said?  'Welcome, and enter of your own will'?"  He grinned at his allusion to *Dracula*, which I  didn't get until an hour or so later because of my exhaustion. "Come in, come in."  He shook my free hand as I stepped through the doorway.

"Good to see you again, Hayden. And thanks."  I saluted him with the beer and took a long pull that drained nearly half the bottle.  Like I said, a tough drive.

"And you, little cuz," he replied, his grin growing as I mock-scowled at the epithet.  "Just don't spill on the carpet, make sure the house always looks unoccupied, and be prepared to evacuate at a moment's notice."

"Nice welcome for someone who's just spent the last ten hours on your damn freeways, which I've already discovered are nothing more than a trick to keep the criminally insane out of your overcrowded jails."

Hayden put one arm akimbo and snorted. "Just the house rules — and I'm glad to see you've figured everything out in your first few minutes on the planet. But it's good to see you, even if you are three hours late. Didn't get too terribly lost, I hope?"

"Not too. Just a quick detour to Tijuana by way of Vietnam."

"Now, now," he said, wagging a finger at me in mock gravity as I stepped past him into the foyer. "As a white man you are a latecomer in these here parts, so show due respect for diversity. Especially now that you are a man of letters, *magister artium*, courtesy of a modern Left Coast university."

"Hey, I just meant the extra distance," I explained lamely, perhaps honestly but primarily trying to avoid a political discussion. For reasons I couldn't fully explain I'd long been convinced Hayden and I were from opposite sides of the aisle.

He snorted again, looking like he wanted to say something but thought better of it. "Whatever," he said, "as they say in these dark days. But let me welcome you to this aggressively unhumble abode." He gestured expansively and I followed the sweep of his arm, taking in two vast rooms, empty of furniture but impressive in their size. He held the gesture a moment then intoned slowly in a voice that suggest mockery of something, "From the deserts to the mountains to the sea to all of Southern California, we are living on plundered land, stolen from a peaceful people so we can erect these monuments to our egos and our acquisitiveness." He paused, laughed softly. "And are we damn glad of it or what?"

"You always were the cynic, Hayden." I said it jokingly, half-raising the beer as though to pledge him but there was something about his declaration that troubled me in some vague way. This *was* plundered land, come to think of it, this house *was* a monument to conspicuous consumption, and he should at least have had the decency to be mildly embarrassed by those combined facts. I was.

He took me on a tour of the house, beginning with the "gallery" in which we stood. At least, I suppose that's a better term than "hallway," given that it was ten feet wide, went on forever, and was indeed lined with pictures (an eclectic mix of Southwestern, postmodern, and who knows what all, all of it second-rate). The entire place, even half-empty of furniture, was an aggressive exercise in pretension on the part of people whose budget far surpassed any sense of taste. Hell, the whole neighborhood was a monument to it: only five houses, each the size of a small castle and virtually on top of each other, on a carved-out ridge-top cul-de-sac that was set a good half-mile up a tiny, otherwise-undeveloped canyon, most of which I later found out was owned by a local college and kept as some sort of field laboratory. Maybe to study the natural behavior of *Homo millionairus*. This house, not even the largest on the block, was overdone in every way. Six huge bedrooms with private baths; a master suite about the size of my parents' entire house and featuring its own private sitting room, two walk-in closets each twice the size of my bedroom back home, a garden-view bathroom with whirlpool tub; vast kitchen with a six-burner Wolf stove and SubZero refrigerator; cavernous family room with a circular fireplace that looked like it belonged in a Swiss ski lodge; huge this and that — it was a monument to Hugeness, a reified paean to Boomer Consumer — gold-plated fixtures in the master bath, for god's sake, like the fucking emir of Kuwait — and I didn't know what to make of any of it. Except that it made me uncomfortable.

Not that I left, of course.

We had a quick dinner in the nearby town and upon our return Hayden led me to the small poolhouse and its refrigerator, generously stocked with various beers. "Knew you were coming," he said with a grin. I gave him a sour look but was in fact genuinely touched. And, by the time I went to bed, fairly drunk.

I awoke the next morning with a slight headache and a serious, if ephemeral, sense of confusion. Not to mention a mild case of seasickness: the bedroom to which I'd been assigned, which that of the youngest son, still kept its waterbed. Apparently Mrs. Parkinson, her youngest now safely incarcerated at Tufts Law, had no need for it. Never having slept on one before I spent a fairly restless night, waking frequently and hoping to hell that Hayden was right when he said I'd get used to it in a few days.

I needed a few extra minutes to get my bearings thanks also to the room's decor: the wall across from the bed was covered, floor-to-ceiling and wall-to-wall, with a larger-than-life-sized photomural of a tropical seashore, the presence of which to this day puzzles me. Why put a mural of palm trees on your wall when you have them in your backyard? I could only shake my head.

Slipping into jeans and T-shirt I wandered out into the house in search of Hayden. It took me a few minutes to orient myself — at one point I ended up just outside the master bedroom before I even realized I was lost —but eventually I saw Hayden outside, briskly sweeping the concrete deck around the pool. The water looked inviting, as the day was already warm and the sunlight stronger than it had any right to be, so I returned to my room and changed.

Hayden was sweeping by the hot tub when I stepped outside. He looked up without breaking the stroke of his sweeping.

"Well, good morning. I thought all you loggers were early risers," he said flatly.

I grimaced. "Logger my ass. I'm in favor of saving the planet, not destroying it for profit. Is it OK if we swim?"

"Oh, that's right — granola tree-hugger." He finally grinned a little to let me know he was joking. If he was. "Swim all you want, if your principles permit you to enjoy a pool here in droughtland, but I gotta warn you: the pool guy says the auto chlorinator isn't working quite right, releasing too much chlorine. And the part needed for repair is on backorder."

I tugged off my shirt, tossing it onto one of the redwood Adirondack chairs on the ramada-covered porch that ran the full length of the house. "Pool guy? You mean we have to pay someone to take care of the pool?"

"Of course not." Hayden finally stopped his sweeping, running a hand across his forehead. As I said, warm already. "The *grand dame* is footing the bill, as she is for the gardener and the lawn service. There's —"

"Lawn service? So we don't have to cut the grass?"

"Nope. They cut, trim, blow, and spray. Stop worrying; there will be little to disrupt your decadent life of leisure."

"Wait a minute. Spray? You mean those guys in the tank trucks dispersing toxic chemicals into the ecosystem?"

"That would be them, yes." Hayden was grinning widely at my dismay now, as though it were less than serious, and not for the first time I half-wondered if I had done the right thing coming here. For all his intelligence, Hayden never seemed to be particularly concerned with environmental matters, and while I'm not a zealot, not by Humboldt standards anyway, I see no need to aid and abet ecocide while living with someone entirely indifferent to what for me is a matter so deeply serious it borders on the spiritual.

"That's crazy," I snorted. "There's, what, maybe three hundred square feet of lawn here," I said, my indignation genuine as I tossed my head in the direction of the small patch of dichondra —a deep, flawless green, I have to admit — that ran from the hot tub deck to the private sitting room off the master bedroom. "What the hell is wrong with this woman?"

Hayden finally laughed outright. "She's filthy rich, of course." He shook his head and returned to his sweeping, then glanced back up at me. "Fitzgerald, wasn't it: 'The very rich are different from you and me.' And Hemingway's response, in 'The Snows of Kilimanjaro': 'Yes, they have more money.' That was 'Kilimanjaro,' wasn't it?"

"Um. . . I think so." I hate it when people ask me literary questions I don't have the answer to, as though an MA in anything literature-related confers total command over every bit of literary trivia ever written or spoken from the 5th Century BCE to yesterday, and if you don't have immediate mastery of it you're either a fraud or a failure. "Yeah, I think that's right," I said again, nodding, not wanting to admit I'd read Hemingway's story years ago but couldn't remember a damn thing about it. To break the awkwardness I plunged into the pool, letting the firm silken shock of the water distract me from all but the sheer physicality of sensation: the gentle pressure, the firm coolness, the hint of buoyancy resisted. I stayed low, a few inches above the bottom, until the impetus from the dive was spent, then coursed slowly upward. It had been a long time since I last swam in a pool and it felt better than I remembered, almost a soft embrace.

Breaking the surface I felt another momentary rush of disorientation: the glass and stucco wall of the house, the dark brown ramada over the porch with yellow-blue haze of sky beyond —all were suddenly unfamiliar, alien, particularly from my low perspective, and for a brief but very clear and memorable instant I felt a brush of that panic that comes with not knowing, not remembering, with utterly losing one's place in the universe. The sensation passed even before I fully recognized it for what it was, but it was so sharply delineated, so insistent, that I can recall it still in all its detail and power. And in retrospect it seems more appropriate than ever, another gesture of foreboding I failed to recognize.

I closed my eyes and floated, hoping I'd reached my disorientation quota for the day. I should have anticipated it, I suppose, but I still find myself being surprised a lot by life. But it truly did not occur to me I might spend the morning of my first day in LA not quite knowing where the hell I was.

"So just where *are* we, Hayden? In relation to LA proper, I mean?"

I could hear his broom on the flagstones, a gentle rasping sweep that made me think, for some reason, of a large animal, peaceful despite its menacing size. And then a pause, filled with the bright idiot call of a mockingbird in the canyon below us.

"I'm not sure there *is* such a beast as LA proper," he said, "but we're about twenty-five miles west of downtown. LA improper." He grinned. "I have a good map if you need one." His sweeping resumed.

I backstroked lazily down the length of the pool. "No, I got a map. I just want to get a mental picture of where I am in this strange land." A pair of palm trees came into view overhead, tall and languidly graceful. "With its strange vegetation," I added.

"Yeah," Hayden drawled. "But the strangest thing of all in LA is the visitors."

I laughed. "Are we going to Disneyland today, dad, or to Magic Mountain?" I turned to catch the look on his face.

He was looking at me as though I was indeed crazy, his mouth open to speak, but when he saw my expression he just shook his head. "You know, I think maybe you've come to the right place after all," he said.


A short while later we were in the "village," as it was pretentiously styled by the locals, of Glendora Hills, at a restaurant called Hakeem's which Hayden assured me was excellent. A true technophile, and one with even more money than I suspected, Hayden drove us in his Porsche, a gleaming black Turbo Carrera with every option and gadget known to the species and a stereo system that alone probably cost more than my pickup. Riding in it felt like riding in some  domesticated smart bomb utterly taken with itself.

"So you're a full-fledged member of the LA car-worship culture," I said lightly as we were seated at our table. Hayden arched an eyebrow, not as amused as I thought he'd be. "Somewhere back in my childhood I earned a degree in electro-mechanical engineering — I appreciate technical achievement and, thanks to the employment opportunities that've been opened by my other degrees, I can afford such a combination of aesthetic and technical excellence." He stared at me, his expression unreadable.

Quick change of topic. "So just what is it you're doing now that you're back in LA? Come to think of it, I can't even remember who you work for now."

"Allied Intelco," he said, his voice suddenly modulated slightly so as not to travel, and I was struck with the impression that Hayden had just taken a small step back from me, withdrawn slightly in some indeterminate way. I waited for more but he said nothing.

"Yeah," I finally said, prompting him with a gesture. " Defense something or other, right? What exactly do you *do*?"

"Defense-related, yes. I can't really go into any detail," he said, his eyes sweeping quickly around the patio, "but generally Allied is involved in what you might call the high-tech end of intelligence acquisition and processing."

I nodded, waiting for more and again seeing that nothing would be forthcoming without encouragement. Hayden's always been less than loquacious, but something else was operative here.

"'Intelligence acquisition'? Spies — You're a spook?"

"Do I look like a spy?" he asked, grinning slightly but his voice humorless and flat.

He had me there. "James Bond you ain't," I said. "But what *do* you do if you're not out doing the John Le Carré thing, seducing women and dashing around the globe and all that? The last I remember, you were teaching people how to do serious military things on computers."

Hayden looked annoyed for an instant, the muscles of his jaw tensing briefly. Tread more carefully, I thought as it suddenly began to appear I knew this person less well than I thought.

"Yes, I've done some instruction, but long ago, when I was working on my second master's, in computer science. What I do now, well, I can't say much." And he looked at me with a look of finality.

"You can't tell me what you do?"

Hayden shook his head slowly. "My married colleagues can't tell their spouses what they do. I hate to sound like a spy novel, but it's mostly classified."

"So you can't tell me what you work on? Not even in really general terms?"

"I can go this far: it's beyond virtual reality."

"What? What the hell is beyond virtual reality? How can you get more unreal than that?"

Hayden laughed briefly. "Not beyond in terms of reality – in terms of technology."

"Well, I don't even have much sense of what regular reality is, let alone VR. Barely even heard of it, to tell you the truth."

"Not a futurist, eh? Not a video game player?"

"No, that computer fantasy crap isn't for me. I'm a dinosaur; gimme a good old fashioned hardcover book any day."

Hayden opened his eyes wide in mock surprise. "Ah, an antiquarian—how quaint. A bit young for that, aren't you?"

"Antiquarian in training," I replied with a grin. "Last of my race. But seriously, I don't believe all that stuff about computers replacing books. People aren't going to stare at a screen for hours to read for pleasure. Computers'll never replace the sheer tactile, physical pleasure of paper, cloth, all that."

Hayden grinned, eyed me intently for a long moment, then laughed aloud. Studied me again and I began to wonder just what the hell was going on. "Good luck," he said quietly. "I think you're going to need it."

I had no idea what he meant and no wish right now to find out. This conversation, this entire moment, now felt awkard, somehow disturbingly at odds with the casual chatter around us, the ordinary sun falling on the low ivy-covered wall just beyond the shadows where we sat, the sleek gleaming cars in the street just beyond.

"So you can't say what you do, huh?" I said lamely, falling back on anything just to move past that sense of strangeness. "Guess I'll just have to drop in on you at work one day, see what you're up to."

Hayden laughed. "You'd be arrested before you got into the parking garage." And laughed again when the surprise registered on my face. "You know, I'm beginning to think you really *are* a bit backwoods, cousin," he said, relaxing a bit as he sensed this topic dying of its own weight. "I guess the humanities will do that to a person, eh?" It was with genuine relief that I saw our waiter approach.

That Porsche hustled into the house's driveway as though it belonged there but Ii was no longer paying attention to the car, watching instead a young woman exiting a black BMW in the driveway next door. I asked Hayden about her.

"Flake," he said emphatically. "Came over last week and introduced herself, but I forget her name. Something weird. But she's a flake, a planethopper."

"A what?" I'd never heard the term.

"Planethopper. Space cadet. Never met her before and in three minutes she's talking new age bullshit and witchcraft and God knows what all idiot nonsense." He looked deliberately at me, his grin wicked. "Of course, maybe you *should* talk to her — you northwoods liberal humanities types probably understand all that mush-brained crap intuitively."

He'd probably have been surprised if I'd told him how much of that mush-brained crap I just might understand because I've read a fair bit about the goddess religions and New Age spirituality and in Humboldt you're going to know folks drawn to that. But I say nothing of that, not after the disorientations of the morning and our restaurant conversation. Tread carefully, I reminded myself.

"She own that house? She looks pretty young. . . ."

Hayden snorted. "She's older than she looks, I think, but her father owns it, a big-name neurosurgeon according to the real estate agent. Planethopper said something about owning a new age store in the village but I really didn't care to get into it. I don't have time for juvenilia." He looked at his watch. "Speaking of time, I need to put in some hours today, so I'm going to brush my teeth and head out to work. I should be back around six or seven."

"No rest for the wicked, eh?"

Hayden nodded sagely. "None whatsoever." Pause. "Which is why those of us working on the side of Good can't take weekends off either."

"Spare me," I said lightly, shaking my head in mock disgust but genuinely beginning to wonder just who he was.


I didn't have long to wait before I met Hayden's planethopper. It was, of course, entirely his fault: he'd posted a list of regular chores on the beer-stocked refrigerator, apparently assured I'd be seeing it regularly, and I decided to do what I could in his absence, thinking to ingratiate myself while at the same time trying to evoke a sense, or at least an approximate semblance, of stability through routine. I was, after all, the guest of a housesitter, a situation exquisitely designed to maximize the sense of both rootlessness and of reaping undue rewards, thereby exacerbating my residual lapsed-Catholic guilt-anxiety over just about everything.

So I set to sweeping the eucalyptus-lined driveway, an unwelcome task in the hot afternoon sun, and by the time I was halfway through I was sweating so profusely that a dip in the pool seemed as inevitable as love's disappointment. A few laps cooled me off and I returned to my sweeping wearing only my swimtrunks and huaraches, in a hurry to finish and return to the pool.

Dumping the last of the leaves into the yardwaste bin I was startled by a female voice behind me.

"You must be the country cousin."

I turned quickly, dropping the dustpan into the barrel, to see the young woman from next door walking with calm assurance up the driveway. My surprise turned to mild embarrassment mixed with fluster: not that I'm a prude but if I'm going to meet strangers while wearing only swimtrunks I'd like to be a little more prepared.

She stopped only a couple of feet from me, closer than most people would find comfortable, and without a waver in her startlingly direct gaze held out her hand. Instinctively I shook it, and she clasped both hands around mine for a long moment. "Nice to meet you is, I believe, the standard suburban formula," she said with a slight smile. "I'm Karita, next door."

I stammered out only my name before she cut me off. "Yes, the one from the far north," she said, nodding. "Your unfriendly cousin mentioned he'd be having some company." She flashed a quick grin. "Before he got so annoyed with me he became too prickly to be around. Not a candidate for Open Mind of the Year award, is he?"

"Hayden? I, well —" Shit, what do you say to that? I was still feeling strange standing there only in swimtrunks.

She held up a hand. "Doesn't matter. His life's its own punishment."

I must have been looking at her a bit more strangely than I figured, for after a moment she laughed.

"Yes," she said cheerfully, "I usually say strange things. Sometimes even stranger—but only if you're lucky." She laughed again, looked at me with an almost disconcerting openness. "You're not much like your cousin, though, that much I can tell."

"How can you tell that? I haven't —"

"Eyes," she said matter-of-factly. "Plus I shook your hand; that helps more than you know."

I realized suddenly that her eyes were a remarkably dark green — contacts? — their color heightened by contrast with her pale skin and short copper-red hair.

"Eyes," I echoed, distracted for a moment, then flushed as I realized I'd spoken my thoughts. To cover my embarrassment I blurted out "Uh, can I do something for you?" And instantly I blushed again at the stupidity of what I'd just said, but what the hell: I was flustered, standing on the driveway of a house I didn't belong in and wearing only swimming trunks talking to an odd      young woman who, I was in the process of noticing, was curiously interesting even if only ordinary in terms of physical attractiveness, and I'd just driven down from Humboldt yesterday and was every day here going to be this odd?

She smiled. "Yes."

Her response startled me, seeming, as it did, to answer my unvoiced question.

"Yes what?"

"Yes, you can do something for me: hold out your hand."

"What?"

"Your hand, your left hand this time. Palm toward me."

Affecting a condescending grin, but beginning to wonder if Hayden perhaps hadn't gone far enough in warning me of her weirdness, I did as she asked, still clutching the broomhandle in my other hand. The sun was beginning to feel very warm on my shoulders and back.

Lowering her lids until her eyes were almost closed, this strange neighbor raised her left hand and gently pressed her fingertips to mine. She held this pose for a moment, silently, as I stood sweating in the sun, hoping no one would see us, hoping I wouldn't laugh at her theatrics.

"Now your other hand."

We repeated the gesture. Another long silence.

"Aries," she said quietly.

I've always taken alternative modalities of knowing more seriously than most people do — personally, I think astrology is the poorly grasped and incompletely understood tip of a legitimate occult iceberg, so to speak — but nonetheless I felt a disturbing tingle of surprise. "Yeah," I said, nodding casually despite my surprise. "April ninth."

She said nothing, her eyes closed completely now. "Have you ever had a full horoscope done?"

I nodded again, then realized she couldn't see me. "Yeah, as a matter of fact —"

"Good," she said, "then you'll know if I'm right: moon in Cancer, Pisces or Sagittarius rising but that one's always tricky," she said firmly. Then lowered her hand and took a half-step back, looking at me expectantly, eyebrows arched in question.

For a moment I couldn't answer, for the day had quantum-shifted on me yet again. A short time ago I was in a familiar place, surrounded by familiar sights and known people. Now — less than two full days? already Humboldt seemed weeks, maybe months ago — I find myself in a strange place with strange people I thought I knew and the most comforting thing I've done is swim in a stranger's pool and now I'm standing here half-naked in a stranger's driveway talking to a decidedly unusual woman whose name I can't remember though she just told me and having known me all of two minutes she correctly identified my full astrological sign.

"Yeah," I said slowly. "Pisces rising. How — but how the hell did you do that? People can't do that stuff," I stammered. She smiled, but before she could say anything the answer occurred to me, and for a moment I felt myself regain some footing in the unstable world I'd somehow lurched into. "Hayden," I said quickly, wanting to speak the truth into being before I lost it. "Hayden told you my birthday and that's how you figured it out, huh?"

Her laugh had the sharp brightness of the flash of a knifeblade in the sun. "Do you really think your cousin knows where and when you were born, down to the minute? Besides, we didn't exchange pleasantries long enough to get around to the matter of your birthday ." She laughed again. Then, noticing either my redness or the sweat beginning to track down my chest, she remarked "Pretty warm out. I'll let you finish up."

"Well, I — no, wait a minute," I said, trying to regain control; "how did you know my sign like that? Really, I want to know. That's incredible. I mean, I believe in astrology and the occult, but you —

that's something else. You must — how did you do that?"

She smiled slightly, eyes focused somewhere beyond me. "Shouldn't you finish cleaning up? Can't have an unkempt driveway when the house is on the market. Curb appeal and all." With that she laughed again, shortly, and spun on her heel, both her hair and a profusion of jewelry I was just now noticing throwing glinting highlights of gold and red in the harsh midday light. She strode off down the drive without a word.

"Hey," I called as soon as I recovered from my surprise. "You can't — you need to tell me how you did that."

"No I don't," she called without looking back, "but maybe I will when I come over for lunch tomorrow."

"You — what? yeah, OK, tomorrow. Lunch. See you." She didn't look back, said nothing, and I watched her disappear around the hedge that separated the houses. "What the fuck have I gotten myself into?" I muttered, shaking my head. "This weird after two damn days? Any weirder I'll be lucky to survive." I laughed at how foolish that suddenly sounded.

Hayden just shook his head when I told him that night, in brief outline, about my encounter with our neighbor, whose name neither of us could remember. "You're a big boy, cuz, you don't need instruction from me," was all he said.

"I agree she's weird, man, but sometimes that's interesting. Just look at you."

Hayden gave me a mock-sour look, said nothing. He looked too tired for a Sunday night.

"Besides," I continued, "I need to find out how she got my sign right."

"It's not that big a deal," Hayden said firmly. "She had a one in twelve chance. Just got lucky."

I realized then, of course, that I hadn't fully explained what had happened and that his disdain for all things New Age kept him from knowing anything about the complexity of a full astrological sign. I decided to say nothing, having already discovered enough unsuspected distance between us and wishing not to make my stay here any more uncomfortable than it was already threatening to become if I weren't careful.

Another topic change, then. I asked Hayden if there had been any inquiries about the house.

"Not that I know. Listing agent stopped by the evening I moved in — I think Mrs. Parkinson sent her to make sure I was here — and she said there'd been no interest yet. Think about the price point; not that many buyers in this range."

"Two point six, right?"

Hayden nodded. "And Mrs. P isn't desperate for the money, so she can afford to wait. Don't worry, cuz — you won't be out on the streets next week."

Oh brave new world, I thought. "That much money is small change to these people?"

"Close, I suspect. But not 'people' — just 'person.' The house is for sale because Dr. Parkinson shuffled off his mortal coil. It's just Mrs. P now 'cause the kids are grown and flown, and she's living at their new townhouse — her new townhouse — in Santa Barbara, or at the condo in New York, or is it the flat in Geneva? I can't keep up, but she's a wealthy widow."

"What did the good doctor do? Another neurosurgeon?"

Hayden shook his head, then smiled oddly. "Lunacy."

"He was a psychiatrist? I didn't know they got that rich."

"He did: started a chain of psych hospitals a few decades ago. Took off like wildfire and he made piles."

"A *chain* of psychiatric hospitals? Like fast-food restaurants? What a concept."

Hayden just shrugged. "What? People need psychiatric help —big deal. You ask me, the world needs a lot more psych hospitals than it has."

"Yeah, I guess building a chain of psych hospitals is a sure financial bet in LA, but somehow it just smacks of commercializing what is really a deeply individual and personal experience. You can't cure people by putting them on an assembly line."

Hayden smacked his forehead in mock dismay. "My apologies. I forgot I was talking to an English major."

I just sneered, willing to let the topic go and wondering how we again got to this point so quickly.

But Hayden had one last dig. "This," he said, gesturing dramatically at the house around us and speaking in a theatrical tone, "is the house that madness built." He looked at me, eyebrows lowered, and nodded once, sharply. "Be thankful," he admonished with mock severity. Then, leaning back in his chair and in a much lighter tone,

"And go have another beer."

I thought for a moment about making the trip out to the poolhouse for another, but as I pushed my chair back I suddenly remembered my encounter with the neighbor, the touch of her fingers and the frank openness of her gaze and the nameless whatever that made me find her interesting, even attractive. "No thanks," I said; "can't be showing up in Iowa with a beer belly."

"Whatever." Hayden had had none himself, in fact had eaten only some of the frozen pre-fab junk with which the freezer was thoroughly stocked. The extent of his indifference to food surprised me, but then I'd read that people who were geniuses in one area could be utterly hopeless in others, like Einstein using a ten-thousand-dollar check for a bookmark. I tried not to think about Hayden at work, saving the free world by developing unimaginably sophisticated computer programs for high-tech espionage having had nothing but diet cranberry juice and a toaster waffle for breakfast.

I'd intended to devote the next day to wandering around the Village, getting my bearings and perhaps some nascent sense of this fabled and faded land, but my lunch date changed those plans. I'd seen a health-food grocery in town on our trip there for breakfast the day before, so I dug out one of the cookbooks I'd brought and procured supplies. Arriving back home I realized I had no idea what time our lunch date was supposed to be; I assumed noon and hoped for the best.

The doorbell chimed three minutes after twelve. "The perfect time, right?" she said lightly as I swung open the front door, an eight-foot slab of some endangered rainforest lumber that probably weighed six times what I did. Without waiting for an answer she stepped lightly past me into the foyer, giving me a chance to take in her costume.

No, that's unfair, but she was dressed in an exaggerated style, as it seemed to me and it took me by surprise. Despite the warmth of the day she was in a black blouse and long black skirt (cotton, I think) with a flowing sash of so many colors I couldn't discern them with any degree of certainty; it seemed almost to defy any attempt to be clearly seen. Even more striking was her jewelry. I can only describe it, probably unfairly, as mock-theatrical: gold pentagram earrings that must have been three inches across, at least half a dozen gold bracelets on each arm, an indeterminate number of gold necklaces of varying description, the most noteworthy being one from which dangled a striking red-gold hieroglyph of a hawk. Pinned to her blouse was a gold brooch in the shape of a spreading oak. I've never been one for jewelry, either wearing or appreciating, but even to my inexpert eye this stuff looked expensive. She looked, I couldn't help thinking, like a rich, over-dressed gypsy, some trust-funded refugee from a Stevie Nicks concert.

"Sorry I didn't dress appropriately," I said with a grin, indicating my own blue jeans and polo shirt, which at least had the decency to be Nautica. "I'm a casual guy."

"Country," she said good-naturedly. But she wasn't looking at me; she wasn't, in fact, looking at anything: although facing the dining room her head was tilted slightly to one side, her gaze unfocused.

"Something wrong?" I asked.

She didn't seem to hear me, but just as I was about to speak she gave a short shake of her head, as though waking from daydream, and turned to me. "The house has some life, at least, but I don't think you belong here, really."

"What do you mean? I'm just staying here for a little while, but —"

She shook her head vigorously, her thick pageboy swaying. "No, that's not what I mean. It's . . . something else." She looked around, as though expecting to see something. She pointed to a picture hanging at the far end of the gallery, a life-size rendering of St. Francis done in the exaggerated vertical style of El Greco. "The energies of this house are . . . without much substance." She abruptly turned her gaze on me. "Your foolish cousin belongs here, maybe, but not you. Not really."

"He's not an idiot, you know," I said. "He's some kind of computer genius, a —"

"That's not what I meant." She twice tapped my chest over my heart with her index finger, firmly, then traced some sort of pattern. "You know." Without further comment she strode confidently down the gallery toward the kitchen but took a turn so sudden it floated both fabric and jewelry and walked briskly into the family room. I followed, not knowing what else to do, my mind drawn to the lingering physical memory of her finger on my chest. It occurred to me "planethopper" was a wonderful term but at the same time there was something more here, something not so readily dismissed, but all I could do was sense its presence, get a dim suggestion of vague outlines in shadow. And wait to see what happened next.

She stood next to the circular fireplace, looking vaguely up.

"Have you been in this house before?" I asked, hoping the question didn't sound as inane to her as it did to me.

She shook her head. "No. Which is why I need to feel it now."

This made sense to me, actually: houses hold the energies of their owners — or so I'd read, and believed. I've never been able to feel it myself, exactly, but the idea seemed right. I read a book once which argued, convincingly I thought, that this is what haunted houses were, buildings deeply impressed with the energies of traumatized former occupants. But for all that I'd read about this, accepted it intellectually, I have to admit it felt more than a bit odd to be standing in a room with someone who claimed to be registering these energies. Remembering the events of yesterday, I knew I wouldn't be saying a word of this to Hayden.

She turned abruptly to face me. "This is the most powerful room in the house. Not surprising, really: These people lived for parties, had them all the time." She nodded, as though being in the room confirmed what she had suspected. "Not the house for you, though. Don't stay long."

I grinned. "Don't worry. I'm leaving early September at the latest, grad school at the U of Iowa, creative writing doctoral program. But why is this not the house for me? And how did you know my sign, anyway?"

She smiled brightly, flipped the sash hanging at her side. "Mystery is a useful thing. But the house . . . its energies aren't harmful, but they could distract you. You're susceptible to them, but they're — let's just say they don't lead down the right path for you. You have to watch yourself, watch the path." She shook her head resolutely, reminding me suddenly of a little girl, petulantly denying or refusing something, but the impression passed as quickly as it came because I suddenly felt, with genuine surprise, a full-blown attraction to this curious woman. I couldn't even recall her name, she was clearly a strange and spacey person though I couldn't just dismiss her getting my sign right, and I had sworn (without much conviction, I confess) not to get involved with anyone since I would be in LA for such a short time and I wasn't at all sure that things were completely over with my girlfriend in Humboldt, though it had in all honestly felt that way. But there's no denying I was attracted to this strange woman. And not just sexually; she wasn't any kind of beauty, although she wasn't unattractive. She was . . . the best word I can come up with is "captivating." Not because of the occult weirdness, some of which surely had to be an act; maybe her parents had ignored her when she was growing up and this was some kind of compensatory attention thing. I mean, the occult stuff, whatever of it was legit, was part of the attraction or fascination or call it what you will, because as I said I take all that more seriously than most people, but there was something else. I realized with some embarrassment that I was staring at her rather frankly, so to cover my confusion I quickly asked her if she would like to eat.

"No, sorry, actually I have to break our date. Jazz called to say she was really out of harmony so I have to go to work early. But I'll make it up to you."

"Wait a sec." I wasn't sure what to process first. "Jazz? You know someone named Jazz? Is that for real? And what do you do, anyway? You have to at least answer that since you won't stay for the wonderful meal I slaved over all morning."

"I own The Golden Oak, down in the Village. See," she said, pointing to her brooch. "This is our sign." Not "logo," I noticed.

I nodded. "Hayden said something about new age supplies."

"It's mostly art, actually. Jazz — yes, that's her real name — is my assistant, and she's out of harmony today, so I have to go."

"Out of harmony? You mean she's sick?"

"I'll give you one of my cards later," she said, ignoring my question. "You'll have to come down and see the place some time."

"Sure."

She stepped up to within inches of me. "Bright child, far from home," she said softly, almost as though it were an incantation. Before I could respond or react she touched me lightly with an index finger on my lips. "Merry part. I'll see myself out." And in a swirl of black cotton and iridescent sash and glimmering jewelry she left.

Caught off guard, by the time I recovered enough composure to call out "Merry part," recalling the formula from books I'd read, she was opening the front door. The chiming of the doorbell — a lengthy chime; it takes about ten seconds to finish — told me she had heard.

I said nothing of this encounter to Hayden, realizing, as we talked of other things that evening, that I was off to a bad, or at least clumsy, start with my cousin. His strange employment, my dissembling, the ideological and I guess philosophical gulf between us — not in LA even a week and I was feeling more, not less, uncomfortable, surrounded already by swirling eddies of dissimulation and pretense, hidden feelings and outright lies. Things were definitely not going the way I had expected, or planned. Not that I had planned much, which I guess was good.

The next day brought more surprises, thereby doing nothing to counter my sense of being moored to a floating island. The first was small but struck me in an almost visceral way, like the somatic shudder of a bass chord too deep for hearing: pinned under my truck's windshield wiper was a business card, matte black with bright gold script: "The Golden Oak / Alternative Personal and Domestic Art / Supplier for Naturopathy and Wicca." And, in the lower corner above the address, the name I'd been seeking: Karita — but no last name. Smiling, I tapped the card and slipped it into my pocket.

Then to the university, a twenty-five minute drive (or would have been had I not missed the correct offramp), a ten-minute walk from the parking lot, and another fifteen minutes to find the office of Professor Isadora P. Seville-Beljanski. Like most professors I'd ever met she had perfected the art of exuding impatience even while being deeply engrossed in work — I was all of twelve minutes late — and as soon as introductions were over she launched into a lengthy explanation of the bureaucratic gauntlet I would have to run to finalize my hiring.

Two hours later, back at the good professor's office, I got another lecture on the work she was doing and how my humble duties — she made it very clear, without ever coming anywhere near saying so directly, that I was a drudge doing a drudge's work — related to her project. To tell the truth I had a little trouble following her, distracted as I was by events in general, the warmth of the day, the office full of books, and the brusque intensity of this woman. She was tall and almost painfully thin, her salt-and-pepper hair pulled back and twisted into a tight bun; her hairstyle was never to vary in the entire time I knew her, but never once did I see the same hairpin. Apparently her travels in the South Pacific had supplied her with an infinite variety: carved from bone and wood and stone, fashioned from clay and hide and feather and grass; dyed and painted and carved with figures strange and sweet — and many of them with jewelry to match, for despite the almost insistent plainness of her clothes, Professor Seville-Beljanski (she never asked me to call her by her first name, although I soon thought of her only as "S-B") always wore bracelets and/or brooches and/or necklaces, all obviously acquired abroad as well, as were the statues and totems and god-knows-what-all mojo curiosities gathering dust in every available nook and niche of her book-piled office. A strange — and, to be fair, exceptionally intelligent and energetic — woman, and I wondered that day if I was ever going to meet an ordinary person in LA.

My work turned out to be even more lackluster and tedious than I had feared. Having explained that the project involved translation, my thesis director — I should have known better than to take him at his word; he could make taking out the trash sound like an epic adventure — had suggested that my talents as a creative writer would come into play during the polishing of translated texts. Well, the project involved translation, all right, but I had nothing whatsoever to do with it at any point. My task was nothing more than data entry, some of it from handwritten (hand-scribbled, I should say) field notes, some of it from cassette recordings that sounded as though they were made underwater on a cheap toy cassette recorder thirty years ago; too much of the work was the excruciatingly tedious addition of various diacritic and accent marks into dozens of megabytes of text already on disk. It was, in short, boring and tedious academic slave work, and did nothing to ameliorate my sense of dislocation: on average I spent four or five hours a day, three days a week, working with the text of a language I did not understand for purposes that never became clear to me. At least, I recognized from that very first day, it was in perfect accord with the rest of my experience in this place.

I spent my first few on the job working closely with Professor S-B — or, to put it more precisely, being frequently watched over by the good doctor — as she showed me, with the redundant and verbose over-thoroughness so prevalent in academia, precisely what it was I needed to do. She scrutinized my work carefully at first, but as I learned my way around the special characters and my work improved she left me on my own, typing away in a windowless broom-closet of an office around the corner from hers.

      I arrived home that first afternoon surprisingly tired, which annoyed me. I'd sworn I would start writing today, but when I could summon no energy. Too much strange newness, I told myself; things so far have been too unsettled, in ways both intellectual and emotional, for me to get composed enough to write. I'd vowed to keep a daily journal, to commit myself to diligence, and that afternoon vowed anew to do something along those lines but before I could make even desultory notes I'd somehow had a couple of beers — damn that Hayden and his refrigerator — and fallen asleep on the wicker settee in the sunroom.

      I was awakened by the sound of Hayden rummaging about somewhere in the house. Groggy and thick-headed from the afternoon sleep and the beer, I stumbled into the kitchen, taking a few minutes, in my state, to notice that it was only 5:45, a good two hours earlier than the time Hayden said he normally came home.

      "Well, well," my cousin said in mock indignation, his eyebrows arched for effect. "The bohemian poet, sleeping away the day, saving his energy for the midnight production of immortal verse."

      "Oh, spare me" I said. "I just fell asleep reading." Another lie, coming easily.

      Hayden only grinned, briefly and without humor. "I'll spare you all the space you need for your decadent liberal lifestyle, at least for the next five days. I'm off to Atlanta. I know it's a bit abrupt, and you just got here, but I told you I'd be travelling. I'll leave a list of the things that need to be done — there isn't much, so I'm sure you'll manage reasonably well without me," he smirked as he pulled a box of microwave pancakes from the freezer.

      I shook my head at his choice, said nothing. "OK, no problem. But what's with this sudden trip to Atlanta? One of your classified junkets you can't say anything about?"

      Hayden looked at me archly. "This happens to be a combination of business and personal. Mostly the former, but there's someone special I know in the  Atlanta area which is why I'll be staying through Sunday."

      I waited for more; there was none. I was tempted to pursue this final point, the only hint Hayden had yet given that he had some sort of life beyond work, but some instinct, aided by recollection of prior experience, told me to let it pass.

"Sunday, huh?  I'll try not to burn the house down before then."

He nodded, liberating four icy disks of modified food starch from their cardboard prison.  "It'll be late."  He glanced at me with a smile dripping irony.  "Don't wait up."

Hayden's plane was scheduled to leave at nine-thirty.  I offered to drive him to Ontario airport so he wouldn't have to leave his Porsche in a parking lot, but he wouldn't hear of it, his faith in high-end car alarms and valet parking apparently knowing no bounds.

In the wake of his departure I couldn't help wondering about the suddenness of this trip.  He'd said nothing else, so I was left to wonder if such last-minute trips were standard or if he had just not bothered to tell me ahead of time.  I made a mental note to ask him about this when he returned; maybe that information wouldn't be classified.  Then again, maybe it would.  I'd probably get no further asking him about the someone he knew, either.  Damn, he could be close-mouthed.  I didn't remember this about him, and wasn't sure how much I cared, but I did think it would be nice to have some sort of substantive connection between us given our situation and the fact we were family.

I couldn't shake the sense there was something strange, perhaps something estranging, going on here, something more than the fact of my very recent arrival.  It was an elusive intimation only, nothing clear at all, but there was a distance, some shadowy rift of recalcitrance I could sense only dimly.  Computers, defense, virtual reality, secrecy — an awkward combination.  Far removed from the world I wanted.  But something else, too, something personal.

Fuck it, I thought finally, heading outside for another beer, too distracted to realize I really didn't need one.  It's Hayden's life; I'm just passing through this demented waystation.  I suddenly thought of Conrad's *Heart of Darkness*, wished I hadn't.

The evening was warm, the sun low above the hill on the far side of the canyon, and I took a seat on the diving board to drink my beer and watch the smog-filtered sun slowly approach the ridge of the canyon, drop below it, journey on.  I remained there in silence, feeling the approaching edge of a tranquility I hadn't felt in days, had no wish to move until I suddenly registered, acutely and discomfortingly, how fully silence seemed to have settled around me, enveloped the entire neighborhood in a stillness that felt freighted with some meaning I couldn't fathom. This sudden shift from calm to deep unease unsettled me and I couldn't remain still; I got up, went to get another beer but lost interest before I got to the poolhouse. Into the house then, thinking perhaps to grab my journal and make some notes but when I picked up my notebook it felt inert in my hands, a dead thing and alien. What the hell, I thought. This isn't like me. I needed to shake this and the only possibility that came to mind was movement, get out of the house for a while, see some life happening around you. I grabbed my keys and drove almost aimlessly for over an hour, unable to think of anywhere to go having lived here for so few days, and the lingering sense of having experienced some strange and subtle unsettling never fully left me.

And yet no sense of foreboding ever touched me.


I'd just stepped back in the house when the phone rang: Karita, inviting herself over. Sure, I said, surprised and delighted — and surprised again a moment later when I realized I'd never given her the phone number here, that I didn't even have it memorized myself yet. She must have seen it the other day when she came over to cancel our lunch date, I figured. Then realized we'd never gone into the kitchen, where the only phone was located.

I asked her about the phone number before she crossed the threshold. Only to hear her light laughter again.

"Always full of questions," she said, breezing past me into the empty dining room where she came to a twirling stop, arms akimbo.

"Always theatrical," I countered, smiling. What is it about her? Just looking at her made me feel good, the unease of an hour ago suddenly forgotten.

"Always?" she echoed. "A sweeping statement to make about someone you've only met twice before."

"Maybe, but you still haven't answered my question. Or told me how you knew my sign exactly." I gave her my best serious look, not easy given the rainbow extravagance of her skirt, dark orange blouse, and what was apparently the usual complement of jewelry.

She shrugged. "I thought mystery was becoming."

"Becoming what?"

"Lame."

I shrugged, smiled. "Want a beer?"

"No thanks. Let's sit outside."

And we did, talking of nothing, watching the evening light slowly dying from the sky, from the surface of the pool, from the glass behind us. Dying in the dirty salmon haze that is the color of choice for sunsets in LA, dying into the thin purple wash of the languid summer evenings that are the stuff of modern nostalgia. Or so I thought.

"You seem lost in thought," Karita said gently after a long moment of silence. "What do you see in that sky?"

"I don't know," I said. "Clichés, obscurities." I turned to her with a grin. "The stuff of postmodern fiction."

She stared at me, expectantly it seemed, but I had nothing else to say. Watching her was more rewarding, more real. In this light her hair looked darker than usual, framing her pale face in a way that somehow emphasized the contours of cheek and jawline; she look almost . . . sculptural, I guess. I forgot the sky.

Her eyes remained fixed, steadily, on mine. "And what do you see now?"

I shook my head, never taking my eyes off hers. And felt bold enough to say, "I'm even less sure. A captivating woman, a strange character, I don't know."

"Good thing I'm not normal," she said, her voice softening as she spoke. "I might be offended." Holding my gaze she slipped easily out of her chair and joined me, almost touching, on the redwood chaise. "Do you see a lover?"

I felt a wave of surprise at her directness, and below that the dark familiar surge of libido. And, coming from somewhere unfamiliar, an answer direct and unflustered. "I would like to. But I'm not sure what I see because I don't know what the hell's going on in my head or my heart right now. Don't know what to trust. After all, I've only been here a couple of days, and . . . well, this place...." I laughed self-consciously. "I feel pretty much unanchored."

I took another swallow of beer, wondered if I was saying the wrong sort of thing, decided to plunge ahead anyway because there was nothing to lose now, and no way back. Sometimes you just have to step off the cliff. "Four days ago my life was pretty routine, and now I'm in this weird place doing I don't know what living with I don't know who and finding myself very interested in a woman who is apparently some kind of new-age witch. And very forthright." I grinned. "And I'll be damned if I know what to make of any of it." I shrugged, gave her my best Lothario look, and took the plunge. "But yeah, I find you attractive and thoroughly captivating and I would love to make love with you."

She held my look with a relaxed confidence, nodded slowly. "Make love *with* you," she repeated slowly. Nodded. "But not just yet." She glanced out at the canyon, up at the hazy pall above us.

"I probably shouldn't bother asking why not yet, huh?"

She looked at me with pert surprise. "Of course you can ask."

"OK, why not?"

"I can't tell you," she said with a laugh, spinning lightly up off the lounge as I reached playfully for her. She finally settled on the diving board.

"Well," I said, "is the reason something arcane and mystical, like the moon isn't in the seventh house, or something mundane like you have a boyfriend?"

She tossed her head and for an instant her eye caught the lights of a jet far overhead, heading east out of LA, toward the old world. "I'm tempted to quibble with your archaic choice of terms," she said with mock condescension, "but let's just say it's more like the arcane and mystical." She suddenly fixed her eyes on me. "You *do* believe in the arcane and mystical, don't you?"

I didn't think she was really serious, because I think she already knew the answer, but I responded anyway. "Of course. I'm a writer, so the mystical is part of my stock in trade, as they used to say. The muse, and all that." Words didn't want to come to my aid on this topic, for some reason; with a quick motion I drained the rest of my beer, got up for another.

"So you don't believe it's all electrons and chemical reactions? Isn't that what your cousin would say?"

"I don't know much about the brain," I said, "and I don't want to think too much about how I do what I do. Inspiration doesn't bear examination, they say, and I'll go along with that."

She nodded, and then with the abruptness that I was beginning to understand was a part of her character, excused herself. On her way out the gate she turned and reminded me she had left her card on my windshield for a reason. I told her I'd be there tomorrow.

But I didn't make it, although not for lack of trying. I had planned to leave work at three the next afternoon; my schedule was flexible as long as I logged my requisite hours per week, but at two-fifty I got a phone call from S-B, who had taken to doing most of her work at home now that I could function without direct adult supervision, explaining in a voice edged with panic that she needed some material on her office computer so she could finish a grant letter or something and snailmail it by noon tomorrow. Like most academics I've known she handled rush situations very poorly although she seemed to spend most of her time in them, and it took her about fifteen minutes to explain to me what she needed me to do, which due to locked office doors and recalcitrant secretaries and a misremembered file name took over an hour and a half.

I rushed out as quickly as I could but traffic on the I-10 proved normal for almost four-thirty in the afternoon, which is to say an utter nightmare of slow grinding progress impeded for no discernible reason; by the time I got to the Golden Oak it was closed. The store was on the second floor of what was once an old Art Deco movie theater that had been converted into shops and offices — jeweler, architect, frozen yogurt, something called Starbucks, realty, all the usual — and was one of the most prominent buildings in the yuppified "village" of Glendora Hills. For some reason it never occurred to me to go upstairs and look in the shop; I could see the "Closed" sign from the patio courtyard and I had come to see Karita, not the usual new-age witchcraft paraphernalia that undoubtedly filled the place. So I went home.

About 9.45 that night, as I was just starting to drowse over my copy of *Kwaidan*, the phone rang.

"Come," I heard a voice say.

"Karita?" I asked hesitantly, not sure if the cobwebs had clogged my ears as well as my brain, but the line had already clicked dead.

"What the hell?" I muttered. It had to have been her voice, I thought — who else knows I'm here but my parents? — so figuring I had nothing to lose but a little embarrassment if her father answered the door I made myself presentable and next door I went.

The house was a striking contemporary, towering walls of glass and dramatic angles, but was almost entirely dark as I walked up the drive past the two unfamiliar cars parked there, but as I followed the path to the front door hidden lights clicked on as I walked, illuminating the sidewalk in front of me. Interesting effect, I thought; wonder how much that cost. A porch light came on as I stepped up to the door — like ours, a huge eight-foot double door but covered with dark copper in abstract geometric designs. It was beautiful, drawing me in so fully the opening of the door took me by surprise. Karita, dressed entirely in black but with twice as much jewelry as usual, gestured me in. "Glad you could make it."

"How could I resist such an invitation?" I wanted to rail her more on her one-word phone call but a laugh from somewhere in the house caught my attention. "What's up? Party?" I was suddenly acutely aware of my worn jeans, scuffed Topsiders.

She smiled. "No, no, very small gathering. Just a couple of people. You'll like them. Come." She led me down stairs that began only a few feet away from the foyer so I couldn't see much of the house, but what I glimpsed would give the Parkinsons a run for their money in the conspicuous consumption derby.

"A basement," I remarked as we descended. "Don't see many of these in California."

"Daddy grew up in the Midwest," she said lightly; "says he can't get comfortable in 'houses without bottoms,' as he puts it. Says this one was worth it despite what the engineers made him spend."

We issued from the stairs into a room that looked, to my untrained eye, like something straight out of an East Coast decorating magazine, but my survey of the room abruptly ended when I saw three other people in the room, seated on the floor around a low lacquered table on which burned a single fat candle, bright in the stagey dimness of the room. My first thought was "'I'm glad there aren't thirteen of them" but as I was hastily introduced I began to feel sure these three would prove plenty weird enough. One was Jazz, the woman Karita'd already mentioned to me. She was dramatically striking in appearance, high cheekbones giving her a model's face and she was model-thin as well, bone-thin really, and even though she was seated on the floor it was clear she was at least six feet tall. Her hair was cut very short and impossibly black, iridescent even in the candleglow. The overall effect: gorgeous. The next was Sharah — "Sarah with an extra 'h'," Karita was careful to explain — short but very compact, contours of muscle evident in her arms and beneath tight-fitting leather jeans; I knew her grip would be strong but like Jazz she acknowledged the introduction only by nodding. It wasn't until some moments later that I realized she had African-American blood, so light was her skin and so poor the light in the room. The male of the bunch, about my height but scrawny and death-pale, was introduced only as Treason; he too sported black leather jeans, along with enough piercings to trigger security monitors from thirty feet away, all set off with sandals and a dark vest made of what looked like crushed velvet. He shook my hand from his seated position, his grip flaccid. I said nothing but wondered, not for the first time, what I'd gotten myself into.

I looked expectantly at Karita, who dropped with the ease of long practice into a lotus position on the floor. Jazz shifted and I sat between her and Karita, who had become intent on the pale candle. In the silence Treason reached deftly into a vest pocket, produced and lit a joint, inhaling loudly. He handed it to Sharah, who without inhaling passed it to Jazz. She inhaled at length but with uncanny silence, then held the joint toward me. I shook my head; I still smoke on occasion but this was already strange enough. Back to Treason, who made no offer to Karita, I noticed.

More silence, broken only by Treason's loud inhaling. I was beginning to wonder if there was a polite way of asking what was going on when Karita, her eyes closed now, reached one hand out to the table, letting her palm rest on its edge. Treason adroitly extinguished the joint, slipped it back into his vest pocket. I could feel an expectancy, almost a tightening of the atmosphere.

"Now," Karita said, her voice as whisper-soft as a dream's remembrance. The others extended their left hands, resting them against the table's edge in imitation of Karita. Uncertain, I hesitated, but Karita spoke my name and I immediately followed suit, feeling more than a little silly. While I have, as I said, read some things about Wicca and goddess religions and even know a few people who practice the Craft, or used to anyway, this was new terrain for me. It suddenly occurred to me I may have jumped to a conclusion: none of the conventional props of witchcraft were in evidence; perhaps this was something else, some kind of new age exploration unfamiliar to me, and a bit offbeat for my taste. Wait and see, I told myself. Wait and see.

"Sharah seeks a smoothing of the way," Karita said in the same soft tone, her eyes still closed. I hoped this wasn't intended to explain what we were doing because it meant nothing to me. "Treason seeks to untangle a web of his own devising. Jazz is balance, reflecting pool into which we look and rising road along which we journey for the calm that Sharah and Treason seek."

"And what of Karita?" I heard Jazz say, obviously catching everyone by surprise because all heads snapped in her direction, all eyes open and intent. Jazz, her head slightly lowered but with gaze directed at Karita, seemed oblivious to the rest of us. "What does she seek in reaching outside the circle? What happens to our balance with the presence of others?" That would be me, I thought. There was no rancor or bitterness in her voice — if anything, she sounded preternaturally calm — but it was clear her question was a serious one. Shit. Sharah and Treason both looked intently at Karita and I prepared myself to make what would surely be a clumsy and embarrassed exit.

"Trust, Jazz," Karita said, her tone matching that of her friend, their eyes locked in a way that made it clear to me a lot of what was transpiring was well below the surface. "Sharah and Treason have welcomed this widening. We've widened circles before and my reasons are the same now: a complementary energy —"

"I don't know that," Jazz said shortly, a trace of tension now in her voice.

I started to rise. "Look, I don't want to get in the way —"

Karita's hand on my arm silenced me, guided me back to the floor. "Jazz has been out of harmony; perhaps I called this circle back too soon. Sharah and Treason —"

"Sharah and Treason will come back when this is worked out," Sharah said, rising abruptly and practically hauling Treason up with her in a way that bespoke not only the strength I noticed before but a familiarity that surprised me. I found it hard to believe those two were together in any way, though I couldn't say why.

They certainly left together, without another word or backward glance. Karita and Jazz remained seated while I felt thoroughly conspicuous.

Jazz's eyes flicked over me quickly, then back at Karita. "Peace?"

"Peace," Karita said, nodding slightly. Jazz rose with a grace that was absolutely mesmerizing and as she did Karita held out her left hand, palm toward Jazz with index and middle fingers extended. "The Mother's womb," she said softly.

Jazz lightly touched her index and middle fingers to Karita's. "The Mother's womb," she echoed before slipping soundlessly out of the room.

A long moment of silence followed. Karita looked intently at the candle flame, her eyes focused on some impossible distance; I looked intently at her. In the soft light she appeared younger than she was and somehow stoically fragile, and for a brief moment I was overcome by a sense of deja vu, that I had seen her in precisely this position, from just this angle and in just this light, sometime before, some long ago and distant point on the spacetime continuum.

She looked at me abruptly, smiled sadly. "Deja vu," she said, and her eyes flashed with conscious delight when she registered the shock on my face.

"How the hell do you do that?" I asked in exasperation.

She only looked back at the candle, her smile fading. "You don't know why you're here." A statement, not a question. "If I seem to read you easily, it's because we travel now and have travelled before together."

"'Travel?' You mean like sympathetic spirits or something?"

She nodded slowly, still focused on the candle. "Our spirits have known each other before, in earlier lives, perhaps many of them, and we continue to travel." She turned to me abruptly, and despite the flash of her eyes it was the candlelight on her red-gold hair I noticed. "We've loved before, perhaps even died for each other before, and we are here again together, and this troubles me."

"Troubles you? Why? Don't the same spirits often return together?" I remembered reading something along those lines somewhere, although I'd never much thought about past lives before, never been sure how much I believed in it.

"Often, yes, but in our case there's something hard that remains to be worked out, and I fear to discover what it is."

"Fear?"

She smiled. "You're beginning to sound like my echo." The smiled faded. "Yes, fear, and I'm not sure why. I've been . . . troubled, in a way, ever since I heard you were coming; I still have a lot of thinking to do, a lot of casting, other things that may answer some questions. We're important spirits to each other, but I wonder if this may be a crux manifestation for at least one of us." She shook her head. "I'm sure of one thing, though: we will meet only this once in this life; after you leave our paths won't cross again. And that too troubles me. I will never share much of this life with any one person, but I can't shake the feeling that we need to do something, or that something important will happen, I don't know what, in the short time our paths intersect."

Looking back on this now I know she registered the sense of foreboding I never did. Perhaps because my mind was elsewhere, because at the time all I did was shift my position and reach toward her though she stopped me with a finger against my chest and a wicked grin. "That, too, northern wolf-child, but not just yet."

I grinned, sat back. "But if something is supposed to happen between us, why not just let it happen? Won't it work out the way it's supposed to?"

"That's all it can do, but how can we know what that is? How do we know that 'the way it's supposed to' isn't the way that involves much labor, or hurt, or even denial? Besides, there's no book of fate somewhere out there that preordains our actions. We're never free from being responsible for ourselves; our choices always shape our lives which then shape our choices, in infinite reciprocity and forward motion. Souls sometimes struggle through dozens of incarnations trying to solve a particular problem. You come back for many lifetimes if you keep making the same mistake."

"And that's what you think we, or one of us, is doing? Screwing something up every time? And this life we only have one brief window of opportunity?"

"It's a possibility. Or maybe it's not a case of screwing up, just something important that needs to happen, to resolve perhaps." She smiled. "And I'm impatient. Our souls are old and have not much further to go; this could be the last hurdle, or close to it. And that's why I brought you here tonight. I know I'm pushing a little, but. . . . "

"Yeah," I said, returning to my earlier confusion. "Just what the heck was going on here, and what was I doing here? This wasn't a coven, obviously, but what was that stuff about the circle? And why did Jazz take such an instant dislike to me? Usually I have to open my mouth before I alienate someone that thoroughly."

"What was going on here. . . . Well, think of it as a kind of informal therapy session. Sharah and Treason and other sympathetic spirits sometimes come and we help each other discover . . . ways of dealing with challenges. Don't worry about Jazz. She's been growing distant for some time now, beginning to move away from the arc of my life toward a path that will take her away from here, perhaps even away from the Mother, I think, but such things happen here on the clay beneath the moon. Like a teenager leaving home, she'll have to alienate me to make her departure possible, and what happened tonight was part of that. There may be other things, as well, but —" For a moment Karita fell silent, let her gaze turn inward. Then an abrupt refocusing. "She's a strong spirit and has been a great help to me in many things, and I'll miss her deeply, but so mote it be."

I nodded, not sure I entirely understood but not overly concerned what someone like Jazz thought of me. Even if she was gorgeous. Then something else registered, my mind apparently being a bit sluggish due to the evening's strangeness. " 'The clay beneath the moon'? Where do you come up with this stuff? Sounds like something out of Old English poetry, *kenning* they call it." A thought suddenly struck me. "You weren't an English major by any chance, were you?"

She laughed. "No, but I took some English classes in college, enjoyed them a lot. The Romantics were my favorite."

"That figures," I said. "All that mysticism and nature worship. Gimme Robert Creely and Ed Dorn any day."

"Who?"

"Poets, contemporary American. My favorites. But I like the Romantics too. A lot of our sense of the natural world comes from there, but the forms are too, well, old."

She just shook her head. "Forms — I love what they *say*. I'll leave the details of structure to you literature types."

"So, what did you major in, anyway? Come to think of it, where did you go to college? You haven't yet told me any of this stuff, or much else about you for that matter."

"You never asked. But since you have, I went to Berkeley. Dual bachelor's, art history and business administration."

"Shit, that's a combo. I guess you knew you were going to end up running an art gallery, huh?" And I told her of my failed visit yesterday.

She gave me a look of smug disdain. "I'm a pretty strange spirit, I know, and yes, even before I graduated I had a clear idea of what I wanted to do. And I probably shouldn't tell you this, and won't go into more detail, but I don't do it for the money."

I nodded; the house in which we sat made it pretty clear money was not much of an issue for her, or at least her family. "As long as we're sort of on the subject, do you mind if I ask why you still live here with your father? I mean, if I had an independent income I sure wouldn't live at home."

"We weren't on that subject, but as long as you're being so inquisitive, I do it because my father and I are good for each other, although he's rarely home any more. I keep an eye on him when he is here so he doesn't work himself to death, which he probably would do otherwise. Right now he's in Baltimore; he's been at Johns Hopkins since January and won't be back until September. Besides, if I didn't live here I wouldn't have met you, would I?"

"True enough." I paused, looking around the room again. "I don't mean to harp on this, but I'm still not sure why you invited me here. Why was I sitting in on a therapy session for people I don't even know. Shit, I wouldn't let strangers sit in on any counseling session I was in."

Karita looked at me. "You already did, or almost did."

"What? What's that supposed to mean?"

"You were here for the psychic energy you could contribute; Sharah is unintentionally very good at drawing out people's stronger psi energies, and your being here would have allowed me to fill in some of the details of my, well, let's call it a psychic profile."

"Psychic profile? I never heard of that."

"Just a term I use for my sense of someone. I read you well, and could fill in all the details on my own eventually, but like I said, I'm in a hurry." She grinned, ruefully. "And sometimes shortcuts turn into deadends," she said, her eyes sweeping around the empty table.

"So this whole thing was a setup so you could scope out my karma, huh?"

She gave me a mock-sour look. "It's not karma, and no, it wasn't a setup. It would have been real for Sharah and Treason too, if Jazz hadn't lost her center."

I nodded, not really sure of anything other than the fact I was way out of my element. "So what now?" I asked. "Plan B?"

"Plan B." She smiled, rose, and took my hand. "Come."

She led the way upstairs, giving me a chance to see some of the house. I don't care much for contemporary architecture, myself — I think my dreamhouse has been standing somewhere in England for about 500 years — but it was clear this one was designed and furnished with impeccable taste and a hell of a lot of money. I said so to Karita, who squeezed my hand and smiled. "Thanks. I did all the decorating."

"That makes sense. Fantastic job."

I didn't have much chance to appreciate her work, though — or, to be more accurate, I didn't have much inclination at the moment because the subsonic throb of libido began to distract me. I did notice a cat — one of her three, Karita said — sleeping on a futon on the upstairs loft. Even in the dim light I could see that the cat's coat was a lustrous and unmarked black; the animal did not wake, although it stirred and made a gurgling moan as we passed.

Into her bedroom she led me, my libido in gear now to the point of distraction: it suddenly occurred to me that some four or five months had elapsed since I'd last made love with Sandy. I felt that slight tension in my chest and shoulders that for me marks the anticipation of sex, an anticipation heightened by the furnishings of her room.

Karita flicked a wall switch as we entered the room, but instead of the usual overhead fixture or floor lamp the room was lit only by a handful of dimmed sconces placed at strategic points along the walls, giving a strangely seductive yet somehow artful quality to the room. Centered on one wall was a queen-sized bed covered with a black silk comforter; an oversized copper and leather chair stood against one wall. A black lacquered chest stood at the foot of the bed, on which rested a tall pewter pitcher and two goblets, etched with some design I could not discern. No other furniture, but lots of art: statuary, pictures, strange multimedia works, some hanging, some stacked and leaning against the wall, none of them clear in the dimmed yellow light.

Without preamble Karita kissed me, hard, her hands to my chest then trailing down to the top of my jeans. I put my hands on her breasts and she responded with a barely audible moan. Then broke away, a wide and wicked grin on her face.

Karita stepped to the chest, poured something into one of the goblets. "Here," she said, handing me the goblet with great deliberateness. I tried not to let my confusion or skepticism show. "This is for . . . travelling in deeper currents."

"What?"

"Drink, prosaic poet."

I let that slide, unable now to shift my interest away from sex. "What is this?" I asked, taking the goblet. It was surprisingly heavy. "Some kind of drug?"

"Not in the sense you mean, no. I never use those."

I grinned. "A love potion?"

She grinned back, seating herself casually on the edge of the bed. A waterbed, I suddenly noticed.

"Not a love potion," she said, a trace of earnestness in her voice. "Never was such a thing."

"What?" I said in mock astonishment. "You mean all the fairy tales were lying?" I groaned melodramatically. "Next you'll be telling me there's no Santa Claus."

She shook her head. "Poor cynical child. Fairy tales all have a core of truth — you're the English major, you should know that."

"Uh, never took that class."

She ignored me. "Old stories of love potions are just exaggerations of reality. There are certain compounds that can lower emotional inhibitions and help people get in touch with their true feelings — that's what 'love potions' were. And are. They don't make you fall in love with someone you can't stand, but they can help people cut through the masks they wear and the customs that distort their inner selves, and then sometimes they realize feelings they've always had but have been denying."

"Sounds like you're talking about booze."

"A primitive and patriarchal substance," she said. "But not entirely unrelated. Too high a stupidity factor, though. Real 'love potions,' as you commoners call them, are much more honest."

I nodded sagely. "So you mean Titania was really hot for Bottom all along?"

"What?"

"Shakespeare," I said, with a dismissive shake of my head. "Bad joke. Forget it. So then what's in this chalice?" I asked, holding it up between us.

"Think of it as herbal tea, plus."

"Plus what?"

She smiled. "Trade secret. Drink already."

I did, taking a small sip of the cool dark tea and feeling rather silly. I was reminded of Mass, something I hadn't thought of since my sophomore year of high school when my parents stopped forcing me to attend. I handed the goblet to her. "Your turn," I said, wondering what her reaction would be.

She took the goblet from me and drank, giving me a chance to see that the goblet was carved with the figure of a spreading oak tree, identical to that on her business card and the gold brooch she wore.

She handed me the chalice again. "Finish." I did, forcing myself to swallow the rest of the bitter tea quickly. My mouth felt dry and puckered already, and I began to wonder if there was more to this foul brew than Karita had told me. As I returned the goblet to her I remarked on the oak design.

She nodded. "My totem, my sign."

"I thought totems had to be animals," I said.

"No," she said. "That's the case only in certain patriarchal systems."

I nodded, vaguely recalling something about Wicca and other forms of natural magic being descendants of pre-historic Mother Goddess nature religions, an idea seized upon by some feminists. One of the two female teachers in my old English department, a feminist theorist, wore an ankh, the Egyptian glyph that looks like a cross with a loop on top — not because she practiced magic (at least not to my knowledge), but because of the ankh's unofficial status as a symbol of feminism. Magic, feminism, hieroglyphs, womb-worship — it all kind of made sense, somehow, and I wanted to say something to Karita about this, but I could feel my concentration faltering as an almost palpable wave of relaxation seemed to flow slowly down my spine. Something more to that tea than rosehips and cloves. Not that the feeling was unpleasant, just a wave of relaxation with the very slightest shading of euphoria, visceral and enveloping. A good feeling, but a weird kind of . . . not helplessness, but a recognition that you don't need to be as concerned about things as you thought. Strange, I know, but that's how it felt.

"Just go with the flow, as they used to say." Karita was looking at me intently, the slight smile parting her lips belied by a look of focused concentration.

I shook my head, smiled. "What've you done to me, witch? Poisoned me?"

"Oh, no," she said earnestly; "the last thing I want you is dead." She paused dramatically. "But a bit of stiffness might not be inappropriate."

We both grinned and I reached for her, our mouths locking and hands groping instantly. The drug had some effect on sensation, too; I felt as though the sensitivity of every nerve had been heightened, every touch receptor keyed to its maximum. I was acutely aware of every quantum of sensory input: the firm smoothness of the silk coverlet, the slow muffled gurgle of the waterbed, the gentle warmth of Karita's body through the thin cotton of her blouse, the eldritch fragrance of her perfume. Every touch of her fingers was electric, and seemed to leave a lingering trace of pleasure on my skin. It was incredible, and by the time we had each other's shirts off I was trembling. She lowered her mouth to my nipples and I moaned, something I don't think I've ever done during foreplay or even lovemaking. The moist warmth of her mouth on my chest and then stomach was an infinite pleasure distilled and focused into a moment, and I felt that I was about to come. I quickly unzipped and pushed Karita's head to my crotch, and moaned again as she slipped away and stood up.

"We have to do this skyclad," she said, slipping off the rest of her clothes.

"Do it what?" I asked, my voice thick as I scrambled to my feet and struggled carefully with my pants, watching her reveal her body in the dim glow, her limbs compact and rounded, breasts full, the dark patch of her pubic hair. I trembled again and felt like heaven was within reach.

"Skyclad. Nude."

"The only way to fuck," I said, reaching out to cup her breasts. But she stepped back again.

"We're not going to *fuck*, you savage northern child."

"What? Then what are you doing?" I stepped toward her, my thoughts dark, confused, and was brought up only by the knife that Karita produced from I don't know where and held up between us. I tensed.

I watched closely, first in apprehension then in growing fascination as she moved the knife — I recalled, incongruously, that a witch's knife is called an athame — toward her, holding the blade vertically between her breasts. (The blade, I quickly learned, was quite dull.) She spoke something in a low voice that I couldn't quite catch, then looked up at me. "Down, boy," she ordered, indicating the floor with her eyes.

Still keeping an eye on the knife I knelt, hoping I wouldn't ejaculate before whatever it was we were going to do. "Flat on your back." I followed her order, my cock rising like some throbbing Tower of Pisa, and Karita stepped over to me. I tensed again for an instant as she lowered the athame but she laid it flat on my stomach, the point of the blade toward my head. I could feel the cool metal of the blade, the fine corrugations of the handle, the rounded knobs at the end of the hilt. I'd never known skin could be so sensitive, so receptive to nuance. From the armoire she produced a cord of some kind, thick but of a soft material and knotted at each end. I thought bondage but she merely draped it carefully across my stomach and over the athame. Karita then placed the goblet from which we had drunk on the floor next to me and knelt down. I reached for her but she slapped my hands away. "Lie still, don't speak," she said, her voice strangely distant, neutral. Or was it the drug, which didn't seem to be getting stronger but remained firmly in effect? She ran a finger across my forehead and down the centerline of my body, stopping at the knife point. I was just about to reach for her again when she stood up and for a second time crossed the room to the armoire.

From it she produced a small cut-glass decanter , some liquid in it which she poured into the chalice. I watched in silence as she moved her hands over it, her lips moving but making no sound.

She came back to me and knelt down again. I put my hands behind my head — the better to watch — as she began to stroke me. Already keyed up, I came much more quickly than I could believe and with a wave of pleasure that seemed for a lingering moment to erase all consciousness, and watched, in a mingled fascination and revulsion I'd never felt before, as she lifted the goblet to catch my semen. Excited by the sexual abandon I nonetheless felt a slight touch of unease. Residual Catholic guilt, I rationalized.

"Don't move," Karita said, then stepped to the armoire again and returned holding something I couldn't see. "Left hand," she said in the matter-of-fact tone of a nurse about to take a blood sample. A brief stab of pain in my index finger then pressure as she squeezed a few drops of my blood into the chalice. She repeated the procedure on herself, then placed goblet and knife on the chest. Standing over me, she held out a hand as though to help me up. I took it and sat up, then pulled her down onto me, kissing her firmly on the mouth, tilting my head down to her breast. She responded for a moment, then pulled

45

back.

"I'd love to play, my bright child-spirit, but I need to work quickly now or everything will be lost."

"Well, then, we'll just have to do it again."

She laughed but slipped out of my grasp and stood, reaching for her clothes. "But we won't have another propitious day for almost two months, so it must be today. We'll explore further soon, don't worry." She grinned. "I want my turn."

There was no point pushing her, and I was, to tell the truth, satisfied. "Can you at least tell me what you're doing, since I was obviously instrumental in supplying necessary ingredients?"

She didn't meet my gaze. "No. To talk about a Weaving is to weaken it. But I can say it has to do with what we talked about earlier."

I wasn't sure I remembered what we'd talked about earlier but it was clear that was as much explanation as I was going to get, and I was a bit amused to realize I was already getting accustomed to her reticence. I guess so little else made sense that another dose of confusion and opacity could do no harm.

"OK," I said, dressing slowly, surprised at the sensitivity of my skin to clothing, a light electric frisson flowing over me as I pulled on pants and shirt. Still under the gentle influence of the tea. "A little bit of mystery's fine by me. Getting used to it ever since I came to this crazed planet. I'm doing weird sexplay with a witch, my cousin's some kind of high-tech spy, and I work on a language I don't understand."

Karita's soft laugh filled the room momentarily. "Welcome to the world, bright child. Far from home."


I could only shake my head in wonder, laughing to myself as I sat in the moonlit solarium a few minutes later, reviewing what had just happened, what I felt about it, what any of this weirdness meant. My final comment to Karita had been a throwaway line, a bit of flip cynical lightheartedness meant at most to cover my confusion. But as I thought it over I realized I meant every word.

I picked up the copy of *The Prince* that lay on the coffee table before me. Meant to start reading it a few days ago, still hadn't begun. I hefted the book, staring at the vague outlines of what was supposed to be Machiavelli's face, drawn in a carefully casual style, red on a black background. And laughed aloud as I tossed the book back on the table with a satisfying plop. Witches and weird sex and pointless work in LA, none of which can fit any goddamn pattern I can conceive. "What would you say to this, Machiavel?" I asked aloud, the resonance of my words strangely lingering in the quiet house. After-effect of the tea, I thought. I went to bed and slept dreamlessly for the first time since I'd come to LA.

The weekend passed uneventfully; I saw Karita only from my bedroom window as she sped off somewhere in her Beemer early Saturday afternoon. Hayden arrived home late Sunday, tired again. I asked him how his friend was and he said only "Fine, a bit under the weather or something" but his tone belied his words: there was some undercurrent of reticence, something withheld. I didn't press. After a few generalities we both retired.

A few days later Hayden came home much later than usual and paused on his way to bed only long enough to tell me he'd be leaving for Atlanta again first thing in the morning. The next day found another card from Karita under my windshield, this one with a strange hieroglyph of some sort drawn in red ink on the back. I got the hint, leaving work early enough that day to make sure I made it this time to the Golden Oak.


I've been in my share of unusual stores – you can't be from the Humboldt area and not have been – so I knew what to expect from a witchcraft/New Age supply store: spacey electronic trance music, ranked jars of incense, black drapery, tacky jewelry, florid posters in overwrought Maxfield Parrish style, crystals, books with lurid covers or pretentious titles written by people with silly pseudonyms like Starhawke and Lady Aragon Mirabella. What I did not expect was what I found in the Golden Oak when I finally went inside late that afternoon.

The decor was not 70s leftover or even 70s retro; the predominant colors were sand and light grey, the music at the moment was Ottmar Liebert, and the artwork, hung and lighted gallery style, was in quality orders of magnitude beyond the lurid rainbow-hued silliness of most fantasy artist wannabees whose work cluttered the walls of typical New Age stores. I was struck by one piece in particular, a large multimedia piece dominated by copper spirals, torched wood and what appeared to be torn aluminum cans, and was eyeing it closely when I was startled by a sound behind me. From a back room issued Karita and another woman, very small, very pale, razor thin, her brown hair crew-cut short except for a pencil-thin pony tail reaching halfway down her back. She was dressed in faded black jeans, a worn baggy black T-shirt, even more worn camo vest, and carried a battered artist's portfolio case. Someone trying to sell some pieces, I guessed.

Karita saw me and immediately moved toward me, drawing the small woman along with her by the hand. I briefly registered a look of discomfort on the woman's face before I turned my attention to Karita.

"Merry meet, and good timing," she said. "This is Summer Despite," Karita said, pronouncing it *despot*. She introduced me. "Summer was just leaving and I'm glad you can meet her. She's a special friend and one of our artists. That piece there" – I followed Karita's gaze more out of politeness than interest, until I saw she was indicating the piece I was just admiring – "is hers."

"Nice to meet you," I said automatically, extending my hand while wondering at Karita's knack for knowing people with unusual names. "I was just looking at that piece. Very nice."

Summer looked at me briefly, an expression of something like pain or contempt on her face, then turned to Karita. "Merry part, love," she rasped curtly, and was out the door while my hand was still out, leaving me feeling somewhere between pissed off and overtly stupid.

"Whoa," I said when the door had closed behind her. "Carrying the sensitive artist thing a bit far, I would think."

"No." Karita shook her head, her eyes lingering on the door. Then she turned to me, and I felt again that almost palpable caress of her eyes. I'd have forgotten Summer if Karita hadn't continued.

"You'll have to excuse Summer. She's had a rough life, and until recently she'd been working out some serious personal issues by getting rather deep into a pretty radical strain of feminism. You've heard of the Lesbian Avengers?"

I nodded, though I wasn't sure I had.

"Sometimes she makes them look like the Junior League. She often makes it a point to offend men, and lately things have been worse for her than usual. She lost her regular job so she had to give up her therapy, and that's been difficult. Now she's lost her apartment, sleeping on a couch at Jazz's. On top of all of that, I'm afraid I've made the situation even worse, at least as far as you're concerned."

"Made what worse? Whaddya mean?"

"Well," she said slowly, and I could feel the moment taking a turn toward the serious, "I've mentioned you a few times in Summer's presence."

"Yeah?"

Karita glanced again at the door, back at me, then taking me by the hand stepped toward the rear of the store.

"Summer has been my lover, and only three or four weeks ago I put our relationship on a different footing. Summer hasn't been happy with that, and I'm afraid you may catch some of the fallout."

I shook my head for a second. "Ok, wait a minute. You're a lesbian? But I, last week – "

Karita took my hand again, smiled mock-sadly. "Poor northern child, raised by wolves." She shook her head.

I got it. "OK, OK, but you – you just surprised me, that's all." I really wasn't that flustered, or wouldn't have been under normal circumstances, whatever those might be. "I don't have any problem with that."

"I know," she said softly. "Otherwise you wouldn't even be here."

I nodded, taking her meaning. "OK, I just, well, I just wasn't expecting this kind of stuff today."

"Oh," Karita grinned. "Shoulda laid it on you next week, huh?"

I nodded, grinning back. "Next week I'da been ready, yeah."

Then serious. "I want to ask you a favor, though, about Summer."

"Ask. I promise I won't beat her up or anything."

"Don't even joke like that," she said, her voice suddenly firm. "She can be rough around the edges, and this is a tough time for her. I need to be there – want to be there – for her in many ways, so you may see her from time to time. I want to ask you to be very patient with her. With a sign like yours patience is not always easy, but Summer will need to be treated carefully. Let her have her say when she needs to; talking out her pain will help."

"OK, I promise. I won't bite. I've known radical feminists at Humboldt and stuff, and it's not like I'm a Young Republican or anything."

Karita nodded almost absently. "Summer's struggling with a lot of bitterness right now. And she wouldn't like it if she knew I told you, but I think it'll help you understand her and be patient with her if you know why. I told you she had a tough life; as a child she was abused for years by her stepfather, and even with years of therapy she still has a great deal of anger and pain." Karita paused, visibly steeling herself. "Then, a little over a year ago, she was gang-raped and beaten." A pause, and I felt her withdraw, move within some inner place I suspected I would never reach. "The details aren't important now, but I wanted you to know at least the outline."

"Shit." I honestly felt sorry for Summer, for the first and last time in my life. "Is she mad at you for breaking off your relationship? I guess it meant a lot to her during her recovery."

"That's when it began, and that has something to do with why it's ended. It's complicated – but you should also know that Summer has never been interested in men, and I have had women lovers before her, and will have others again." Another pause. "You've heard of synchronicity?"

"Yeah, sure, Carl Jung – and Sting."

"The time was right for Summer and me to stop as lovers, and you must have been the reason."

Our conversation was cut short by the muted electronic chime of the door sensor: two women, early-middle-aged yuppie academic types with serious demeanors, conspicuously graying hair and expensively casual clothes. The kind of folks I always automatically distrust: people who take themselves very seriously. The kind, I realized even as Karita bid me goodbye with a lingering touch on my arm, that may well have been the lifeblood of her business. I left quickly.


Karita was incommunicado the next few days; at least, I got no answer at her front door or calls returning the messages I left for her at the Oak, and time passed slowly. I explored Glendora Hills and the university, drove into the mountains only to be repulsed by the crowds and the thick miasma of smog that filled the spreading valley below. My job was quickly acquiring the patina of drudge work and Hayden's absence kept things quiet around the house: chores, reading, thinking, desultory attempts at writing. Nothing really catching fire. I managed to begin my journal, trying to make sense out of Karita and LA and myself. Hopeless all around, I was beginning to suspect.

Then Sunday afternoon Hayden returned. And paradise, so newly promised and only barely glimpsed, began to fade. And still no sense of foreboding.

I'd been away from the house for awhile on account of an open house, and as I pulled back into the driveway that afternoon my jaw dropped: a huge dent in the passenger side of Hayden's car, his beloved and pampered Porsche – a deep and ugly metallic crater, paint scraped to grey undercoat and polished steel. Jesus shit, I thought. Hayden is going to be pissed. He loved that car like only an unsexed technophile can. Damn.

It got worse.

I felt it the moment I walked into the house. Tension, something seriously askew, tectonically out of place; surprisingly I found myself thinking of Karita and her reaction to the house. "Christ, Hayden, it's only a car," I muttered, trying to steel myself for the inevitable. I heard a splash through the open patio door. By the pool. I stepped quickly outside.

And saw what made the splash: centered below the ripples on the pool's surface was a beer bottle, drifting with a comically exaggerated rocking motion toward the bottom. Other bottles were already down there, three of them, resting on their sides or rolling slightly with the pool's currents, deformed aquatic creatures from some demented nature show.

A noise from the poolhouse told me where Hayden was. I opened my mouth to call out but just then Hayden stepped through the doorway, and I froze, my words forgotten. Something was obviously wrong: the tension in his face, the set of his jaw, the narrowing of his eyes – like nothing I'd ever seen. Like no one I'd ever known.

He raised his bottle when he saw me, the classic drinker's salute, and the remote mocking irony was obvious from where I stood. I've never seen Hayden drink in anything other than the most casual way, and rarely more than a few swallows; he now tossed off half a bottle of St. Pauli Girl in a single swig.

Then laughed softly, at nothing, at some half-recognized despair, at the blue distance, and lobbed his half-full bottle into the pool. Only he didn't throw it far enough and the bottle caught the edge of the coping, shattering with a dull thwack and a spray of golden liquid and green glass. Incongruously, I wondered how we were going to get the glass shards out of the pool.

Hayden mumbled something and returned to the storage room. From inside he swore loudly. Surprise and curiosity surrendered instantly to anxiety and I started briskly toward the sound of his voice. Only to come up short as Hayden popped out of the doorway, another bottle in hand, just as I stepped onto the threshold. He pledged me again with his beer.

"Hayden, what's up? What are you doing? The pool – " I stopped short as I noticed blood trickling from a cut on his thumb, drops of deep scarlet pooling on the concrete below. "You're bleeding." I looked around for a rag or towel.

"Stand back," Hayden said with a sharpness, almost an edge of panic in his voice, that caught me off-guard. "I'll clean it up."

I moved a half-step back onto the patio. "What's going on, man? What's the matter? It's just a few drops of blood."

"It can fucking kill you, that's what's the matter." Hayden practically spit the words at me, then suddenly hung his head, shook it as if to awaken from a clinging dream. He raised his eyes to my face but it seemed to take him several moments to focus, even to recognize me.

"Sorry," he said; "I'm pissed off, I know, and I'm over-reacting, but let me clean this up. I just cut myself on the bottle cap, being clumsy and drunk, but I don't want you to clean it up. No need to take the risk."

"Whatever," I said as Hayden set his beer carefully on the floor and pulled out a handkerchief to staunch the flow of blood. "But it's no problem. I – wait, what do you mean, 'kill me'?"

Hayden shook his head as he stepped out of the pool room, carefully locking the door behind him. "Well, little cuz, it seems I owe you an apology," he said slowly, walking unsteadily toward the house. "You came for fun and life lessons and I'm afraid I've brought you death lessons instead." He paused at the edge of the redwood deck, sitting down heavily, tension shaping the contours of his face.

"Death lessons? What are – did someone die, Hayden? Your parents, are they – "

"No, no one's died. Not yet. And it's not my parents." He set down his beer, turned to face me, his eyes red and everything about him radiating a tense weariness. "I was going to explain this to you in the next week or two, after you'd been here a while and I had a better sense of how best to do it, but, ah, it appears the timetable has changed."

Nervously, not even realizing he did it, he clamped his free hand firmly around his wrapped thumb, squeezed it fiercely. His gaze shifted between me and the hilltop across the canyon. Someone there was running a lawnmower.

"To begin with, I'm gay."

I looked at him evenly, shrugged. "So? I – why did you think you had to break that to me like it was some awful thing?" I was genuinely miffed. "I don't care about that at all, man. You – "

He silenced me with a wave. "I gave you enough credit on that account; as I said, that's only the beginning. I'm also HIV positive."

"AIDS? Hayden, you have AIDS?"

"No. Listen to me: I'm HIV positive. I carry the virus that causes AIDS, known about it for almost 3 years now, but I have no symptoms. I'm lucky," he added bitterly, "because I'm one of the tiny percentage of HIV positive people who are symptom-free without being on any meds or antiretroviral therapy. Long-term non-progressor, they call us; with a high T-cell count and very low HIV levels, we're likely never to get AIDS and no one knows why."

I nodded to cover my confusion, my mind racing. Somewhere in there I must have had some stupid thoughts, for when my eyes came to rest on the pool Hayden spoke sharply. "And don't worry, you can't get AIDS from the pool. You probably wouldn't even get it from cleaning up the blood, but no need to take that chance. And no, you can't get it from using dishes and glasses, which I always put in the dishwasher anyway, as I hope you noticed."

"Hey, I know all that — I — look, you're just takin' me by surprise here, and this bothers me only because you're my cousin, you're family, and you could —" I paused, not knowing how to say what I was thinking.

Hayden help up his hand again, imperious in his trauma which, I realized with a start, he hadn't yet explained. "I'm not dying," he finished for me, "and won't be anytime soon. What has most immediately gone wrong is that my partner, Joshua, is dying, now. He was diagnosed with Kaposi's sarcoma some months ago, and won't be alive a few months from now. Thought he was protecting me with his damn secrecy."

"That's what your Atlanta trips are about, then?"

"In part. Some real business, too, but yeah, mostly him."

"I'm sorry, man. I wish I knew what to say. Never really lost anyone — like that. Just a coupla grandparents, and that's not the same thing, I know."

Hayden's strained expression told me he knew.

"I don't know what to say," I repeated, proving my point. "Especially since I don't know the, I mean, it's gotta be tough enough, and – "

"Quit while you're only this far behind, cuz," Hayden said, but without rancor. "I know what you mean: hard enough to lose someone when you're straight, imagine what it must be like when you're gay. But it's not different. It's the same pain anyone would feel, same grief, same anger, same despair. Our hearts are as human as the rest of us." He paused, a bitterly wicked grin flashing across his face. "'If you prick us do we not bleed?'" He lifted his bottle to his lips but paused at the point of drinking, set the bottle down gently. "I shouldn't even be drinking," he said more than half to himself.

"I'm sorry, Hayden, for my stupidity and for your pain. If there's anything I can do, let me know."

"I appreciate that. In fact I may have to impose on you a bit. I'll be out of town more than I thought now, so you'll have to do more of the work around here, I'm afraid. I'll do what I can when I'm here, but with this and my project – "

I waved him off. "Forget about it, man. I'll take care of things here – hell, it's not like there's that much to do anyway. No problem."

He nodded his silent thanks.


There was palpable change after that. Hayden contracted, in a way, losing a good measure of his sense of humor, his sense even of presence. He's not an imposing physical figure but his intelligence and intellectual dynamism have always been forward, as though he radiated some elusive form of mental energy. But not now. He started giving me the impression he could be overlooked in an otherwise-empty room. He worked more, ate less, said little. The next three weekends in a row he spent in Atlanta, and between that and the longer workdays he was pretty much off my radar.

Karita wasn't, though. I sought her out a lot after Hayden's disclosure, and although I now knew where to find her I never felt comfortable getting into personal discussions in the Oak. For one thing the place was busier than I expected; while I never once saw anyone actually buy anything it was rare for ten minutes to pass without someone coming in, and every few days there would be new pieces of artwork on the walls, new titles on the shelves. In a small semi-public conference room next door she often hosted seminars and guest speakers, what she called "gatherings" for holistic workshops or discussions of New Age spirituality, Wicca, feminism, whatever. But for over a week I couldn't catch her at home; twice she failed to appear, as promised, for dinner.

I began to get frustrated. Partly for the sex, of course, but more because I needed to talk to someone. I couldn't call my folks, for though Hayden told me his parents had known for years of his homosexuality I had never been able to ask him if I should mention it to mine. Just felt like an awkward question, schoolyardish in some vague way but a question I needed or wanted to avoid nonetheless. What I most needed was to talk to Karita, who I realized was becoming important to me in ways I wasn't sure I grasped yet but who I knew would be someone who would understand. At first I was surprised, thinking back on it, that she took such a quick dislike to Hayden, but on second thought I realized my first thought was a stupid one: just because she's bi doesn't mean she has to discover a soulmate in every gay man she comes across.

But it wasn't Karita I ended up talking to about this. Apparently I had some profound psychological need to dig myself into a deeper hole than the one I was already in.

And I succeeded.

About a week after Hayden's revelation and a day after Karita again failed to show for dinner (but left a note on my truck windshield saying only "Sorry bright child / The Mother's business") I was working later than usual. Scrambling to meet some self-imposed deadline, Professor S-B was pushing me (and herself, to tell truth) pretty hard to complete a section of stories that had some relation to a conference presentation she was about to make. I'd long since given up trying to understand the details of what she was doing, which seemed always to have some impossibly byzantine relation to a series of NSF grants, conferences, journal deadlines, sabbatical applications, special arrangements with the Provost and god knows what other bureaucratic bullshit. It was nearly five o'clock and the building was quiet as a tomb – standard for a commuter campus in summer – so I was startled by the knock on my half-open office door, banging my knee pretty hard against the underside of the desk as I jumped in my surprise.

"So you're the source of all the difficulty," I heard a female voice say.

And the instant I turned around I knew I was in trouble.

She wasn't attractive in a mainstream sort of way, I suppose, but then the pursuit of conventional beauty is far too cliché to be my style. She was, well, a Japanese-American version of my style: nearly my height, very bright root-beer-brown eyes, slightly rounded face, thick wedge-cut hair as black as one of Poe's worst moods, "pneumatic" (I love that from *Brave New World*) but with grace, vaguely upscale punkish in an academic-feminist way – she reminded me, ancestry aside, a little bit of Sandy, although Sandy could never have gotten away with such earrings, or so many of them. I must have been looking at her like the dope I was, for she looked at me evenly and said "Did I shock you or are you always this introverted?"

"Ah, both, I think," I stammered, rising like the dutiful child I once was. "What difficulty?" I managed. And then, slowly regaining use of my brain, "Whatever it was I didn't mean it, probably."

"Famous last words," she said, taking a step into the room. "I'm Kyoko. Starting second-year TA in English." Her handshake was very firm.

I introduced myself, again asking what I had done.

She leaned back out the door, glancing in both directions down the hallway. "Looks safe enough," she said quietly. Yet she closed the door before dropping into the only other chair in the room.

"Has S-B given you any heads-up about the politics around here?" she asked bluntly, her gaze steady and direct. I half-registered a twinge of guilt as I thought about Karita, her eyes capable of the same sense of penetration and dominating presence.

"No," I said. "She's pretty focused. But I'm glad to hear you call her that too."

"Everyone does," she said dismissively. "I didn't think she

would, 'cause that's not the sort she is. But from what I hear you're about to run into some good old-fashioned petty academic politics, if that isn't redundant, which it is."

"How? I mean, I haven't done anything; I don't even go here. Hell, you're the first person in the Department I've met except for the secretary and the Chair and S-B."

"You didn't need to do anything. You're here, S-B's famous, we have a crazy lady in this Department and a worthless Dean. That's the only problem: bad chemistry and worse luck."

"Whoa," I said, raising my hands defensively. "I kept out of that faculty warfare crap at Humboldt, and I sure don't want to get involved now. I'm only here another six or eight weeks anyway. Going to the doctoral CW program at Iowa." I'm not quite sure why I felt like bragging.

"Well, it might be that you'll be headed to The Bland Land sooner than you think," she said. I was beginning to feel a bit uncomfortable, wondering if perhaps she wasn't a bit of a crazy lady herself, barging in here and laying irrelevant political crap on me. I was beginning to think maybe she wasn't so interesting-looking after all.

"You probably think I'm crazy myself," she said, and not for the first time did I feel my world realign itself with a slight but insistent jerk, "but I'm just pissed at the way grad students like us keeping getting turned into pawns, and it seems to me you're in an especially exposed situation. Thought I'd try to help."

"I appreciate it," I said, not at all sure that I really did, "but I still don't know what's going on, what I've done, or how you know about all this."

"Like I said, I'm a second-year TA here. Did my BA here, too, so I've been around these folks for a while." Then she grinned, wickedly. "Doesn't hurt that the Dean's secretary's my aunt."

I laughed.

"But," she continued, instantly serious, "you may have kicked the hornet's nest without meaning too. What are you doing here, anyway?"

I pointed to the computer and began trying to explain the project but she waved me down. "No, no, what are you doing in this department, in Southern California. You have your MA, I know, you say you're going to Iowa soon, so why are you here?"

I explained, hastily, the housesitting and my thesis director's old friendship with S-B and my enrolling as an unclassified grad student to get the job.

"Bad karma, I guess," she said. "Look, S-B gets a lot of what she wants around here, you know?"

"Yeah, I saw her vita. Part of a grant application she had me print up for her; thing went on for pages. Hell of a scholar, even if I don't understand a word of it."

Kyoko nodded. "She's big-time. International rep. If it weren't for her husband's job teaching at UCLA she'd have moved on years ago. Just another victim of the patriarchal academic culture, ya know?" The wicked grin flashed quickly. I nodded with as much apparent sagacity and compassion as I could muster at the moment.

"Anyway," she continued, "her rep gives her a lot of clout with the Provost, who's a dim bulb but knows grant money when he smells it, and S-B brings in buckets. So she gets leave, release time, sabbaticals. Never costs the university anything, but that's not the point. Point is we have our own honest-to-goddess madwoman in the attic up on the third floor. Lit professor named Hilda Finkhel. You haven't met her, huh?"

I shook my head. "No, I'd definitely remember if I met someone with a name like that," I said, smiling.

"Yeah. Old Midwestern ditz, drank her brains away years ago. Students can't stand her; even the undergrads can tell she's an idiot. Ain't tenure wonderful? Anyway, she and the Humanities Dean – you met him?"

"No."

"Luck's on your side. You met *anybody* here?"

"Like I said, just S-B, the Chair once, couple of secretaries, friendly woman named Virginia in the personnel office, you. That's it."

"Anyway, Finkhel and the Dean, who probably have a combined IQ of 100, are very good pals. *Very* good, according to some, though personally I try not to think about that."

I nodded. And thought, shit, I don't need this same old.

"When Finkhel found out S-B pulled strings to get you a job here she went ballistic. Seems she has her first grad student disciple in a billion years, and he's such a screw-up they wouldn't hire him as a TA and no one wanted him as a research assistant or anything. But Finkhel figures he should have your job, and now she's making a stink with the Dean, who's passed the buck in the direction of the Provost, who has the backbone of a jellyfish. And you're in the line of fire."

"That's ridiculous. I'm here for only the summer; this whole arrangement was temporary from the start; S-B told me she got a waiver signed by the Graduate Dean and the personnel people had no problems with it. We got all that clear, I thought."

She shook her head, rising slowly. "Leave logic out of it, this is academia. Finkhel's close to unbalanced, everyone knows it, and she can be nasty. I'll spare you the details, for a million different reasons, but I just wanted you to know the fire's lit underneath your kettle. And don't underestimate the cowardice of academic bureaucrats, or their lack of principle. Your job's on the line. And S-B's leaving for a conference next week, right? So you won't have anyone on campus in your corner. Not, I think, that it would matter much at this point."

I stood, since she was obviously leaving, wanting to say something because I suddenly had the urge to see her again but I was confused by thoughts of Karita and even more by what Kyoko'd been telling me. "Thanks for the warning. I have to admit we never had to get involved in this kind of crap at Humboldt. Must've gone on, I guess, but we never knew."

She arched an eyebrow. "You guys raised by wolves up there or something? No academic politics, huh? How do you get prepared for the profession?" She snorted. "Hell, what do you do for fun?"

And then my brain kicked into gear without bothering to give me any advance notice. "We go out to dinner. Join me?" I said, surprising myself – not even sure, for a moment, who had spoken. Where the hell did that come from? I wondered, even as the reverberations still lingered.

I surprised her too, and she took no pains to hide it. There was an awkward moment, and with surprise I felt that electric intimation of hollowness you feel when you're a split second away from being rejected. Then she flashed a smile captivating in its elegant asymmetry. "Yeah, if you think you can handle it."

"Sure," I said, having no clue as to what she meant.

She nodded. "How about Friday?"

"Sounds great."

"How about I meet you here, five o'clock?"

I was scheduled to work only until two, but said "Sure, perfect."

"OK. I know a good place. I can fill you in on the rest of the dirt."


Only it wasn't the rest of the departmental gossip I got that Friday. Well, yes, actually it was, but I did most of the talking somehow, fueled by the two-for-one Cuervo margaritas we drank in the bar of a hillside restaurant called the Pomona Valley Mining Company, both of us getting half-drunk and discovering a mutual love of Jamaica Kincaid's fiction and Elizabeth Bishop's poetry and watching the traffic snarl and clog and crawl on I-10 below us, a dense lethargic ballet of glinting metal and slow poison. After a couple hours of drinks and appetizers Kyoko directed me to the foothills where we found a spot she knew from her high school days, a dusty turnout where we parked the car and hiked up the firebreak of a nearby hill. The fire ring and the piles of trash – discarded beer cans, junk food wrappers, used condoms – attested to the popularity of the place, but at the moment we had it to ourselves.

I'd told her about Hayden during dinner, told her more than I'd intended to about myself and the weird sense of being unanchored that had so far been the defining element of my summer in LA. She hadn't said much at the time, shared the pain of a friend's death in a motorcycle accident three years ago, seemed very understanding. As we sat on a rough granite block and watched the jewel-grid of the valley lights struggle through the sunset curtain of smog she returned to the theme, asking me why I'd come to LA, why I'd accepted Hayden's invitation.

I told her about Hayden's "life lessons" comment. She nodded understandingly, the soft clang of her metallic earrings audible in the warm dusk.

"Good choice for a writer," she said. "Guess you got what you came for." She snorted her laugh. "Like those old Greek oracles, you know? Tell you what you're gonna get and it sounds wonderful, but then it works itself out in some awful way and someone hands you your head."

I laughed despite the small wave of melancholy that rose up at the thought of Hayden's comment. "I have to admit this business about Hayden's kind of depressing. He's a weird guy but he is my cousin, an' I feel pretty sorry for him. Bad enough not being able to live your life the way you want 'cause a shit you have no control over, now he's gotta suffer for it too. Seems like he's gettin' cheated outta the main part of the deal."

"He's got a lot of company," Kyoko said, turning to look at me with a directness evident even in the gathering gloom. "Don't forget them."

"No, no, I realize that," I said, feeling a kind of juvenile earnestness rise up within. "It's a shitty situation." Then, realizing I had nothing else to say about it, "I wish I could do somethin' for him, but there's not much I could do under the best of circumstances, and now, ever since I've been in LA, I mean, it's like it's all I can do to not lose my own bearings." I turned to Kyoko and smiled. "You live in a crazy place, ma'am," I drawled.

She punched me lightly on the arm. "You live in a crazier place, Mr. Humboldt-to-Iowa-via-LA."

"And where might that be, pray tell, m'lady?" I said in my best – well, maybe not my best, after the margaritas – Renaissance manner.

"In the big inbetween, the wild meanwhile. You pulled up anchor and sailed into a whirlpool, so don't wonder if the lighthouse isn't in sight."

I looked at her a minute, my brain laboring to dredge up something. It came to me. "You read much Poe?"

She gave me a sour look. "That little boy lit? Hell, no. Get outta here. Gimme Djuna Barnes an' HD any day." And took a playful punch at me again, which I ducked and blocked, causing her to fall across me. I caught her, and as my hands closed around her upper arms – surprisingly firm muscle – I registered again, instantly and without effort, the quiet assertion of those libidinal energies Karita also called forth. I had always cultivated a contempt for those men, those overgrown boys, who pursued a lot of women for the sake of sex only, who thought a lot about sex, let it rule their lives; I've never been a prude and have always, if I can be pardoned the pun, risen to the occasion, but to foreground sexual pursuit, to let it loom so large, was always anathema to me, demeaning, not worth the sacrifice of so much else. So the meat markets and the smooth moves were never my domain, but when Kyoko fell across me it was the most natural thing in the world that I would kiss her. And her response was real but, I could instantly tell, restrained and limited, her energies held close in some way. Is this me suddenly living out some standup comedy routine, I thought, the lust-crazed male who'll pursue any woman who gets within arm's reach?  Have I suddenly become a cliché, a joke?

Somewhere these thoughts registered although at the moment I sought only to make some elemental connection, to pour energy, need, longing into this woman who attracted me but who I barely knew and to will her to have sex with me, make love with me.  This was a part of me I did not well recognize, at least not in this situation, but I cannot deny what I then was.

Kyoko pulled back, gracefully and with a laughing exhale, and as I moved toward her she put a hand firmly on my chest, stopping me in midbreath.

"I was right," she said with an arch smile.  "You *were* raised by wolves."

I took a deep breath, seeking control, mostly found it.  "No," I said, forcing a smile as I swept my hand toward the valley lights below us.  "It's the magic of lotus land: earthquakes and smog and Cuervo and a captivating woman – " I stopped quickly, wondering at the unbidden thought that I should apologize, thought better of it.  "It's a strange alchemy, and I find you interesting and attractive and – "

"Stop while you're only this far behind."  She stood, smoothing her clothes.  "I like you, Mr. Northern Exposure, and I think you mean well and I feel sorry for you what with your cousin and the crazy lady after your job, but I can't help you in the strange alchemy department. I – "

"I know, I know," said, rising also, feigning an injured weariness I did not really feel.  "I'm only here a few more weeks and you have a boyfriend and I think I'm some slickass – "

"Actually," she said, a hint of archness in her tone, "it's nothing to do with you at all."  I strained to read her expression in the starlight but could see little.  "And it has nothing to do with a boyfriend."

She paused; I waited.

Her wicked meteor grin in the moonlight.  "It's my girlfriend I'm worried about; Sammi's a third *dan* black belt and she just might tear off your head."  She grinned again, faster, more wicked still.  "And I don't mean the one on your shoulders."

I laughed despite my confusion, or maybe to cover it.  "I'm only a green belt, so I surrender."  Then, more seriously, "I'm obviously a rube in the land of the operators here, 'cause you're the second woman I've met since I've been in LA who has really caught my attention but turned out to not be straight."  I decided not to explain any further about Karita, but that decision made me realize something. "When I kissed you, I thought you responded, and since you had agreed to go out to dinner, and suggested coming up here...." My voice trailed off as Kyoko's soft laugh spread across the hilltop.

"Raised by *stone-age* wolves, no less," she said. "Shit. Come on, ace, since you seem to be missing so much on a regular basis I'll explain on the way to the car." She set off surefooted down the firebreak we had ascended, talking all the while as I followed a few paces behind. "In this century we have a new math: dinner no longer equals fuck. I went out with you tonight because my instincts told me you were a good person who needed a connection, and my instincts are never wrong." She halted abruptly, flashed the grin over her shoulder at me. "Sometimes things get a little garbled in the translation, though. Your idea of connection was about three feet below mine. But I still think you're alright, for a straight white male."

"Thanks," I said wryly, watching my footing as I followed her down the rock-strewn firebreak. It hadn't seemed this steep coming up.

Kyoko started forward again then halted almost immediately. I came up beside her to see her pointing down toward the traffic turnout where we had parked my car. Another vehicle, an old VW bug, was in the turnout, lights out but engine running and parked just a few inches away from my truck. There'd be no way to get in on the driver's side. I was still wondering just what was going on when the VeeDub's engine roared and the car quickly scooted backwards, its lights still out, and headed down toward the main road back to the valley. We never saw its lights come on.


With Karita absent and Hayden in Atlanta again the weekend crawled by. I finally managed to spend a lot of time writing in my journal, hoping to begin making sense of something but really only coming to a clearer sense of my confusion. Rudderless in the sea of stars.... I finished reading Wordsworth's *The Excursion*, reading being the only thing coming easily to me now it seemed; I cleaned the house and yard thoroughly, left during an open house and got lost looking for a used bookstore I'd seen written up in the *LA Times*, a subscription to which Mrs. P had kept up – not so much for us, as Hayden explained, but because Mrs. P felt that a paper in the driveway helped make the house look occupied.  What, I wondered, were housesitters for?

I spent Monday half-hoping Kyoko would stop by the office, though I wasn't sure why.  Maybe I needed some closure to Friday night, needed to somehow force something to make sense.  Hell, a lot of things need to make sense around here, I thought.  But Kyoko never showed, and in a state of increasing frustration I overcame my reluctance to see Karita at her shop.

She was with customers when I walked in, so I stepped over to the bookshelves to wait.  I picked up a copy of *When God was a Woman*, a book I owned but had never quite gotten around to reading, and was a couple of pages into the introduction when Karita touched me on the shoulder.  The customers had gone and over Karita's shoulder I noticed the closed sign was up.

Karita kissed me lightly on the cheek.

"You've been scarce the past few days," I said casually.  Karita's look was carefully neutral, almost vague; she said nothing.  I went on, "I don't mean to crowd your space or anything, but I was hoping we could talk.  Some bad news about Hayden."

"Come," she said, taking my hand and leading me to the back, into her office, where I had not been before.  It looked much like the store itself except for the piles of paper, in various stages of disarray, covering the desk and shelves.  But my attention was arrested by the small cubicle across from her office, where two computers sat humming.

"High-tech witchcraft, huh?" I asked, gesturing to the machines.

"One's for accounting and inventory,  the other's mainly for our email list and stuff."

"Wicca mail, huh?  Cool."

"Not just Wicca.  Homeopathy, alternative healing, communal sympathy, psi powers—everything in the Mother's world, including the art and literature that celebrate it.  Jazz and Simone are the computer experts."  She slipped into a chair, gestured me toward the other.  "Your cousin.  He's ill?"

"Worse than that," I said, my attention all on her now.  She looked tired, somehow; the lines around her eyes, maybe the fluorescent lights. . . .  For maybe the first time since I'd met her she really looked like someone in her mid-thirties.  Not that I knew, I suddenly realized, how old she actually was.  I shook it off, told her about Hayden.

I don't know what I expected; not much, I guess, given the sort of instinctive dislike she took to Hayden, but wondering if her own non-mainstream sexual preference might prevail, might be enough of a nexus that she felt some compassion for him. But I was surprised by her silence, the long pause during which her gaze was turned in my direction but focused nowhere I could ever see.

After more than a minute of silence, and with the suddenness of an unexpected gunshot, Karita focused and looked at me directly, the pressure of her gaze nearly palpable. "Speaking of webs, the whole world's a tangled skein of powers and energies," she said, her voice soft but backed with adamantine conviction. I could hear, with a strange clarity, the rustle of her clothes, the clink of her jewelry as she shifted slightly, a noise from the street. "A vast interweave of forces, most of which we can't sense at all, or even imagine; some of which we glimpse imperfectly, a handful of which our science detects and measures to its pompous self-satisfaction. The rest of those forces are magic and mystery, ghosts and dreams and love, and most people are content to leave them to the artists and the nutcases and go their merry way thinking they know all they need to know and all that matters."

"And you?" I asked, not quite sure what I was asking but knowing it sounded right despite the fact she seemed to be ignoring what I'd just told her about Hayden.

Her eyes unfocused again. When she spoke her voice was even softer than before, the merest shadow of velvet.

"I'm like you in some ways," she said, looking not at me but at a point somewhere no human map could ever show. "Lost between the threads of the material web."

"That doesn't seem right to me, but if it is, that such a bad thing?"

A half-rueful smile. "Not bad, not good – just is. Like the color of someone's skin, like the death in an amanita mushroom, like the arc of a wave. Live with it, die with it." She glanced at me quickly. "I'd rather live there than anywhere else I see people living." Her eyes took in the world. "Living on the flow of power, living off the blood of the living – oh yes, much better to hang between the threads of the web. Besides, we don't really have a choice."

"Yeah." I nodded but not even close to sure I understood. " Does this have something to do with my cousin dying of AIDS?"

"I thought you said he was HIV positive."

"Yeah, that's what I meant."

She nodded abstractly. "You know, I don't think you told me about Hayden because of Hayden. You told me because of you. *That's* what I'm talking about. You, between the threads, like an artist living in the vacant spaces left over from the world's business, but a newcomer there." She smiled, sadly. "Poor northern child. With my eyes your cousin looks like a worldly fool and if you expect me to care about him you'll have to be disappointed, but your pain I register. Only it's not really pain." She shifted forward in her chair, almost rising from it, her eyes glittering. "Your cousin's loss is part of your childhood's end, part of your summer. You're the English major, you know the symbolism: summer is the early ripeness of adulthood, the journey beyond the village bounds, the young man's pride in his erect phallus and the maiden's budding desire to bear children. The blood rites that mark our passage to full membership in the tribe, however lost it might be. Hayden's illness is part of you, part of your passage. See it for what it is. Be like a swimmer when she comes to the wall: push off from it, turn it from barrier to benefit."

I shook my head, wondering again where she came up with this stuff. "Yeah," I said slowly, "I see what you're saying, but this is my cousin, after all. It's not like, 'Well, Hayden, sorry you got AIDS but at least it's a life lesson for me.' As odd and distant as he is he's family, you know; it hurts me to think he might be dying. Although I guess he isn't. But he's hurting, he's losing someone he seems to love deeply. So it hurts me too, in a way."

"Of course it does," she said earnestly. "I'm not saying you shouldn't hurt or care and I'm not saying anything can or should change that. The pain's real and nothing anyone can say can alter it or shield you from it in any way. All you can do is face it. That's my point. But don't let it stop you; don't let the pain become a refuge, a hiding place." She shifted even further forward, her voice dropping. "I know you, northern lover; I have bound you to myself for this short time and I know you are such that a pain like this could freeze you in your tracks. You could drink beer for a month and rage at the world and feel righteous in your anger – don't look like that, you know you have it in you – and when you were done you'd have done nothing but wasted a month of your time and the Mother knows how much of your psychic capital. And I don't want to see you do that. Accept the pain and acknowledge it fully but let it pass through you, let it pass on into the well of experience where it will remain with you forever but not impede your progress. This summer is a crux moment for us both and all cruxes are supremely delicate; they can be undone by a look, a whisper, a glass of wine. Stay with the path you've begun to follow."

"I thought you said I was living in the wrong house."

"Not the right house for you, sure, but it's a fair price to pay for the season – if you're careful and work to stay on the right path."

"You sound like you know what's happening to me this summer," I said. "I'd appreciate it if you'd let me in on the secret. I'm starting to feel like a whitewater rafter heading for some unmapped falls without his paddle."

A trace of a smile, the merest hint, crossed Karita's face. "You're better off than that; you've given yourself to the moment, like the dancer who's given herself to the dance so thoroughly she doesn't need to think about the steps; they come as they are meant to, as they must. Follow where the season leads; trust the flow of forces to take you where you need to go, even when the road looks dark beneath the boughs. Trust your strength, be true to it."

She paused, and for a moment we simply stared at each other, me trying as usual to understand how she knew to address me in words that didn't quite make sense on the surface but which nonetheless struck exactly the right chords. My eyes wandered to the steel filing cabinet behind her, the richly trailing spider plant flowering profusely in this windowless office, the stack of invoices on the desk between us held down with a thick pewter pentagram. Back to Karita's face, somehow softer in its outlines, abstracted, her eyes calmly expectant. 'Who are you?' I thought with a rueful melancholy, and suddenly wondered if I meant her or me. There was no answer.

She stood, took my hand, leaned across the desk to kiss me, wetly. "My house tomorrow, midnight."

I grinned. "The witching hour. Isn't that kind of obvious?"

She shrugged, grinned back. "Sometimes clichés are valid."

As I pulled my truck away from the curb I saw her friend Summer crossing the patio courtyard toward the building's entrance, dressed just as I saw her last time, still carrying her battered artist's portfolio. Despite the warmth of the day I shivered.

The driveway was dense with cars as I walked up to her house that next night. I had anticipated something like this, something larger after the misfire of that circle session with Sharah and Treason, so I wasn't surprised. The lights on the walkway sequenced their greeting as I approached the front door, which stood open to the still-warm night air.

Electronic music – Tangerine Dream, I think – pulsed softly through the dimlit spaces of the house. I stepped into the great room where a cluster of people stood engaged in earnest conversation, nodding a greeting to the young man – the boy, really; he looked like he was maybe sixteen, with a portwine birthmark that covered maybe half of his left cheek – who acknowledged my presence with his index and little finger extended and "Blessed be." I wondered if there were thirteen people here.

"Karita?" I asked. He tilted his hand, pointing the horns toward the kitchen.

She was there, in close conversation with Sharah, the woman from the other night, and the two of them formed a striking tableau. The kitchen was done in a very contemporary style, everything stark white except the black granite countertops, while off to one side stood Karita and Sharah, both dressed completely in black except for Karita's explosively hued scarf, their skin tones a striking contrast: Karita's lightly freckled paleness, Sharah's heavy-on-the-cream coffee. I suddenly wished I had a camera, then remembered some feminist criticism I'd read about the penetrating and controlling male gaze. Felt briefly guilty.

Their conversation finished, Sharah passed me without recognition; Karita gave me a lingering embrace and powerful kiss. Libido woke up.

"Glad you could make it," she said brightly.

"This isn't some kind of group therapy session or anything, is it? I didn't do much for your last get-together and I don't want to screw this one up as well."

"Not to worry, then. Just some friends, here to relax."

"Not a coven?" I asked offhandedly, my tone belying my seriousness. I had been wondering if she was part of something organized; had to be, I thought, she's too good at this stuff and knows too much about it.

"Not a coven." Then a sidelong glance. "Why? Interested in

joining one?"

"Not sure it's quite my style."

She nodded. "You're right, it's definitely not. Your path doesn't lie through that sort of magic this time around."

"But yours does?"

"Apparently so," she said brightly. "Why else did I come back as me?"

I laughed. "Whoa! Ontological meltdown. I need a beer after a statement like that." Karita nodded in the direction of the fridge.

From the kitchen I followed her out to the pool, only slightly surprised to discover that it looked much like the one in the Parkinson's yard. There were three or four people clustered around the diving board, the unmistakable heavy sweetness of hashish redolent in the warm night. Someone in the group said something I didn't quite catch, causing Karita to step over to the group for a moment of hushed conversation.

"So," I said when she returned, "just who are all these people? Are they all witches?" I peered into the darkness. "And warlocks?" I added, seeing one or two males in the group.

"So many questions still." She took me firmly by the hand, leading me toward the far end of the pool. "I prefer to think of them as friends, but yes, many of them have deep interest in and commitment to the Craft."

I fell silent as she led me past the fieldstone wall that curved by the hot tub, the steady low churning of its jets a pleasant counterpoint to the music from the house. In the half-light it took me a moment to realize the tub was occupied: two women, one of them not so young, locked in a complicated embrace, one moaning softly. Motion and muffled noise in the house's yellow-lit angular spaces of glass and wood were lost as we followed a stepping-stone path through the xeriscape garden behind the hot tub. We came to a fence, eight feet of stout wrought iron, but Karita reached into the bushes to active the electric gate, which opened with a soft click. Through the gate into vegetation beyond.

Her father's house was at the very end of the cul-de-sac; behind was a few more yards of ridgetop, chaparral-fringed and dotted with yucca and, oddly, eucalyptus. A few paces away, screened from the house by a thick growth of manzanita and wild buckwheat fragrant with its characteristic dusty pungency was a small clearing, perhaps twenty feet across. At its center was a small platform – a rough wooden altar, I realized as we approached it. The streetlights cast only a faint sodium glow back here, revealing no details. I tried to recall what I knew of Wicca and witchcraft, but my mind seemed uninterested in responding to the demands of memory or logic. All that came to mind, for some unfathomable reason, was an image of the Druid's wicker men, filled with human bodies and set aflame. Karita stopped next to the altar and turned me so that we stood facing each other, parallel to the length of the rectangular altar top. She pressed my left hand between both of hers, eyes half closed, lips betraying the slightest hint of movement. Her eyes opened abruptly, she smiled – and I shivered involuntarily as I saw in her face, for a fleeting moment, someone I did not know, could never know or understand. More than a stranger, fully Other. But in less than the time it took to think that half-formed thought her smile changed and she began to kneel, pulling me with her. On our knees the altar's surface was shoulder level.

"Now, northern child, next step."

Before I could force some witty response past the confusion she raised my hand to her mouth and began sucking on my index finger, her tongue moving with practiced dexterity. And to the expected effect: I jerked with the sudden onset of erotic longing, my erection almost instantly beginning to press against my jeans. Karita laughed low in her throat and the vibration excited me further. I don't know what embarrasses me more: the fact that, through what must have been some great cosmic oversight, no woman had ever done that to me before, or that simply having a finger sucked can make me so excited, begin to lose myself so thoroughly. Whatever. At the time my only thought was the predictable one, and with my free hand I began fumbling with the buttons of Karita's blouse.

"Not so fast," she said, taking my finger from her mouth. I stopped as she ran the tip of her tongue the length of my finger. I literally trembled. She laughed again, and slowly unbuttoned. She was braless, and as she was undoing the final button I lurched forward, clasping my mouth firmly over her left nipple. Instantly she pressed both hands hard against the sides of my face and pushed me firmly back. My breath was coming hard by this point and I said nothing, just looked up into her face, trying to let my eyes do the talking. Not that there was much that needed to be said as far as I was concerned.

As though reading my mind she pressed a finger to my lips and

70

immediately I followed her lead, taking it into my mouth and sucking firmly. She briefly smiled up at the smog-dimmed stars.

Karita then fumbled with her free hand in a pocket of her open blouse. She took my left hand again and suddenly I felt a sharp stab of pain in my left index finger.

"What the!" I pulled back, more surprised than anything until I remembered our previous session. Can this woman not have sex without blood? I wondered. How weird is that? Karita had a firm grip on my left wrist but instinctively I had twisted my arm free. I saw the dim glint of metal in her hand before I saw the cut on my finger. "Again? What's up with the blood thing?"

She smiled. "Ghosting the vampire," she said, her voice casual. Despite the deep strangeness of the moment I noticed a slight shift in her posture, a squaring of her shoulders ever so slightly, causing her blouse to pull back, further revealing her breasts. I became acutely aware of my erection again.

I glanced quickly at my finger – a small cut, only a few drops of blood – then back at Karita's breasts. Her words finally registered. "'Ghosting the vampire?' What the hell is that?"

"Ghosting the vampire. . . . Flirting with primal energies, with blood and its binding power. Just a name, not the real name, for a ritual of linking, binding our psychic energies for a time." Her eyes unfocused slightly and she looked into the canyon darkness to her left. I had no real sense of what she was trying to say, and the thought occurred to me that maybe I should go back inside, that maybe this whole business was a bit more over the top than I suspected. But Karita raised a hand to her breast with seeming absentmindedness and began to stroke her left nipple. I shifted, feeling the stir in the depths, moved closer to her. Still looking away she took my left hand. I must have flinched slightly, for she looked at me, her eyes steady and veiled with something I did not know, and whispered "Strength, child. Are you willing to follow me on the path?"

"I am," I whispered back, not knowing or caring what she meant, my voice husky with lust. "Let's do it."

She held up a scalpel blade, studying it with a practiced intensity, and then to my relief stabbed her own finger before tossing the blade onto the altar. She stared hard into my eyes for a moment, searching for something, and I fought to hold her gaze. She extended her finger toward my mouth, blood dripping, a few drops falling onto

71

the dusty ground. I surprised myself by taking her finger again, sucking the blood (quickly losing the taste of it) but more confused than anything. A brief thought of Hayden's blood on the floor of the poolhouse and his urgent warning, doubting the wisdom of this but unable or unwilling to hold the thought.

After a few seconds she withdrew her finger, then she again raised my index finger, the one she had cut, to her lips. I thought she was going to lick the drops of blood that still clung there – thus the "vampire" nonsense – but instead she leaned slightly back, pushing her left breast forward, and moved my finger until it was just above her nipple. With surprising force she squeezed my finger and a trickle of blood fell onto her breast, trailing down the aureole to the tip of her nipple. I felt disoriented, disconnected. This was a bit too strange to be happening, but it was obviously very real: the vague throb in my finger, the painful tightness in my crotch, my very real desire to crawl naked with this woman into whatever bizarre sexual strangeness she could conjure.

She pushed her breast up toward her face and, reaching toward her nipple with her tongue, quickly licked a few drops of my blood. She then took my hand and squeezed more blood. Still without a word she reached out, cupped a hand behind my head, and drew me slowly forward to her breast. With a reverence that came from a place I did not know I had I lowered my mouth onto her and sucked, again barely noticing the blood, barely noticing the utter weirdness of what we were doing. But registering, with at least some straining portion of my brain, that there was decidedly something very strange here, exhilarating in its perversity. And just before the id declared total mastery I wondered, with a fast-receding part of my mind, just what I was getting myself in for.

I sucked and fondled for what seemed like five minutes as Karita moaned softly deep in her throat, and began to moan myself when she reached for my crotch. I stood, crouching, so I could keep my mouth on her breast as she freed my cock. She then pulled back, leaning against the altar.

"The blood is the life," she whispered, her lips against my ear as she began to stroke me, "and so is the semen." And she bent her head to my lap and took me in her mouth.

On our way back to the house we paused at the iron gate, watching the movements of the people, fewer of them now, in the house. The hot tub was empty.

"You know," I said, "I have to admit I don't fully understand you."

"Good," she said distractedly, a half smile on her face but her eyes still fixed on the house.

"Seriously," I continued, half turning her toward me. "On the one hand you talk with incredible compassion about Summer and her problems and then you do this 'ghosting the vampire' stuff." She turned abruptly to face me, her eyes glinting in the light from house and yard. "I'm not knocking it," I continued quickly, "but it just seems kinda, well, dark, in a way." Her brows had lowered and I knew I had said something stupid, although it was a legitimate question for me at the moment.

"I told you," she said evenly, "it's a ritual of binding. It summons elemental energies and weaves them into a nexus that joins us, our astral selves. It's not dark at all." She shook her head, a stage gesture as was her way. "You are a poor northern child," she said after a moment, "but you watch the sea, don't you?"

I nodded, wondering what that had to do with anything.

"Waves taller than these trees or a surface as flat as glass — same ocean. Woman is Maid and Mother and Crone – same woman. Compassion or binding – same love even if different people." She shook her head again. "There's nothing dark about blood, it's the fluid of our lives, the river of being. This is not a casual ritual, not an everyday perversion or some Goth posturing."

"Did you do that with Summer?" I asked, knowing the answer.

"Yes." A sudden pause. She gazed directly at me, her eyes sparkling. "That excites you, thinking about it? Me and Summer?"

I shook my head. "No, I don't think it does. Well, maybe a little, but she's not, uh, well, she's kinda offputting – for me at least."

Karita laughed. "You see so much and yet so little, northern child." She kissed me, hard. "But fret not. Your vision will expand before you leave us." And she led me back into the house.

My grandmother always used to say talking of the devil is a sure way to summon him: when I followed Karita back into the kitchen there stood Summer, all 5-foot-zero-scrawny inches of her. Still dressed in worn black but minus the camo vest, her scowl darkening as

73

she looked past Karita and our eyes met for the briefest of recognizable moments. 'Oh, Christ,' I thought. I was relieved when Karita took her into another room.

I got myself another beer and took a self-guided tour of the house, vowing this time to see all of it. Like the Parkinson house it was reified conspicuous consumption, decorated with degrees of style and money I could not get my mind around. Somewhere in the back of the house I found what must have been the good doctor's study: a book-lined room dominated by a huge and elegantly graceful desk made of several woods I could never hope to identify in front of floor-to-ceiling windows that looked out on the night across the canyon. I flicked off the lights and stood for a long moment by the glass, watching the silent glimmer of the few lights across the way. 'Fucking strange-ass place,' I thought, taking a long pull at my beer. 'And rapidly getting stranger.'

A noise behind me: I turned quickly to see Karita silhouetted in the doorway. She crossed the room, touched my arm, and I felt the night wrap around me in a curiously comforting way.

"I need to talk to Summer," she said, a half-suppressed sigh somewhere behind her voice, "and I think it might take a while. Didn't want you to think I'd abandoned you, but I need to do this now." She glanced away. "Things aren't going well for Summer; this might take some work."

"Understood," I said, wanting nothing to do with Summer and her difficulties, wishing the little rat would fill her pockets with stones and walk into the ocean. "I'm tired anyway." A kiss, lingering, and I followed Karita to the door oblivious to the hum of music and conversation around me. Outside I walked slowly down the drive, beer in hand, trying to pick out the constellations, any constellation, from among the handful of stars piercing the smog. Fewer cars in the drive now, and one that hadn't been there before, a Volkswagen Beetle, its astonishingly decrepit state evident even in the glow of the low-pressure sodium lamps. I was tempted to toss my beer bottle in through the open window, thought better of it.


Thursday was a bitch at work, beginning with a note taped to the door when I arrived – they had never gotten around to assigning me a mail slot – from the Dean's secretary, Kyoko's aunt, asking me to make an appointment with his worship at my earliest convenience.

Christ, I thought, crumpling the note and tossing into the recycle bin, looks like my spending money's going to dry up sooner than I thought. I thought about calling the Dean's office right then and pulled out the directory, but then thought better of it. My earliest convenience ain't here yet, yer highness; if you're going to fire me I see no urgent need to make it easy for you.

But my concentration was shot, and it was only after entering a good twenty pages of text that I realized I'd been consistently using the wrong diacritic marks for certain phonemes and would have to do a lot of painstaking editing to clean up my mess.


The Oak closed at 5.30, I knew, so I timed my departure to arrive just at closing time. The "Closed" sign was up but the door unlocked when I arrived, and as I stepped inside I could hear voices coming from the back of the shop. Stepping to the rear of the offices I peered around the door of the conference room and saw chairs and table pushed into a corner, a group of people sitting in a loose circle on the floor: Karita, Jazz, Summer, three or four other women I didn't recognize and that weird guy from the circle, Treason. Karita motioned me in; against my better instincts I slipped into the room and sat just outside the circle, almost seeming to join in, making sure I couldn't see Summer's face. After a few moments Karita introduced one of the women as Jana, a part-time history teacher at a couple of area colleges. Then she introduced me, much to my dismay.

"This gathering is part of our ongoing discovery," Karita said, mostly for my benefit; "some of us have been meeting to talk about Wicca and the sister arts and their historical value."

"Ah," I said, looking cautiously around at the others, "sounds great. I took a comparative religion class once and we had a class period on witchcraft." I felt stupid as soon as I said it.

Summer snorted derisively. "Right," she said acidly. "Give women's great achievement one day and spend ten weeks on the forms of phallic oppression."

I nodded, recalling Karita's request for tolerance. "Unbalanced, I agree," I said hastily, "but it wasn't really a class on feminism or gender or – "

"Well it needed to be," she snapped. "The history of witchcraft is the history of women, which you'd understand if you weren't handicapped by your dick."

I flinched but let it pass. She clearly was, as Karita had explained, bitter to the point of hatred. I could sympathize to some extent, given what had happened to her, but hell, other women get abused and raped and don't go out of their way to insult and provoke males at every opportunity. But I just nodded. And wondered what Karita ever saw in her.

"It's my parents' fault," I said with a weak grin, hoping she would just shut up.

She did, but only after giving me an icy glare before turning back to look at Jana.

"Wicca can only be understood as a gift from the Mother Goddess," Jana said, the inflections of academia clearly evident in her cadence. She wore a large pewter ankh at her neck. "The gift of a healing art. Witches were the village wise women, herbalists, healers – they were the pharmacists and doctors of their time, for centuries."

"The medical establishment before men claimed it," Jazz said. "Woman as nurturer."

I nodded. This was familiar ground.

"These women," Jana continued, "with their power to dull pain and turn illness, were exactly what patriarchy could not and would not accept: women with power. You can't see viruses and bacteria with the naked eye, so when these women made their teas and extracts and people got better, which they didn't always do but they did often enough, they were exercising power not only over people but over the unseen, the unknown. What patriarchy called the magical, the supernatural, eventually the demonic."

Summer snorted in derision, nodded. "Leave it to prick-think to believe there's a place where nature stops. If you can't fuck it, eat it, kill it or trade it, it must not be real." I began to suspect this was all for my benefit; I looked at Treason, who seemed to be under the influence of something and paying no real attention at all, wondered what he thought of Summer, why he was here.

Jana's smile seemed a bit forced. "So patriarchy did to wise women what it does best when it comes to women: marginalized them. Made them outcasts, freaks, worse. Codified woman's Otherness and patriarchy's misogyny in the *Malleus Maleficarum* and thousands of other tracts and books and sermons just like it. The Halloween image of the wart-nosed witch in the pointed hat is the modern, trivialized, commercialized outgrowth of that early exclusion."

"But, you know, stereotypes sometimes have an element of truth to them," I began and immediately regretted it as both Summer and Jazz instantly turned steely glares in my direction. I suddenly forgot what my point was going to be, wished I had kept my mouth shut.

"What bullshit." Summer growled the word out between clenched teeth, looked like she wanted to say something more, glared at me briefly, then spoke in response to Jana's words but clearly aiming them directly at me. "Women became figures of fear because the prick always fears what it can't understand, which is why it's always piling up money and weapons and power: takes all that shit to keep real life at arm's length."

Jana held up her hand. "Fear, yes. Women with power were feared, so ancient cultures demonized the wise-woman, even though they needed her. Just as with prostitutes and mothers: men surrounded sexual woman with cultural baggage that gave her just enough space to breathe, because they needed her services, but didn't give her enough space for autonomy or freedom. But the wise woman was mistress of the unknown, and that was too much, so they finally had to bring in the big guns, to use one of their favorite phallic images." She smiled. "Having sex and raising babies, men could understand and needed those, so the control they had over hookers and mothers" – both of these words sounded equally denigratory as Jana pronounced them – "was, while strict and denigratory, not usually fatal immediately, at least in most Western cultures. But Wicca was too much for them, so they played the greatest of all male trump cards." She paused, nodded. "The Man-God. Demonized the wise woman—'she consorts with Satan,' they said. 'She rides his ice-cold dick in the night and makes our cattle to die. Kill the witch. Kill the bitch.' And it of course was bullshit, because Wicca had nothing to do with the desert religions, with Jesus or Satan or salvation. Nothing at all – Western patriarchy just imposed it, invented the connection, to justify their prosecution and their powerlust."

"Kind of like what happened to *Beowulf*," I said, still struggling to be a good interlocutor. "Pre-Christian story that had Christian elements grafted on, an overlay of language and imagery that sought to co-opt it for Christian culture."

Jana shook her head. "I'm not so sure that's an apt metaphor.

*Beowulf*'s really a perfect document for Western patriarchy: kill it, screw it, acquire it, lord it over other people by virtue of brute strength. The Anglo-Saxon tradition was in many ways a perfect fit with Christianity. Adding Christian elements to that worldview is just icing a cake you would have eaten anyway. Wicca was the *enemy*."

"Well, so was Anglo-Saxon paganism. They – "

"Not the fucking same," Summer growled again; "shut up." When I looked at her she was staring intently at Jana. It was disconcerting arguing with someone who wouldn't look at you, as though you were a petty annoyance that had to be dealt with before anything substantive could happen. 'Fuck you again,' I thought. To my relief Jana cut in.

"The desert religions and warrior cultures were made for each other – look at all the killing in the Bible, the warriors of the Hebrew Bible and the violence of the New Testament and the Quran. The Mother religions, Wicca, they're about something entirely different, something a lot further away from Christianity than a bunch of chest-beating warriors from Scandinavia."

"Even you should be able to see that," Summer added quietly though without looking at me. I said nothing, giving up on any attempt to participate. Karita reached toward Summer, touched her on the arm, but Summer just flinched, looked back at Jana.

With a strained look Jana continued. "So the Christian powers-that-were associated the wise woman with the greatest evil they could think of: their goat-devil, grand enemy of their sheep-god, and launched what amounted to an all-out crusade against Wicca as well as other heresies. Turn the healer into a demon-fucker, turn her cat into her demon-lover, turn her power into the evidence of her corrupted nature."

"It's always sex when you're a prick." That from Summer, staring straight ahead at nothing. I could feel my jaw clench, deliberately waited a moment to relax.

"Inextricably linked to sex," Jana said, nodding calmly but looking increasingly uncomfortable. "And so, of course, with power and control. Whether they were wise women or not. Read the histories and you see they were killing old widows, cripples, cat lovers, some old farmer's wife who'd cheat you a few pence on vegetables. Didn't matter, marginal women still don't count for much. Burn them, drown them, hang them, violate them in the name of the Prince of

Peace. Persecute, deny, harass, victimize – a successful strategy. Turn their power into an evil, make them ashamed of it, deny it to them so power accrues to the men in control. It's the story of all women for far too long. Like prostitution: used to be done in the temples, back when people realized the magic of sex. Patriarchy turned it into a crime, now pimps and the law control it so woman's body is just another commodity in male hands. The healing arts of Wicca too. And all this right at the same time the so-called Enlightenment was beginning, when modern medicine began developing; can't have women stealing patients from male doctors. Midwives still face difficulties today. The male-dominated medical profession portrays midwives as little better than a bunch of hillbilly housewives, or witches, and you're at major risk if you don't do the sanitary hospital ob-gyn routine when you give birth."

Summer's glare returned to me for an instant. "Get all that, professor?" she sneered.

I felt helpless for a moment, target of an anger I did not merit. "Hey," I said, against my better judgement, "I agree with this. I never thought of witchcraft that way, but what Jana just said makes sense." I nodded, wondering how to make a quick exit. Not that this wasn't interesting, but I was sick of Summer's abrasive bitchiness, her condescension and hostility. Feminism's supposed to be about bridging gaps, not widening them.

Summer was staring straight ahead again. Out of the corner of my eye I saw Karita move her head fractionally to the side, the barest hint of a negative flashed in my direction. I looked away from Summer, saw Jana lift her arm and give her watch a theatrical glance, a gesture for the gallery. "Sorry, dear," she said to Karita, "I need to run if I'm going to make my class tonight." Karita nodded, issued a general thank you, and almost in unison everyone rose, the discomfort and tension in the room dissipating as everyone left. As she passed me Karita touched my arm, lightly and unobtrusively, and went to Summer, put an arm around her shoulder and led her toward another office. I left as quickly as I could and knew I would never return.


A few days later the strangeness escalated again, this time into a range I could never have been prepared for and was sure I wanted nothing whatsoever to do with. And the invisible walls of LA pressed around me more closely still.

Saturday morning: Hayden in Atlanta again and I was very slow getting up. Kyoko had stopped by my office late yesterday with a quart of Jim Beam in her fluorescent pink knapsack and some microwave popcorn, and we ended up getting fairly drunk, talking for hours about department politics and literary studies and Djuna Barnes and sushi, which I hadn't eaten in years. Yet I couldn't shake the feeling Kyoko had something more on her mind than filling me in on the latest gossip and the imminent end of my employment and the aphrodisiac properties of *wasabi*; in fact I had the impression she was maybe thinking of cheating on her girlfriend, experimenting or indulging in some hetero sex. Or maybe, now that I think about it, that was probably just me, some vestige of a primal male ego – or more likely id – refusing to admit final defeat. At any rate I behaved myself, despite the urgings of Mr. Beam.

Between the whiskey and thoughts of Kyoko I was pretty distracted driving home; despite my fascination with Karita and my *faux pas* with Kyoko in the mountains the other night I had to acknowledge to myself that I continued to find myself very interested in Kyoko, drawn to her both sexually and otherwise. Maybe it was something self-defeating, although I'd like to think that sort of quirk isn't really my psychological style, and as I drove home I kept returning to the nagging suspicion that Kyoko might be interested in me. Vanity, perhaps, and likely the whiskey, as I said, but the thought was there, and the idea of having sex with Kyoko and then with Karita – on the same day? – was predictably exciting.

To say nothing of deeply stupid and depressingly cliché.

Thus my distraction and my not noticing the battered Volkswagen Beetle parked near the end of the cul-de-sac. But when I stumbled out of my truck I saw it, parked at the edge of the streetlight's yellow nimbus. And a second later saw the slight figure emerge from around a hedge at the corner of the property. It took my alcohol-dimmed brain a moment to fully register the sight, and when I did I tensed instantly: Summer, striding with awkward determination up the driveway directly toward me.

She stopped a good ten feet from me, her hands clenched into fists held rigidly at her side and visibly vibrating with anger. She'd startled me, I admit, but seeing her this close I relaxed. At perhaps five feet tall and maybe 90 pounds she was hardly a threat; I'm six-one and one-eighty with a green belt in shotokan karate; I could toss her halfway down the driveway without even trying. So I just stared back, wondering what the hell kind of weirdness was about to unfold now.

As my eyes further adjusted to the gloom I could see her occasionally shiver, blinking rapidly. I was just about to say something when she finally spoke.

"Why don't you just fucking leave?" she said abruptly, her whiny high growl of a voice making her sound like an asthmatic twelve year old in a very bad mood. "Everything was fine until you came. Just fucking leave and everything will be OK again. Just leave." Her voice was taut with rage, a whip of anger in the warm night.

I sighed inwardly; even through the Jim Beam I could recognize the self-pity and emotional instability. And projection, making your own problems the fault of someone else's actions. Psych 101 in the driveway, I thought; I really don't need this. Karita's repeated reminders about Summer came back to me, and I thought only about ending this as quickly as possible.

"Look," I said, "I'm sorry things haven't worked out the way you wanted, but there's nothing I can do about it. Talk to Karita, not me. Besides, I've had a long day and I'm tired so I think it's best this conversation end right now."

"No," she said sharply before I could even turn away. "You fucking listen to me, you prick. You need to leave. Karita's mine. Things'll get back to normal if you leave so just fucking leave. I fucking mean it!" Her agitation was growing as she spoke, the cords of her neck straining against her pale flesh and her thin arms jerking almost involuntarily as her voice rose. I began to think she might really charge me.

"I told you," I said, deliberately modulating my voice so my words wouldn't travel, "this isn't my problem, and I'm tired of you acting like I'm some kinda damn monster. Karita told me you guys were…close, but she also told me she broke it off – " that was the wrong phrase but I was too drunk to think of another – "before I got here. So quit blaming me; that doesn't make any sense. And go home." I turned toward the house, began walking away.

"NO!" she screamed. "You fucking PRICK!" I could hear her move and whirled to face her, almost losing my balance, but she'd only taken a single step toward me. Out of the corner of my eye I saw lights flick on in the backyard of the house next door. "Karita and I would be back together if you were gone. Take your fucking cock the hell out of here!"

I rubbed my face wearily, then pointed at her with calculated suddenness. "For the last time, take your problems somewhere else. I'm not responsible for what happens between you and anyone else, I'm leaving on my own damn timetable, and unless I miss my guess the police will be coming by soon because the folks around here like their quiet. So get the hell off of this property and out of my life, you fucking little runt." I regretted that last phrase as soon as I said, Karita's caution about her history and treating her with patience coming to mind just a bit too late to do me any good.

She took another step toward me and I could see her face white now with anger. She was trembling from head to toe and I could feel my own adrenaline spiking. "You've been warned, you fucking prick," she said in a gravelly whisper. "Leave now with your cock or you might end up leaving without it." She spit at me but missed. I remained tensed, half-expecting her to try something physical, but she turned and ran awkwardly back to her car. I didn't move until she'd sped off down the ridge.

Turning back to the house I felt a wave of revulsion and anger. My stomach was in a knot, I suddenly realized, and I felt vaguely troubled. This shit's getting way out of hand. I suddenly changed my course, walked over to Karita's house to tell her what had happened. But no answer.

I walked slowly back to the Parkinson's, half-expecting to hear the characteristic buzz of a VW returning, but there was only the hum of cars in the distance, the far-off hollow roar of a jet, the insistent chirping of crickets. Strangely deflated, I went straight to bed but lay awake for a very long while.

Thus it was that I was pretty much unprepared for anything at all when the doorbell clanged a few minutes before eight the next morning, waking me out of a troubled and restless sleep. By the time I fumbled into some clothes the chimes had rung three more times, their clangorous echoes grating directly on some major nerve endings. As I approached the door I had the sudden thought it might be Summer, and her threat echoed in my head.

No. Through the peephole he looked ordinary, about my age and height, black hair against very pale skin, slender, something kind of nervous in his eyes but not threatening. Probably selling something, I thought, probably religion; shoulda stayed in bed. I flipped the deadbolts and swung the door.

"'allo," he said with a curious duck of his head, his French accent as thick as cold brie. "I am lookeeng for Monsieur Don-yel Parkeensohn."

We must have looked at each other in mutual bafflement for a good twenty seconds before he decided I needed to hear his greeting again. But this time he looked genuinely nervous, and by now I having caught the tone of his voice through the mental fog I realized he was reciting a memorized phrase in an unfamiliar language. And my heart sank, because if he had to memorize something that brief and basic then I'd just opened the door to a load of unnecessary grief. I'd taken a year of French as a high school freshman before switching to Spanish but remembered almost nothing of it. I have no foreign language gift; the Spanish and two years of college Latin had knocked most of what little French I'd ever learned out of my head. And who the hell was Donyel Parkinson?

Oh shit. Through the lingering miasma of the hangover it came drifting to me: Daniel Parkinson, the youngest of the Parkinson kids, the one Hayden had told me was at law school somewhere back East.

No fucking way, I thought. Not today. Christ.

I looked again at the young guy in front of me. He was beginning to look seriously uncomfortable, no doubt wondering what sort of strange American rudeness he was being subjected to now. He glanced at a piece of paper in his hand, held it out to me, saying something in French. I understood nothing but the much-traveled scrap of paper he handed me bore the name Daniel Parkinson and the correct street address.

"You're in the right place," I said, handing him the paper, "but I'm afraid we have a problem."

The look of blank incomprehension on his face stopped me short. I groaned inwardly, opened the door wider and gestured him in, sighed aloud. This was going to be a bitch I did not need.

"Maison, uh, damn, what's the word? Maison juste, no, uh, bon – maison bon, but no Daniel Parkinson."

He winced at my French but I think I got my point across. Setting his huge Kelty softpack on the marble floor he again pointed to the scrap of paper, rattled off something in French. I caught "Daniel

Parkinson," "mon ami," and what sounded like "visit," which didn't tell me much but told me enough. Mostly that I had a pretty big problem on my hands and Hayden was on the other end of the damn country. My first thought was to call him. I led my visitor to a chair and dialed the number Hayden had left. Answering machine. I left a slightly panicked and probably incomprehensible message – suitable for the occasion, I thought – and hung up.

The sight of a nervous stranger at the breakfast table inspired me to take drastic action: despite the early hour I dialed Mrs. Parkinson's Santa Barbara number. To my surprise she answered the phone on the second ring, and with a rush of relief I explained the situation to her.

My heart sank again when she told me she had no idea who this person might be or what he was doing in her kitchen. She said she would call her son, interning for the summer at some prestigious Boston law firm she was careful to name, and find out what she could. At the same moment we realized we didn't know the stranger's name; fortunately I remembered "nom" and after supplying him with a pen and paper got the necessary information: Jean-Pierre Barthes. On the cheery note that she would send some money to cover expenses if Jean-Pierre had to stay for a while, Mrs. P hung up and left me to my very limited French devices. Recradling the phone it occurred to me I should have asked her if she spoke French; I thought about calling her back but couldn't bring myself to do it. Wondered who I knew that spoke French, realized that the only name that came to mind was Sandy, my (ex?) girlfriend in Humboldt. It struck me this was the first I'd thought of her in what seemed like a very long while. How the hell did that happen I wondered, and immediately "Karita" formed in my mind. Shit. I could no more call Sandy now than I could a total stranger, I thought carelessly, and then *that* thought struck me, palpably. She was truly a stranger now, already. Or was it me? Then it occurred to me I just *had* called a total stranger, and that was a lot easier than trying to call Sandy.

"It's too early in the day for this shit," I said aloud, rubbing my temples as I dropped wearily into a chair across from Jean-Pierre. "Sinking into the maelstrom. Or is it the pit under the pendulum?" I spoke carelessly, still hungover and half-asleep, knowing my guest wouldn't understand and not especially caring, so I was stunned at Jean-Pierre's response.

"Le pit et le pendule ," he said excitedly. Then something else in even more rapid French, ending with "EdgarPoe."

I look at him in what I can only think of as confused amazement. "Poe? You read Poe? You can read English, is that what you're telling me? You just can't speak it, right? Oh, man, I'm saved." I grabbed the pen and paper, scribbled "Can you read English?" on the top sheet, pushed it to him. He looked at it closely, pointed to the word "English," said "Anglais, oui?"

Shit again. "Poe. How can you read Edgar Allan Poe if you don't read English?"

"EdgarPoe," he said, nodding cheerfully. Then something more in French and I caught "Baudelaire." It hit me with a load of embarrassment: translations. The French symbolists loved Poe; his work's been accessible in French since forever. Christ, I can be dense sometimes. Or hungover. Or both. I rubbed my temples again, silently cursing Summer and Kyoko and the sinister Mr. Beam.

"Monsieur," I heard. I looked up, watched Jean-Pierre point at me with great deliberation and utter "nom." I nodded, stuck out my hand and introduced myself.

"Now we're on speaking terms." I grinned wearily, lapsing back into a funk composed of equal parts hangover and confusion.

Jean-Pierre, the stranger in a stranger land, showed considerably more self-possession. "Sprechen zie Deutsche?" I heard, and while I most certainly did not, I at least recognized the phrase, shook my head. Then, taking his cue, I offered a desultory "¿Hablas español?" Jean-Pierre looked at me blankly. "Too bad you don't speak Latin," I mumbled, then brightened as it occurred to me he just might. Not speak it, of course, but at least write it. I grabbed pen and paper – and couldn't for the life of me figure out how to ask "Do you speak Latin?" in that language. "Latin?" I asked plaintively. Nothing from Jean-Pierre. I groped for a phrase, anything that might spark recognition. Out of nowhere came Julius Caesar's classic opening line, "Gallia in tres partes divisa est." I gave it my best Ciceronian oration. His eyes brightened momentarily at "Gallia" but all I got was a shake of the head.

"We're fucked," I said. "We need a goddamn dictionary."

"Dictionnaire," Jean-Pierre said promptly, and immediately rummaged in his backpack. Of course: a bilingual dictionary or phrasebook or something. In my excitement I stood just as Jean-Pierre flourished a pristine paperback dictionary: French-English only. I sank back to my chair with a groan. Who the hell would publish such a worthless thing?

But then I immediately brightened. This was the right track; a trip to the bookstore should ameliorate if not solve our problem. "A la bibliothèque!" I declared, rising quickly to get myself presentable and too excited to wonder how I'd managed to remember that word. Jean-Pierre seemed comfortably resigned to whatever madness I might be leading him into – I guess you have to be heroically flexible when you travel in a country where you don't speak the language – and in a minute we were in the carport. It struck me as odd, for a moment, that he had no car; I was tempted to ask him how he had gotten to the house, which was pretty far off the beaten track, but our language barrier made that impossible.

We were just getting into my truck when movement by the street caught my eye: Karita, putting something in the mailbox. I was tempted to call out to her when Jean-Pierre suddenly rattled off a long and rapid string of French in which I could have sworn I heard "la sorciere," a term I remembered only because I embarrassed the hell out of myself once in class trying to translate a paragraph on witchcraft. I looked at him in astonishment, then quickly over at Karita, who had seen us and was headed our way. "La sorciere? How the hell...?" I shook my head, feeling the world slip again into a deeper strangeness.

"Morning," Karita said brightly. "You look like crap this fine day."

"He called you a witch," I blurted, "and he doesn't speak English. He just fucking got here and no one knows what he's doing here. And I need to talk to you about Summer."

Karita gave me a level stare, smiled as she shook her head slowly. "You are making absolutely no sense whatsoever. And if your friend doesn't speak English how can he call me a witch?"

"French, he's French. Jean-Marc or something. Just showed up at the door looking for one of the Parkinsons and he doesn't speak any English. I called Mrs. Parkinson and she's trying to find her son and in the meantime I was gonna go get a dictionary so we could at least communicate a little."

Karita nodded, turned to Jean-Pierre, standing at the open door of my pickup looking thoroughly baffled, and rattled off a long stream of what sounded to me like beautifully fluent French in which I caught "sorciere" three times. He responded with comparable volubility, and I just stood silent as the conversation flowed for a good five minutes. At last Karita turned to me.

"A simple matter. Jean-Pierre met Dan Parkinson – who's an arrogant smug asshole by the way, a perfect lawyer type – when Dan spent his next-to-last semester in Paris. They became friends. Dan invited him to drop by anytime he came to the states, and here he is."

"What? No one just 'drops by' another country. You don't just show up on someone's doorstep after six months and say 'Oh, hi, I was in the US this morning, thought I'd stop by for a chat.'"

Karita laughed. "Apparently some folks do. And it wasn't six months; more like two years."

"What? That's ridiculous. No wonder he didn't know they'd moved."

"He's figured it out now. He would, however, like to know where you're dragging him off to, and he also wants you to know he's starving. And he'd like to go for a swim, if that's OK."

"Jeez, he's a demanding foreign bastard. Tell him we're going to the bookstore for a bilingual dictionary. Then we'll eat. And yeah, he can swim all he wants."

She spoke to Jean-Pierre for a moment, then turned back to me. "Why don't I meet the two of you at Hakim's for breakfast? I'll translate for you before I have to open my store. Better than a dictionary." She gave me a quick cheek kiss.

"Definitely so," I grinned. "But can you ask him one thing: how did he know you were a witch?"

She gave me a quick wink. "He didn't, really. He just said I remind him of his sister, who's Wiccan. See you in a few."


Despite the fact I never had a chance to talk to Karita about my encounter with Summer last night breakfast went reasonably well, although J-P, as I came to think of him, seemed interested primarily in telling lengthy stories of his travels through the States. From the parts Karita translated for me, he was impressed mainly with how lousy American food and manners were. Between his haughtiness and the difficulty of having everything translated I said very little, in fact began to wonder if getting a dictionary was a good idea. Maybe the less I talked to this snob the better. But the thought of the awkward silences overcame my better judgement and we picked up a bilingual dictionary on the way back. I was delighted to see the answering machine blinking merrily.

First message: a morose Hayden telling me to call Mrs P. as there was nothing he could do from where he was.

Second message: a perky message from Mrs P telling me she'd been in contact with her son and he had explained everything and would call shortly.

Third message: the real estate agent saying she was bringing someone to see the house at 11.00 so could we please make sure it was straightened up and empty?

No fourth message: what the hell was keeping that legal-assed son of a bitch?

I looked at the clock: 10:20. Shit. When in doubt, panic, I thought, and called The Golden Oak. No Karita, Jazz reported; she left just a few minutes after arriving.

Double shit.

J-P, who'd been waiting impatiently at the kitchen table, pointed to the pool, said something in French; I nodded distractedly. Just don't drown, you asshole; I'd never be able to explain that to the police.

As I was pondering my next move, or at least trying to get my brain in gear enough to do some pondering, I heard a car pull up in the street and stop. "Shit, no!" I shouted. "They're fucking early." I ran to the bedroom Hayden was using, once the maid's room, since it has the best view of the street and peered through the blinds just in time to see an old Volkswagen Beetle scoot quickly away. "Fuck!" I practically shouted. Summer. "I don't fucking believe this. I've landed in the middle of a goddamn lesbian *Fatal Attraction*." I was half-tempted to chase after her for no coherent reason but before I even finished formulating the thought the phone rang.

Daniel Parkinson. I was saved. He talked to me long enough to explain he'd already booked Jean-Pierre on a flight to Boston, and if we would be kind enough to drive him to LAX for his 9:20 flight tomorrow morning he'd really appreciate it and would I please put Jean-Pierre on the line? Smug asshole lawyer for sure, I thought, heading for the pool to summon J-P, already splashing merrily and nude to boot. I spent the next fifteen minutes frantically cleaning with half of a conversation in French as my background music, and only at the last possible second remembered to ask for the phone back. I quickly explained to Parkinson that we had to vacate the house, and asked him to communicate this to J-P, which he grudgingly did.

It was a close call: on our way down the canyon road we passed a Volvo with 2 passengers and magnetized realtor signs on its doors. Unfortunately this was the most excitement we had for the next two hours: I thought a drive through the San Gabriel mountains would kill some time but the smog was heavy, rendering the views of the valley below disturbing, almost nauseating, and even at eight thousand feet the air was thick with heat and hydrocarbons. Every turnout seemed filled with squalling children and beer-drinking picnickers with boom cars, and the parking lots at the few trailheads we passed were full. Every tree, every ridge, every rock looked tired and attenuated as though in the process of losing what sense of presence and solidity remained, fading under the heat and the relentless human pressure. My mood sank even lower than the fading hangover and silent companionship warranted. Even before I'd left Humboldt I counted on the scruffy, stony mountains of the San Gabriels for some consolation during my sojourn in LA, but every time I'd come up here something had been amiss, missing, and now I knew, incontrovertibly, what it was: nature. Even here at the end of the road, the crowded parking lot for the ski lift up to Mt. Baldy, under the steep canyon walls and heavenclimbing pines, there was too little nature, too much humanity, the sheer psychic pressure of too much human thought (and, paradoxically, thoughtlessness) driving away any sense of the consoling, abiding presence of nature. That sense of being quietly, subtly enwrapped in something other than the noisesome clutter of human daily life was thoroughly absent, chased from even this semi-remote place by the upwelling tide of humanity. I felt tense and tired in an unfamiliar way as I pointed my truck back down the mountain.

We'd been home ten minutes when Karita called, suggesting we meet her at the beach: surf was up due to a tropical storm off Mexico, she said, which made for interesting sightseeing. It sounded desperately good to me, so I put J-P on the line for the French version and he seemed reasonably enthusiastic. From mountain to beach in a few hours, I thought; how Southern California can you get, although going from skis to surfboard was probably the only way to fully realize the experience. I thought of trying to explain this to J-P, who apparently was part dolphin, given his fondness for the pool, but I couldn't find "surfboard" in the dictionary I'd bought. I left him to his laps while I went inside to read a few more chapters of *Les Miserables*.

Karita's directions to Balboa and the Wedge were impeccable, even included a shortcut she said would route us around the worst of the traffic, but if that was a shortcut I'd hate to see the long way: what should have taken an hour took nearly two, for no discernible reason, and by the time I found a place to park, nearly a mile from where we wanted to be and only after cruising Balboa's unimaginatively named side streets for twenty minutes, I was ready to kill someone. J-P must have sensed my tension for he hadn't even attempted to say anything since we'd gotten onto the Newport Freeway – I seemed to have recently developed the habit of swearing aloud when I drove, a development which surprised me not at all – and he now seemed almost to be keeping his distance, staying half a pace behind me as we walked toward the Wedge, that narrow angle of beach on the upcurrent side of the Newport Harbor jetties, renowned for its spectacular but dangerous body-surfing conditions. I'd heard of it on previous trips to SoCal, and visited once though my parents had always preferred Dana Point.

It was nearly five by the time we got to the Wedge, and as I surveyed the crowd I wondered how long it would take to find Karita for beach and jetty were packed with spectators, many armed with camcorders and telephoto lenses. The waves thundered dramatically – I heard someone say ten foot crests – and the dozen or so bodysurfers in the water were the object of constant speculation and almost frantic scrutiny. I've never been much of a water-sports person, and while I couldn't see much attraction in body surfing, particularly given the jagged proximity of the jetty's dark glistening boulders, the scene was undeniably compelling: the blowing salt spray – one of the most invigorating sensory experiences in the natural world below ten thousand feet – the visceral trembling of the sand under the pounding waves, the muscular grace and fearless intrepid skill of the bodysurfers. Pretty damn cool, in short. I became caught up in the moment entirely, watching with more than a frisson of apprehension as surfers rode the primal power of the dark urgent waves in toward shore, and so was startled by the hand on my shoulder. Karita.

Giving me a quick cheek peck she turned to J-P and spent the next ten minutes in animated conversation, during which I caught "sorciere" at least three more times. At one point Karita stooped for a

90

handful of sand, holding it before her face, touching it gently with an index finger as she spoke intently in French. J-P extended his left hand, just below hers, and Karita poured half of the sand into his palm, speaking slowly as she did so.

My puzzled look caught Karita's attention. "Jean-Pierre was telling me about his sister's coven, which has a strong ocean affinity. I was just explaining to him some of the ideas involved in that, since he seems interested."

"The ocean? I didn't know witches were into that."

She gave me one of her "poor northern child" looks. "Why would they not be? It's your momma's amniotic fluid, you know."

Something came to me. "'Mother and lover of men, the sea,'" I intoned before I quite knew what I was saying.

"What?" Again the glance askance.

"Swinburne," I said, "Weird British poet, dead white guy. 'I will go down to the great sweet Mother, Mother and lover of men, the sea.'"

She closed her eyes in brief exasperation, sighed. "More northern wolf-boy fantasies, huh? Ocean as lover and mother – seriously disturbed." She tapped me lightly on the chest, smiled. "You sailor boys never did get enough, did you?"

"Hey, I don't write it, I just read the assigned pages and it sticks in my head."

"Ah. Just another victim of overeducation in the humanities."

"Art major back at ya."

"True, but at least I have a job."

My retort, which would have been devastatingly clever, was washed away by a huge wave that sent water rushing up the beach, causing a minor panic among onlookers trying to keep their feet and video gear dry. As we regrouped on higher ground I pursued the question that had been troubling me for hours.

"You know," I said, moving a step away from J-P and drawing Karita with me, "this is just too weird to be real. Some total stranger from half a planet away shows up at the right house which is the wrong house and doesn't speak a word of English and you just happen to walk by and it turns out he's into magic too?" I shook my head as though to rid myself of an annoyance, the impossibility of it all fully occurring to me for the first time today. "I couldn't invent something like this in a work of fiction. No one would believe it; agents and publishers would scoff."

Karita looked at me seriously. "Well, it's his sister, not him, but in one sense you're right. World's full of people with nearby horizons, isn't it?"

"I guess that means me too, huh? 'Cause I'm having trouble with this. Hell, I'm still waiting for you to explain how you knew my sign back there in the driveway a thousand years ago and why that lunatic Summer is stalking me."

Karita reached a hand to the side of my head, her thumb gently tracing the top of my ear. "You're so close." Her look was direct, firm yet soft and shaded with a trace of rich melancholy. "You look over the edge and you fall in love with what you see, but you can't jump. You sense the spirit, the nearness of the veil, and you're reaching out, but at the last instant you pull back your hand, afraid to see the things that will change you forever."

"Damn I wish I had your gift for metaphor, but what are you talking about?"

"I think you know, or will soon." She turned, pointed her chin at the sea. J-P stood a few feet beyond her, his back to us, absorbed in the sight. "You feel the elemental magic of the sea, the pull – "

"Yeah, but so do millions of people."

"And unlike most of them you know the reality of that magic means the reality of a thousand other magics, the reality of imagination and ghost and dream and witch, the reality of Wicca and spirit and Gaia, and you know from this and from your books and your life in the redwoods that there's an overarching context for all of it, a context that embraces us all and is the Way and the Art and the Raft and all those other metaphors you don't seem to like. But the final step, the little step that is the biggest leap anyone can ever make – you haven't made it yet."

"The proverbial leap of faith, huh? Didn't make it despite the nuns and the priests and all their threats. Guess I've always been just a bit too pragmatic for my own good."

Karita laughed, surprising me. "Pragmatic? You? Mr. Iowa-bound M.A. in creative writing hanging with a witch? Oh yeah, they're ready for you on Main Street." She laughed again. "You're many things, northern child, but not pragmatic. Not really. Just reluctant, just got a tighter grip than you know on that fragment of the universe the Western world markets as the whole deal and you're having trouble letting go. You want to be like the Fool in the Rider Tarot deck but unlike him you're genuinely afraid to step off that cliff. But that's what you have me for," she said with a playful tap on my chest.

I pulled her to me for a deep kiss, and as I released her saw J-P looking at us, smiling. "I knew there had to be some reason why we ran into each other, but here I thought it was because I needed a translator."

"You did, but you need a Beatrice more."

"A wh – ? Oh, yeah, Dante, Divine Comedy. The lady who leads him into heaven."

"But that was a million years ago; we have a much more interesting place to go now."

"Where's that? What do witches call their heaven, anyway?"

"We don't have that limited a vision, as you know perfectly well. Besides, I didn't mean that sort of thing at all. I meant Angelo and Vincie's."

"Who?"

"Best pizza in the Southland, and an atmosphere that will give our *ami* here something to tell the folks back home about. Come on."

Karita called to J-P as we turned to leave – and tensed immediately.

"What?" I asked instinctively. I followed her gaze: Summer. She stood about 20 yards away, staring straight at me with an intensity that even after last night still caught me by surprise. Karita called her name and the sound seemed to strike her physically, for she shook her head as though collecting herself, took a step forward, then broke into an awkward run away from us. Karita took a few steps after her and called again but Summer was quickly lost to sight in the crowd.

"I told you!" I practically shouted as Karita returned and took my hand. "She's whack. I don't fucking believe this. She followed me here, I know it." And blurted out, to my great relief, a quick version of last night's driveway encounter.

Karita looked at me, her look distant, troubled. "I'm not sure what's going on; Summer's been avoiding me these last couple of weeks. But I agree it's not good. . . ." And her voice trailed off, disappearing under the aural friction of crashing wave on sand.

We spent the next few hours at Angelo and Vincie's, a multilevel barn of a place on Harbor Boulevard that was furnished in a decor that beggars description. Christmas lights, giant suits of armor like something out of a Horace Walpole nightmare, a fabric rainbow of flags, old tavern signs, Halloween decorations, trapeze mannequins caught forever in mid-act like figures from Keats's urn if Keats had gone to the circus instead of the British Museum – an eclectic extravaganza that kept me somewhere between astonished and bemused for hours. The pizza was phenomenally good, though I'm not really much of a pizza fan, but Karita identified herself as a Master of Pizza and declared repeatedly that this was the best to be found in the Western Hemisphere. I had somehow forgotten this morning's hangover enough to help J-P polish off two liters of chianti and get so drunk that Karita refused to let me drive, so the three of us piled into her BMW. I was asleep before we hit the freeway.

I have no memory of arriving home that night, but I still recall the hangover that I awoke into at 5:15 the next morning when the phone refused to stop ringing. The next thing I remember Karita was at the door, pulling us merrily into her car again for the drive to LAX and J-P's flight to Boston.

"Why did you let me get this drunk?" I moaned as we sped down the canyon road at what was clearly an excessive rate of speed intended only to increase my bone-deep misery.

Karita laughed. "You Vikings never listen to women once you start drinking. Must be a guy thing."

With some effort I turned to look at J-P, already lost in sleep again, sprawled comfortably across the back seat. No help from that quarter.

"Well," I said, "I'm never going to drink again anyway, so it's a moot point. Can we stop for caffeine?"

We did, twice, yet reached LAX in what Karita declared was remarkably good time. J-P awoke as the car came to a halt, as chipper as ever, and was voluble in his farewells, especially to Karita, who of course could understand more than "merci beaucoup" and "au revoir." By 11:00 we were back at the parking lot of Angelo and Vincie's to get my truck.

And a rude surprise: the rear window of my truck had been shattered, rounded fragments of safety glass scattered across seat and dash, glittering merrily in the bleached morning sun. My stomach, already in sad shape, sank, and I wondered if the sense of oppression I felt wasn't from the heat but from the frustration and anger at being the victim of random vandalism here in the too-big city.

Random? I suddenly pictured Summer at the beach yesterday, running from us as awkwardly as any schoolgirl. And the episode in the driveway. And the rudeness at the Oak. I looked at Karita and could see she'd already had the same thought.

"It was Summer, wasn't it?" I asked, leaning against the truck and rubbing my eyes wearily. I did not feel like cleaning this mess up, I did not feel like paying for a new window – I felt like punching that psychotic bitch in the face and told Karita so in those words.

Karita stepped closer, put her open right hand on my chest just over my heart. I stopped in mid-diatribe, looked at her expectantly.

"We can't know for sure that Summer did any of this, but we both know she's dealing with  very serious issues right now, and there's no denying she thinks you are at least partly to blame for her pain, but I've known her a long time and for all her anger I don't believe she's truly a violent person."

"She was at the Wedge yesterday, undeniable fact. She threatened to castrate me the night before, undeniable fact. Maybe she wasn't violent before, but she's gone off some kind of deep end and she needs serious help. And I'm not gonna put up with this crap."

"I know," Karita said, her eyes unflinchingly locked to mine. "I'm not trying to say there isn't something serious that needs to be addressed. I'll make sure I talk to her today because it's clear she's desperately struggling and has a long way yet to go to come to terms with her life now. But your anger will only get in the way, make it worse. I'm going to talk to her, definitely. But please, let me deal with it. Try to release your anger." She stepped closer to me. "You'll be leaving far too soon, and I don't want the static of your anger between us; it will pollute what we still might achieve."

"And what's that?"

She smiled, and the edge of my anger dulled at her energy, her presence, the play of sun in her hair. "Parking lots are no place to talk of such things. Come on, I'll help you clean up."


But Karita did not talk to Summer that day, or the next day, or the day or week after that. Summer's at none of her usual spots, Karita reported, but not to worry. They would talk and things will be OK. I could find no comfort in such assurances; something felt treacherously wrong, as though matters had slipped into a darker register.

Yet no proper sense of foreboding occurred to me.  I should, looking back now, have been fully alarmed, but I simply and inexplicable was not.  Concerned, yes, annoyed and even angry that some irrelevant stranger was making it harder than it already was to find some sense of solid footing in this place.  Even without her disruption LA was feeling to me like nothing more than a constellation of instabilities bound together by a Gordian knot of concrete and asphalt, some unapproachable construct that shifted shape every time you tilted your head to get a better look.  I don't know, looking back, how I could not have felt some entangling nightmare approaching, but I did not.  No foreboding.

A few days later, my windshield replaced and my checkbook a few hundred dollars lighter, I dragged myself into work in the company of a fairly serious hangover, having somehow gotten carried away with Zin – a welcome change from Hayden's refrigerator of beer – while watching Frank Langella in *Dracula* last night.  I knew I was beginning to drink too much here in LA, though the realization did not surprise me.  I think, in fact, I would have been surprised to find my alcohol consumption *hadn't* increased.  Waiting for me, taped to my computer screen, was a memo from the Dean's secretary, requesting me to report to the office of the Dean at 2.00 o'clock that afternoon, reminding me I had so far neglected to contact his office as requested.  Crumpling the message I wondered if I should leave a farewell note to S-B.  Fuck it, I thought, she's been as friendly as a salesman at closing time, communicating only via email and handscribbled memos.  I hadn't even seen her in three weeks.

I spent the next few hours halfheartedly doing the good Doctor's drudge work, deliberately waiting until a few minutes after two before setting out for the Dean's suite.  I'm normally the sort who regards himself as late if he's not five minutes early, but my normal self seemed to be fast becoming little more than a passing acquaintance.

I'd been to his office once before to get something signed when I first arrived – it seemed like months ago now – but I'd met none of the handful of Deans it apparently took to run a college of liberal arts.  The Dean himself was in now, however, and after keeping me waiting ten minutes he buzzed the secretary, Kyoko's aunt, who with a look of sympathy ushered me in.

He was facing his computer screen, his back to me, as I stepped into his domain.  It was huge: a corner office with window walls, it

96

commanded a beautiful view of a small artificial lake and grove of eucalyptus, backed by one of the hills that marked the northern edge of campus. Two leather couches lined one wall; a credenza that looked to me like antique walnut was on the other. I had just glanced at the artwork when the Dean swore loudly. He turned, gestured me over to his desk, which also appeared to be walnut with some sort of elaborate inlay work. On his monitor was a small animated figure, a male wearing only a black jockstrap, tugging comically at a locked door, an exaggerated look of frustration on his face as balloon-sized drops of sweat flew from his head with every jerk.

"How the hell you get that Heather Hooter to open the door?" the Dean growled jovially in a gravelly Southern drawl. "She wants a hot love phrase and I've tried everything." He shook his head, looked at me as though I had only that instant come into focus. As I realized he was playing some sort of pornographic computer game I fully expected him to blush, look startled, make some stumbling excuse but he only stared at me all the more closely. "Know how to play this one?" he asked, jerking his thumb at the screen behind him. "'Long John Clarence'? Damnedest thing; piece a cake 'til now."

I just shook my head, opened my mouth, said nothing. I suspect I was blushing enough for both of us, but the Dean didn't seem to notice. Just waved me to a chair in front of his desk, turned back to his computer, tapped a key to bring up a screensaver; I was relieved to see it was only the university's logo.

He looked at me in silence a moment, his gaze sharpening, slowly running a hand over his hair, thick and an impossible shade of black, curling slightly at the collar, heavily weighted and glistening with sort of gel. What a throwback, I thought. Then he slowly tilted back in his chair, hands behind his head, and lifted his feet onto the desk. I was suddenly so close to his cowboy boots – cowboy boots? I wondered. In an LA university? – I couldn't help noticing they appeared to be very expensive, as did his suit. It took conscious effort for me to not shake my head.

"Seems you have a bit of a problem, son" he said slowly. "Mighta heard something about this?" His eyebrows, as black as coal streaks, arched into comical bows above his eyes. I felt the urge to laugh begin brewing; he was some bad Hollywood caricature, surely, a lost character actor from some forty-year-old B movie.

But I just nodded. "Yes, one of the TAs here — "

"Like to get the word out ahead a time," he said with a wink. "Circulate a little rumor or two, helps people get ready for the inevitable, know what I mean?" He cleared his throat with deliberation, then added, in a stage whisper, "Got myself a secretary – whoops, executive assistant nowadays – what's great at that. Better at rumors than coffee." He smiled, pleased with what apparently passed as humor with him. I was beginning to feel that now-familiar sense of unreality begin to close in again, a slowly rising tide filling the room, filling my life, closing my throat, burying any sense of the pathetic humor of this situation. "What a fucking ass," was my main and recurring thought.

"Ya see," the Dean resumed, leaning back even further in his chair, his eyes drifting to the ceiling, "we like to make certain accommodations here when we can, an' I think you know what I mean, for certain faculty who are deserving of, well, certain considerations. 'M sure you understand. That's why you're here, frankly; Isadora has a lot of pull around this place. Lot of pull. Not without reason; does fine scholarship. NEH grants like clockwork. But our Provost – fine man, very fine man of principle and integrity– gets uncomfortable when accommodations go beyond the bounds. Know what I mean? Does what he can, winks at certain things when it's possible and in the interest of the University, but sometimes a line has to be drawn." He slowly lowered his boots and sat upright in his chair, hands on the edge of his desk now, vulture stare directed straight at me again. "Line got redrawn and you're on the wrong side, son; 'fraid your employment here has been terminated." He stood suddenly, extended a hand. "Nothin' personal," he boomed jovially; "enjoyed havin' ya here, but ya see how it is, I'm sure. Feel free to take the rest of the afternoon to pack your things. Can get your final paycheck next Friday at the Bursar's office. And don't worry about Isadora; I've sent her an email, and I'll talk to her soon as she's back."

Flustered, I stood, and – like the idiot I can too often be – shook his hand. "Sure you don't know how to play this game?" he asked again with a broad wink.

"Sorry," I mumbled. And with that his back was to me and I found myself without a source of spending money. Only a couple of hundred dollars remained in my checking account and less than five hundred more set aside to cover my expenses getting set up in Iowa. I returned to my office, sent email farewells to S-B and to Kyoko (adding the house's phone number at the last minute), and walked slowly out to my car. The parking sticker caught my eye: $45 for a summer permit and I'd gotten about only half use out of it. Thought about asking for a prorated refund; yeah, right. Drove home.

Only to find a note from the real estate agent on the kitchen counter: "Great news, guys!!! Very interested buyer; think he might make an offer! Let you know soon!! Give me a call if I can help you find a place!!" Two of her business cards lay under the note.

Real estate agents. I sighed. "Of course," I muttered aloud. "Lose a job and a house in the same afternoon. This is fucking *worse* than a bad movie."

By the time Hayden came home that night I was already on my third or fourth beer and feeling pretty sorry for myself.

"So, Hayden, whaddya know?" I slurred, saluting him with my empty bottle.

"I *think* we'll be moving out soon, but I *know* you're three sheets to the wind. Again," he said, his voice oddly flat and with something else behind it; he didn't care about my drinking or his beer. It was, I knew even in my condition, the same unspoken concern that was behind almost everything he said, behind his eyes every time I looked at him. But right now, yeah, three sheets to the wind – who the hell says that anymore, I wondered? – I was well past concerning myself with his opinion of my actions. And was a little surprised that he cared one way or the other.

"Any wise man can see that," I said carelessly. "You, on the other hand, are an even wiser man, so you must know something more in'eresting than the fact of my current mild inebriation."

Hayden's gaze remained flat and he sighed.

"Come, cousin, come," I insisted. "Pearls before swine, perhaps, but I must know what you know. Speak, mighty oracle."

Humorlessly he spoke, missing my point altogether. "I know that spiders spin," he said, catching me off-guard. Then, after the briefest pause, "And that stars collapse. That because locality fails action gets spooky at a distance." Another pause, a wan version of his Harrison Ford grin. "And that chaos abides."

I nodded mock-sagely, not looking at him, not wanting to give away the compounded surprise and puzzlement that surely must have been showing on my face. "Profound, cousin oracle. Very profound." Not that I would have had any idea what he was talking about even if I were sober. But I forged ahead anyway. "So, pray tell, where does chaos abide? I get the impression LA is a likely home."

"Everywhere. I told you, locality fails." A trace of a sneer. "Forget your quantum mechanics already?"

With just a bit of unsteadiness I sat up, and as I did so the unvoiced thought "Falstaff" formed in my mind. I hadn't thought about Shakespeare's Henry plays in years, not since I'd had to read them in a junior-year class, and even through the beer's fog I did not like the fact I was suddenly thinking of Falstaff now. Definitely did not like it.

"Everywhere," I echoed, mostly to cover my confusion.

It must have sounded like a question. "Yes, everywhere," Hayden said. "It's the fundamental power in the universe, the dynamic that impels all things."

"'Rolls through all things . . .'" I said, pointlessly. "Wordsworth."

"Wordsworth, as I recall him, was a self-important sap who rarely deigned to actually talk to the people whose lives and culture he claimed to be most interested in," Hayden responded, warming now to the discussion. He flopped into one of the white wicker chairs, his eyes starting to flash. "Which is to say, a humanist."

"Well," I said, trying to get serious but not feeling very good about my chances, "what about you? You're not a humanist, you're not a Christian, you're not anything as far as I can tell. So just what are your beliefs? You can't be an existentialist, can you? That's passé."

"I'm a gay man with HIV," Hayden said calmly. "Doesn't leave me much, does it?"

I flinched, and the atmosphere in the room suddenly closed in. What could I say to that? Come to think of it, what did he mean?

"Pardon the self-indulgent morbidity," Hayden said after a moment. "I didn't mean to close down the conversation, which finally seemed to be taking an interesting turn. To answer your question, I'm a Pragmatic Entropist."

"A pragmatic whatropist?"

Hayden held up a hand. "No, no, with capital letters: Pragmatic Entropist."

"Ok, ok, Pragmatic Entropist. What are you talking about?"

Hayden's smile was somewhere between malicious and delighted, a shark closing in for the feast. I suddenly wished this conversation hadn't started, that I had another beer, that I was somewhere far from LA.

"You're familiar with the concept of entropy, the laws of thermodynamics?"

I nodded. "Increasing disorder, or something. Energy required to order a system and maintain order. Somethin' like that. " It was very foggy, coming from a little reading done a long time ago.

"Yes, very good," Hayden said with attempt to hide the irony. "Energy is required to organize systems and maintain organization, yet energy is a limited quantity and some is always lost to unusable forms. One of the few truly fundamental facts of the universe, and that's where my system of Pragmatic Entropy begins."

"*Your* system? You made this up yourself?"

Hayden arched an eyebrow in mock indignation; he was having more fun than I was. "As a man of letters you are undoubtedly acquainted with William Blake."

My turn to act supercilious. "Yeah, I got that one: 'I must invent my own system or be enslaved by another man's.' From 'The Marriage of Heaven and Hell,' I think."

"Close — from *Jerusalem*," Hayden said. "If you can even get past their anthropocentrisms, which personally I can't, you realize belief systems are just that: founded on *belief*, on unprovable hypotheses, on slippery chimeras like faith and dubious ancient documents." He shook his head emphatically. "Religions are a crapshoot because they require faith there's a god, with nothing for evidence but a mishmash of reworked myth and legend. Secular humanism dispenses with the fairy stories but still requires faith in humanity, and that's a road I can't walk."

Although I was pretty sure Hayden was wrong about secular humanism I waved it off, getting interested in where he was going with this and not at all confident of my ability, at the moment, to offer any sort of rebuttal.

"I begin with one of the fundamental precepts of the universe, one of the foundation-stones of all existence: the laws of thermodynamics. They are irrefutable, and they tell us, to put it in the layman's vernacular – as, I think, Isaac Asimov once did – that we can't win, we can't break even, and we can't get out of the game."

"That pretty much means we lose then, I guess."

"Precisely. We lose because of entropy: our ordered systems

cannot remain ordered because according to the inescapable laws of thermodynamics we always waste some energy, yet we cannot create more. It's a zero-sum game that must ultimately end in the decay of order and organization, a return to the lowest energy levels. We are, in short, inevitably and irreversibly headed toward chaos, disorder, and decay."

"But that's like over a cosmic time scale, right?" I hiccupped loudly, surprising myself. "You can't really apply that to human lives."

"Why not? If we're talking metaphysical systems, we're by definition concerned with the supra-human, the eternal." He smiled. "If it's all going to hell in a handbasket – although it's more correct to think of it as going to something near absolute zero – does it really matter if only some humans live to see that ignoble end? Not that they'd live to get anywhere near that end, but you know what I mean. The point is the fundamental governing principles in the universe are those of decay and disorder, or at least what humans in their arrogance insist on calling disorder. From there it is a small step to the realization that, as far as human endeavor goes, none of it ultimately means shit."

"Well," I stammered, searching for something familiar, "that's just another version of nihilist despair, then."

"No," Hayden said. "This is a pop metaphysic based on one of the fundamental truths of science, not on the drivel of chain-smoking French pinheads who could never get real jobs so contented themselves with collecting disciples like dung beetles collect shit." He repeated the Harrison Ford grin, wickedly this time. "Philosophy with an attitude."

"I need another beer." Although I was pretty sure I did not.

"I'll join you," Hayden said. We went out to the poolhouse, opened a couple of bottles, then by some unspoken agreement took seats on the deck. Across the canyon ridge-top houses were backlit by a sun made wan by the customary chemical miasma of the LA sky. Entropy, I thought. And felt sadder than I had in a long time. I wondered where Karita was.

"OK, Hayden," I said after a moment, "I can't argue thermodynamics and entropy with you, because I don't understand that stuff very much. But if everything we know ends in some kind of meaningless chaos, if that's not a redundancy – "

"It is."

"— then what's the point of living. Why not kill yourself?"

"You're overlooking the first part: *Pragmatic* Entropist. What redeems the meaninglessness of existence is the fact we're alive. Why people think there has to be a point to life is beyond me, just an expression of intellectual and emotional weakness, I guess. Death avoidance, a metaphysical whistling past the graveyard." He paused for a sip of beer. "As a Pragmatic Entropist I believe that as long as we're here, as long as a series of chemical accidents produced the evolutionary deadend known as *Homo sapiens*, we may as well take advantage of it. So do what you can to maximize your time here."

"Whoa," I said, jerking in surprise and spilling some of my beer. "Wait a minute. This is anarchy-meets-Epicurus, or – or something like that. Self-interest and hedonism."

He smirked. "Leave it to a humanist to think hedonism is the only form of pleasure."

"Whaddya mean? You're talkin' intellectual pleasures, then? Yeah, OK, I grant you that, but aren't you still overlooking a whole bunch of life? I have a master's, I know how gratifying the life of the mind can be, but there's also the life of the heart, Hayden, and the life of the body. And the soul."

"The soul," Hayden intoned, as though repeating a wearisome lesson, "is an escapist fiction. The body is meat. The heart, as you mean it, is a vestigial evolutionary mechanism that causes a hell of a lot of trouble – and I certainly don't except myself. Emotions, particularly those involved in sexual relationships, are a survival mechanism, a means by which natural selection aided the species by establishing communal bonds. Like monkeys, only we write poetry about it. And some of us get yanked, since we feel the emotions but have nothing to do with reproduction." An ironic grin, a salute with his bottle. "But Pragmatic Entropy acknowledges the absence of fairness in this our grim and futile cosmos."

"Jesus, Hayden, you're grimmin' me out." My voice trailed off, for the next words were ones I did not want to say; the gulf between us would have become an open rift. I decided to change tack. Seizing on his mention of fairness, I told him about my job disappearing. Or was it me disappearing?

"Doesn't sound like your day," he said when I'd finished. "I drag you all the way down here to Shaky Town only to see you unemployed and unhoused in a matter of hours." He paused, smiled, glanced in the direction of the lowering sun. 'O, what a rogue and peasant slave am I.'"

"For a techno-guy" – I'd almost said 'techno-geek,' which he probably would have regarded as a higher compliment – "you sure remember a lot of literature."

"Cursed with a very good memory," he said distractedly. Then, after a moment, "Come," he said, pouring his beer into the pool, "doctor told me not to drink this wonderful stuff. Let's go for a drive; I need a Boswell, if I might be allowed another literary allusion." In a moment we'd left our canyon in Hayden's still-dented Porsche; after a trip into town for gas, during which time I sobered up slightly and began to wonder if Hayden had been serious about all that Pragmatic Entropy business or if it was just posture and play at my expense. To this day I'm not sure.

After gassing up the Porsche Hayden pointed the car back toward the foothills. Only a few miles east from where our own canyon lay he turned up another canyon, darkening now as shadows began to gather like mute warnings under the live oak and sycamore which crowded the narrow asphalt roadway. A few twists and turns and a sudden left into a steep driveway and Hayden had killed the motor before I was quite sure where we were. At that moment a photocell clicked and lights came on beside us, illuminating a large brass and stucco sign: "Thomas Webber Preparatory School. Founded 1922."

Hayden was already out of the car, his face lifted to the streaks of pale orange fluorescing above us. I was about to ask him what this place was when the answer drifted up from some chasm of memory: Hayden's high school; it occurred to me I'd even been here for his graduation, long ago.

Hayden was looking at me, could see I remembered, and gestured silently for me to follow him. Wishing I had another beer, I set off beside him as he headed uphill. The school was set into the side of the canyon and was consequently quite hilly; thickly planted with oak, sycamore, eucalyptus and liquidamber, to name only the species I recognized, the setting was bucolic. The various buildings were vaguely Spanish style, their whitewash making them almost glow in the gathering evening. We walked in silence for nearly fifteen minutes, and between the heat and the beers I'd had I was beginning to sweat fairly heavily while my curiosity turned to I was on the verge of protest when Hayden suddenly stopped on the asphalt path, looking around as though seeing the place for the first time.

"Been a long while," he said.

"Yeah, memory lane." I nodded. "I was here for your graduation; I don't remember this place being so large, though. How many acres this school have, anyway?"

"Feels small to me," he said, ignoring my question. "Small and long ago."

I felt myself sobering up – a condition in which I had no interest after a day like this one – and was now genuinely regretting coming along on what was clearly shaping up to be an odyssey of self-indulgence but I forced myself to feign polite interest. "You were here for grade school too, right?"

"Seventh through twelfth," he corrected me absently. Then, staring into some distance only he could see, shook his head again. Clearing the cobwebs of memory, I thought. I'm not much of one for personal nostalgia, or nostalgia of any sort for that matter, and was somewhat surprised to find this streak of sentimentality in Hayden. But I caught myself: he *is* HIV positive, I reminded myself, and his lover is dying; if those aren't sufficient reasons for nostalgic melancholy I guess nothing is. Thomas Parnell, where are you when we need you? I try to grant him the indulgence but still I regretted being here; despite my flush of sympathy for him Hayden still felt like a stranger, resident in a land where I was alien.

Hayden pointed to the northeast, where through a thin stand of shadowed eucalyptus I could see the vague dark shapes, smog-blurred and disappearing into the evening gloom, of the eastern San Gabriel Mountains.

"Thunderheads over Baldy," he said, lifting his eyes to the towering masses of clouds, the highest of them still tinged pink and pale orange by the setting sun, gathered above Mt. Baldy.

"Yeah," I said slowly, wondering what his point was. "Rain, I guess."

Hayden shook his head, smiling sadly. "No. That's my point. Thunderheads over Baldy always look portentous, like they're bringing God's own deluge to this parched paradise." Pause. "But they never do. Never rains. Lots of promise but nothing substantial, nothing life-affirming, ever comes of it." He turned, and I could see his eyes flash in the gloom. "Kind of like LA itself," he added after a snort. Then, quietly as though to himself, "my favorite LA metaphor." Without warning he turned and walked briskly back down the asphalt path. So much for nostalgia. I followed in silence.

On our return to the house it was clear even before Hayden had killed the engine that something was amiss. Hayden felt it too. "Lights are on," he muttered, clambering awkwardly out of the car. The backyard was ablaze with light; pushing through the gate we could see that every porch and yard light had been turned on in our absence. My first thought was that our ditzy real estate agent had come through and simply forgotten to turn off the lights, but then I saw the pool. The underwater lights there were on as well, providing backlight for the dark mass floating on the pool's surface.

"What the fuck?" Hayden said, walking slowly to the edge. "Clothes," he said wonderingly.

I looked, closely, and my heart sank again. "Son of a fucking bitch! My clothes!" I must have sworn, probably incoherently, for thirty seconds before I realized Hayden had disappeared inside; with a forlorn glance at the pool I hastily followed him, the adrenalin pumping as the anger filled me.

He was just coming down the gallery from the direction of the master bedroom. When he saw me he shook his head, waved dismissively. "Nothing," he said; "nothing else has been touched. Not even my laptop." He shook his head. "Can't believe I forgot to set the alarm. That's what I get for rushing off like a damn fool."

I suddenly thought of my own laptop, of my novel in progress and my notes, none of which had been backed up since I'd arrived in this cursed town – and with a flash of hope recalled that I'd been using it that afternoon in one of the eastern bedrooms because of the coolness there. The laptop was where I'd left it, on the floor, screened from view by the unwanted canopy bed Mrs. Parkinson had left behind.

The rest of my possessions did not fare so well: I stepped into the room I was using – already I'd stopped thinking of it as "my" room, since it appeared we'd be leaving soon – and was brought up short by the total disarray. Every drawer in the dresser was standing open and empty, as was the closet, and with a sinking feeling I noticed that the three boxes of books I kept in the closet were gone. I raced back outside to the pool; sure enough, there in the deep end and largely hidden by the floating clothes were the boxes, weighted down by the books within. I swore again, and more in dismay than anything grabbed at a shirt floating near the edge. It hung strangely in my hand as I pulled it out of the water; holding it up at the shoulders I could see it had been slit down the front. A pair of jeans I pulled out: slit. A T-shirt. Swearing another blue streak I grabbed the skimming net and began lifting clothes out of the pool. Everything: every single piece of clothing I had brought with me, except the jeans and polo shirt I was wearing, had been slashed, ruined.

I had removed most of the clothes when Hayden stepped out onto the deck and yelled at me to stop. Freezing in mid-motion, I looked up at him in stupid surprise, looking at him out of the depth of my anger.

"Leave it," he said wearily; "I've called the police; they're on their way and they'll want everything left as it is. We've also got a broken slider, in the sitting room. Whoever it was threw a brick – crude but effective, I guess."

"I know who the fuck it was, " I sputtered. "That bitch Summer."

"I wondered what you meant by that," Hayden said; "you've been yelling about Summer all along and I had no idea what you were talking about."

"You don't want to know," I told him, the bitterness almost palpable on my tongue.

"I suspect you're," he said, "but the police will feel differently. So tell them the story and I'll get it then."

And I did tell them. A couple of police officers young enough to make me feel old and with enough aloof officiousness to alienate anybody showed up half an hour later, and after looking through the house in a surprisingly casual manner and taking only a few pictures they listened, making desultory notes, to Hayden's story and my suspicions. With great deliberateness one of them began to fill out a report; I was delighted that he asked me again about Summer, for I wanted that bitch arrested. I told him of every encounter, of the windshield, everything, and in my relief felt the words tumble out almost frantically. I regretted having to drag Karita into it – I gave the officer her name since she would know what I did not: how to find Summer – but saw no choice. Things were getting out of hand; Summer was seriously out of control.

After the police left Hayden phoned Mrs P and the real estate agent but I wasn't interested. I sat at the edge of the pool, kicking sometimes idly and sometimes angrily at the clothes that I'd tossed back into the pool before the police arrived and getting drunk again. At one point I wandered over to Karita's house but there was no response to my repeated buzzing; I took my revenge on her absence by pissing on the bird of paradise that grew by the front porch. When I returned poolside Hayden was busily at work fishing my clothes out of the water, working with a focused energy that even in my inebriation I could see testified to his annoyance, some of which I was sure was directed at me for getting involved with such people in the first place. Fuck you, I thought; it's not my fault the neighbor knows a nutcase. Without a word I headed for the house, paused when Hayden explained, tersely, that the police didn't need the clothes for evidence and he'd throw them in the trash if I had no objection. "No objection," I sighed, suddenly feeling drained. Within minutes I was asleep, sprawled across the waterbed fully dressed.


I awoke the next morning to the ringing of the phone and the cartoon-cheerful voice which responded to my malevolent mumble: our real estate agent, explaining that everything was taken care of and a repairman would be by shortly to fix the slider and could we please be out of the house between four and six because her client was coming by for a second look?

Hayden had already left for work so after a shower that failed to assuage the pressure in my head or the general sense of unease that had settled into my very joints I left a terse message on his work voicemail. I was on my third cup of coffee and second helping of antacids when the doorbell rang, startling me for an instant. Karita? I thought, before I remembered the glass repair. I dragged myself to the door and admitted a pirate.

That's the vibe I got from him, anyway: tall and lithe in worn black cutoffs, sandals, a bright red shirt, thick black curls that hung down to his shoulders, ferocious mustache, a three-day growth of beard and at least three gold earrings. Where's the parrot? I was tempted to ask, but he immediately launched into a friendly rapid-fire monologue and I found myself pleasantly amused, warming to him despite the theatricality of his appearance. I remembered, vaguely, that

Karita struck me the same way at first, though I'd quickly become so accustomed to the exuberance of her clothes I had long ceased to find them unusual or even striking.

The pirate, who introduced himself as Max, hadn't stopped talking and it took me a moment to catch up, to realize he wanted to know where the damaged slider was. Shaking my head to clear the cobwebs I led him to the master suite. He chuckled as he followed me. "Tough night, eh?"

"You could say that," I grumbled as I led him into the atrium. Hayden had swept up the shattered glass but had touched nothing else; a delicate hint of breeze from the shattered door, bringing with it the forlorn scent of warming chaparral, was like the touch of a loving, half-forgotten ghost on my skin.

Max nodded as he took in the damage with a quick glance. "No prob," he said, rubbing his chin; "lemme get some dimensions and run back to the shop real quick, I'll come right back and in a coupla hours you'll be good as new." Then, with a sly glance at me, added "or at least your slider will be." He chuckled again as he drew a tape measure from his toolbelt and stepped to the shattered door. I aimed a silent snarl at his back and returned to my waterbed, where through my listlessness I tried to read more of *Desolation Angels*.

I was awakened from the dream-haunted sleep into which I'd fallen by repeated calls of "Hey, dude." Startled and groggy, a dream still half before my eyes, I slipped out of the waterbed and crashed loudly to the floor, swearing as I stood up.

"Hey, you all right?" Max stuck his pirate's face around the doorjamb.

"Yeah, fuckin' slipped," I growled, rubbing my knee; "damn waterbeds."

"Sorry, man, didn't mean to wake you; just wanted to let you know I'm finished, you're all set. Didn't get an answer when I came back so let myself in. Door's good as new, man. That one-piece single-pane's a breeze."

He peered at me solicitously, a look of what appeared to be genuine compassion shaping his features. "You look pretty crapped out, man; musta been a helluva party." I opened my mouth to say something, to explain, but realized I had neither the energy nor the desire. Max appeared not to notice. "I can tell ya what, though; I seen a hell of a lot worse in my line a work. One window ain't nothin', 'specially if there ain't no blood. I once hadda reglaze three sliders and a coupla skylights at a place up in Pasadena – monster house, man, you shoulda seen it – dude there was tellin' me they had two ambulances up there, plus a coupla other folks they hadda drive to emergency." He shook his head, clearly impressed with the memory. "Some fuckin' folks, man, party like the devil's up their ass and twirlin' that pitchfork."

"Nothin' like that here," I said vaguely.

"Tell ya what though, man, you still look pretty whacked; since I woke ya up and all, and since ya didn't bug the hell outta me lookin' over my shoulder like some folks do, lemme help ya out. Hang on just a sec."

I shuffled out to the atrium, wondering what sort of help he was talking about. I glanced at the slider he'd repaired, which looked fine now, when he returned from outside.

"Here ya go, man," he said amiably, holding out a small gold tube. At first I had no idea what he had given me but then I noticed in his other hand a small round mirror, a little pile of white powder in one corner. "Nothin' special," he said, "just regular blow, but you sure look like you could use some help." With the dexterity of long practice he used a razor blade to quickly stroke out a few lines. He held the mirror toward me. "Go on, man, on me."

And to my surprise I did it. Surprise, I think, not because I did the coke – I've used it maybe a half dozen times before, found it entirely pleasurable but so unaffordable I never thought much about it – but because of the strange sense of detachment in which I seemed to float even before I bent to snort the cocaine. This was as surreal as anything that had happened to me during my time in LA yet felt as normal as a puzzling dream. But when I caught a glimpse of my eyes in the mirror in Max's hand, a witchwork tracery of capillaries surrounding hard iris and shrunken pupil, I was almost startled – I probably would have been genuinely alarmed if I hadn't been so hungover – by the strangeness, the Otherness of those eyes, of the hand holding the coke straw, even the sound of my sharp snort as I snorted the powder. I shuddered slightly, and wasn't sure if it was the rush of the coke or this latest brush with a recurring strangeness, a persistent sense I was being haunted by some Other who was myself and who kept showing up more and more often yet was never expected, never fully recognized. I blinked hard and snorted another line then handed the straw to Max. He did a couple of lines, then returned the straw to me for two more as the buoyant rush hit me, lifted me like a benevolent ocean swell.

"Thanks," I said, beginning to feel as though I might have the energy to get through this sour day.

"Don't mention it, man," Max said as he cleaned off the mirror with his forefinger, sticking it into his mouth to get the last grains. "You look better already, so I did a good deed today. But I got another job so I need to cut." He slipped his paraphernalia into a pocket. "Take it easy, man." He held out his hand, which I shook. "Been real, man. Adios."

"Adios," I echoed. Adding, after he'd closed the front door behind him, "but it's most definitely not been real."

I spent the next few hours aimlessly banging around the house, practicing my *kata* and twice jumping into the pool to do laps in a vague and listless attempt to burn off the energy of the coke, which made me energetic but didn't do enough for my mood. I left a message for Karita both at home and the Oak, and some hours later, once the coke had worn off, fell asleep again. Only to be awakened again by the ringing of the doorbell, and as I stumbled down the hall – excuse me, the goddamn gallery – I realized it had probably been ringing for some time.

Karita. I think I'd blurted out half the story of the previous night's events even before she stepped inside the house, and would have kept on babbling if she hadn't pressed a finger to my lips to silence me.

"I know," she said; "I talked to someone from the police department this morning; they told me all about it."

I nodded. "Come on in, then; I think we need to talk."

She shook her head, glanced at her watch. "Can't stay. Jazz is covering for me at the Oak and I told her I'd be back by four-thirty."

With a sudden flash of panic I suddenly recalled the phone call from the real estate agent that morning. "Shit," I cried; "what time is it now?"

"Four-ten. Why?"

I told Karita about the return visit – this was, I suddenly realized, the first she'd heard about the possible sale of the house – as I rushed into the kitchen to set everything in order. I'd been too hungover to make much of a mess that day – the only moment in my life I've ever been glad of a hangover – and in two minutes had grabbed my wallet and keys and half-dragged Karita out the door. I was still thinking we could go to her house and talk, for it suddenly felt as though we had a very great deal to discuss, but she was firm in her insistence on returning to the Oak.

"OK," I said, "then I'll drive you. We gotta talk about this shit or I'm gonna fuckin' explode."

She shook her head. "I have a better idea, and if you'd quit acting like the crazy male you are I could make you the offer I came here to make."

"OK," I said, "offer away."

"I have someone coming by the Oak for private instruction tonight, so I'm not free till 8, but if you meet me then I'll drive you to Wormwood's for a bite and we'll stay for the poetry slam. It's all on me."

"Wait a minute. Poetry slam? We need to talk. Christ, I've lost my job, I'm probably gonna have to move in a few weeks, and your psych – " I caught myself – "Summer's mistaken me for the antichrist and you want to go to a poetry slam? I'm not sure I'm up for it. And when the hell are we gonna talk?"

"It's forty minutes to Venice; we'll talk on the way."

"Shit," I moaned, burying my face in my hands. "How LA...."

Karita's laugh sparkled incongruously. "Poor northern child," she said, lightly touching my cheek. "It'll be fine. I've got to get back to the store, so go buy yourself a funky shirt to wear. Gotta be hip, hipster, we're going to Wormwood's."

"Yeah, and I almost forgot: I'm damn near broke, too, or will be now thanks to Summer. And what the hell is Wormwood's and why a poetry slam, tonight of all nights? You don't really strike me as the poetry slam type, and I sure as hell don't strike me as the type either. I've been to a couple and they're mostly self-indulgent crappy poetry with a dash of quirky exhibitionism. So why you wanna go?"

"One of my artists," she said quickly. "Wenceslaus Perlmutter. He – "

"Wait a minute," I laughed despite myself. "Wenceslaus Perlmutter? That's a joke, right? That can't be his real name."

Karita shrugged. "Never asked. If that's what he wants to be called, that's all that matters. Anyway, he makes absolutely exquisite jewelry, I can't keep his stuff in stock. He does spoken word as well, and keeps hounding me to come hear him. If I put it off too long, he makes himself very scarce, so once or twice a year I have to do my duty. I promised him – months ago, before you came – I'd be at Wormwood's tonight. His first time there. You understand."

I waved dismissively. "Biz is biz, yeah. But what's Wormwood's?"

"Currently the hottest spot for spoken word this side of New York." She smiled impishly. "Don't tell me that even you literati are out of touch up there in the northern reaches. My, my, my. Well, after tonight you'll have some tales to tell in Iowa. Eight, remember."

"Eight," I mumbled as she moved quickly to her car.

I was there, new shirt and all, although only because I needed new clothes anyway and had to be out of the house until six, at which time I returned for a quick snack and more antacids. Hayden arrived home just before I left, looking even more harried than usual, and I asked him to check into the possibility that Mrs. Parkinson's insurance might cover my losses.

He nodded curtly and disappeared into his room.

Karita was waiting outside the Oak when I arrived, which struck me as curious, and she was so buoyant that some twenty minutes had passed before I could talk to her about last night. I told her what had happened – it now sounded much less dramatic and significant than it had felt, for some reason I couldn't determine – and then asked her directly if she'd told the police where to find Summer.

She shook her head but before my anger – dismay? – could spill out she said "I couldn't tell them because I don't know. I told you the other night she wasn't at any of her usual spots; she's really gone underground or something. A few weeks after you arrived she moved out of the apartment she was sharing, and since then has been living with a couple of different friends, a few nights here, a few nights there; no one seems to know where she's living now, and I've been in every club and studio she normally goes to, and that's not many, asking for her. No one's seen her. I don't know what else I can do, and I'm worried."

'About her or me?' I asked silently, quietly surprised to find myself wondering if Karita was telling the whole truth, if there wasn't perhaps more she didn't want me to know. In that moment I could feel the mooring lines, as loose as they were for me already here in LA, slipping even further. I looked out the window for a long moment, the glass-fronted strip malls and tediously beige apartment buildings slipping repetitively past in the fading light, and felt for the first time a sense of aloneness so sharp it seemed a hollow space ringed with knives, just enough room for me to stand and observe but every move would bring blood.

"Besides," Karita added in a silence that had, I suddenly realized, grown awkward, "the police said it would be very hard to prove it was her, what with the house being for sale and all, people coming through and everything. They didn't – "

"They don't give a shit," I burst out. "They didn't even dust for fingerprints or anything; said the recent open house made that irrelevant."

Karita looked askance at me. "This isn't Iowa, darling; the police have more serious things to attend to. They told me they'd try to talk to her though, if they could find her, see what they could learn."

My laugh was edged with a bitterness I barely recognized. "I know a brushoff when I hear one. Yeah, who gives a damn about some slashed clothes? Except me." I shook my head. "But what about you?" I turned to Karita. "We both know it was her. What the hell's going on and what am I supposed to do, watch my back every second I'm in La-La Land?" I sat back hard in my seat, suddenly angry at the casual absurdity of the events that swirled around me like a psychic postmodern version of Poe's consuming maelstrom.

"I told you," Karita said, something in her voice suddenly remote, abstract; "Summer's blaming you, projecting onto you a lot of anger and hostility that isn't your fault or your responsibility." She put her hand on my leg momentarily, which only reminded me we still hadn't had sex in any sort of normal way. I almost laughed aloud at the idea of normalcy. "I know that's shitty," she continued – far too reasonably, I thought; we need some fucking anger here: do not go gently into that good nightmare – "and I know it's not fair, but I don't know what else to tell you. Summer's very troubled, even more so than I thought. I mean, I never imagined she'd react quite this way."

"Or else you wouldn't have broken up with her, huh?" The edge in my voice, calculated to cut, surprised even me. And my words sounded stupid the instant I uttered them.

"Don't," Karita said, her eyes locked straight ahead. "Don't talk foolishly about things you weren't part of. Summer's behavior isn't your fault or mine. It's her responsibility, and hers alone. I'm not her keeper. Sometimes lately she's been almost as mad at me as she's been at you."

"Doesn't slice up your clothes, smash your windows, threaten you with bodily mutilation," I observed.

Karita ignored me. "Neither of us can help what she is and what she's been through, but we can try to understand, try to deal with it. She needs a great deal of help and it's going to take a big push from outside of her to get her to understand and accept that."

Crushing her trachea sounded like a good way of dealing with it, I thought. Then, annoyed at myself, wondered where that came from. I turned abruptly to face Karita, though she continued to focus on the road before her. "Would you call the police if she suddenly showed up?"

Karita's sigh was sharp. "It's not like she's a wanted criminal, you know; it's not like she tried to hurt you or anything. Besides, that's not the point."

"Is for me. She's damaged my truck, threatened me, followed me around, trashed my belongings – she's got some serious anger directed at me and she has some serious issues in general. I think – hell, I know – she's broken the law, and I'm afraid I'll be the one in jail by the time this is over because if I see her I'll probably beat the hell out of that damn little stalker."

Karita turned to me, her eyes wide. "You wouldn't dare touch her," she said anxiously, angrily. "She's half your size. Aaaah!" She shook her head fiercely as I realized I'd made a huge mistake: next time keep it to yourself, man. "You – how can you even think – "

"No," I said quickly, hoping to cut her off. "I wouldn't really. Sorry," I said. "I'm tired, hungover, pissed off: I'm over-reacting, OK? But – fuck, I don't know what. Damn!" I pounded my knee so hard it genuinely hurt. "I don't know," I said again, "too much weird shit happening – way too much weird shit happening in too short a time. Maybe I just need to leave." I shook my head, looked out again at the strip malls and apartment buildings – had we moved at all? – crawling anonymously past. "This has been one weird-ass summer."

"It's been what it should be," Karita said softly, and I could tell by the tone of her voice she wanted to turn the conversation away from Summer. "This is life in its full flow and chaotic tumble. The stream doesn't complain about the eddies and the falls and the rocks, and it can't avoid them; they *are* the stream, and without them the stream wouldn't be what it is."

I looked at her a long moment, saw her turn and flash a quick if half-hearted smile.

"Where do you get this stuff?" I found myself asking yet again, willing to let the conversation take a new course. But I knew something else had changed, something unspoken, unfaced, yet making its presence felt like a shadow in the doorway.


Wormwood's turned out be a jammed-to-the-rafters dive of a bar in a seedy part of Venice, if that's not redundant; from the street its cracked, faded stucco and dirty glass gave the place an aura of futility and wearisome failure, but a step into the darkened bar changed that, primarily by glossing it over with noise and chaos and fevered energy. Definitely not my kind of place. We waited nearly 30 minutes for our reservation, me drinking what tasted like overpriced Gallo while Karita had only water. We said too little. The food was indifferent at best and the music ear-crushingly loud; the only positive for me was the crowd, and that because it was an entertainingly eclectic collection of the most unlikely looking literary types ever assembled. And I fit in not at all: no piercings, no tattoos, no black clothing, my hair its natural color. With considerable if somewhat pallid amusement I pointed this out to Karita, who laughed. "And you told me you were a writer," she cried in mock dismay.

The energy in the place was the high-tension brittleness of the insecure that seems to be the ambient psychic atmosphere of choice in Anglo LA; it was one of those below-radar "see and be seen" kinds of places that took itself and its hyper-trendiness too seriously. I sighed inwardly, out of nowhere recalled Byron's lament: "O ye shades of Pope and Dryden, have we come to this?" I knew I was being deeply judgmental but my mood was too sour and my reservoir of goodwill and tolerance was as dry as the rocky forgotten creekbeds of the San Gabriels. I was about to make some scathingly witty remark to Karita about the pretense and posturing around us when we were accosted by Lurch.

Well, no, it wasn't really the laconic butler from "The Addams Family," but it could have been. He must have been nearly seven feet tall, bone-thin and pale with a William Burroughs face that went on forever, looming over our table like some sort of hyperthyroidal junkie nightmare.

"What a good little girl," he boomed, his voice an astonishingly deep rumble, as pure in tone as a double bass and carrying perfectly, probably by direct vibration of bone, despite the noise in the bar. "You came to hear me." He reached his arms out to Karita, who stood and gave him a hug, her head coming not even to his chest.

"Of course," she smiled. "Wouldn't miss the debut for the world."

He looked down at her archly. "You lie like a dime hooker bitch, doll. Must need more of my pieces. What this time? Earrings? Lip studs? Bracelets? More of those to-die-for platinum labia rings? Be happy to put some more in for you, darling." He winked broadly, a grotesque gesture that seemed to occur on a geologic time scale.

Karita laughed. "Anything and everything, Wence, as always." She introduced me to the giant, who angled his massive skull just enough to give me a quick, dismissive glance before turning his full attention back to Karita. I don't need this shit, I thought, and wished yet again I was elsewhere.

They exchanged unpleasantries for another ten minutes – Karita later told me it was all normal behavior for Wenceslaus, think nothing of it – when the abrupt cessation of the music and the sudden pop of floodlights on the bare wooden stage marked the start of the slam. A table of four black-garbed heroin-waif wannabes was announced as the judging panel and with only a perfunctory introduction from a bored and vaguely Asian-looking kid with a very long ponytail the slam got under way.

The crowd, apparently intent on taking "slam" literally in its vernacular sense, got quickly into the spirit, interjecting raucous, rude and irreverent comments even during the readings of the poems, driving the first three poets – too grand a term for them, really; their stuff was sophomoric, self-indulgent crap – off the stage in a matter of minutes. The fourth poet got through both of her pieces, but almost burst into tears when one of the judges, instead of holding up a scorecard, simply stood and ratcheted the zipper of his leather jeans a few times. I smiled when she regained enough composure before leaving the stage to flip him off.

Karita had mentioned this was an invitation-only session but the poetry was as trite and vapid and cliché-ridden as any I'd ever heard at the few open-mike poetry nights I'd been to in Eureka and Portland, or in the poetry writing class I took at Humboldt. I was struggling to stay focused when Perlmutter lumbered into the spotlight, looking comically misproportioned there on the tiny stage which creaked audibly under his feet. But the crowd actually quieted down after he began booming his poem, and by the time he finished I could tell that the atmosphere had subtly altered, that a small space had been granted to at least the possibility of the power of words; some of the people in the crowd thought they heard real poetry. The judges did too: Perlmutter got a 38. But I was troubled; his poem – he read only one because of its length – sounded vaguely familiar. It sounded very much like something by Wallace Stevens, in fact, and I turned to Karita to make some comment to this effect.

And saw her frozen in mid-gesture, her hand extended toward me as though to touch my arm but arrested in mid-air, held immobile as she looked intently and unblinking toward the back of the crowded bar. I followed her gaze.

Summer.

The instant I recognized her scrawny elf-form wedged into the crowd by the entrance I could feel the adrenalin surge. With the vague intent of confronting her I lurched to my feet, one knee knocking our flimsy table so hard our glasses went tumbling to the floor and I stumbled, falling. I threw my arm in front of my face as I fell, hoping to absorb the blow, and clambered back to my feet as quickly as I could, ignoring the shouts and protests around me as I started again for the door. I bumped into a couple of people, several of whom shoved back rudely, and after one particularly sharp blow to my right forearm I became aware of a strange stinging. I put my hand there only to feel a warm stickiness that I knew without looking was blood. I stopped for a moment, confused, wanting to get Summer – still not sure what I'd have done if I reached her – but reflexively knowing I needed to check my arm. The gash was surgically neat, only a few inches long but there was a lot more blood than I expected.

Just then a hand touched my shoulder, and as I turned I brushed against someone who had been jostled next to me. He screamed and jumped back as much as the press of bodies would permit. "You son of a bitch, you got blood on me!" His screech was almost a falsetto; I just looked at him blankly. "Shit, you probably got

AIDS, you prick."

I still felt confusion, mostly, although it was dawning on me that it would be a real good idea for me to get out of this bar. But from somewhere, some psychological terra incognita whose presence had always gone unglimpsed before, came my response: I glared evenly at the guy in front of me, who seemed almost to flinch, and said very calmly and with a casual shrug, "Well, the man I live is HIV positive, so I guess that's possible." He did flinch visibly this time, looked for a second like he was wanted to hit me but instead just moved back into the crowd, dabbing carefully at his sleeve with a napkin.

The touch on my shoulder was repeated, more firmly this time: Karita. Her eyes were unusually wide and even in the stark half-light of the bar I could see she was pale. "Come on," she said, her voice solicitousness layered over a very real nervousness. "You're leaving a trail; we should get you to an emergency room." She guided me outside.

I looked around for Summer, of course saw no sign of her. Karita was silent as she wrapped a scarf around my arm to staunch the blood, then a blanket to keep this particular vital fluid off the leather seats of her Beemer. A quick check of the car's nav system gave her the location of the nearest hospital and in an hour I was getting a few stitches and giving thanks I was still on my parents' health insurance.

Karita had been mostly silent throughout this episode, talking – in fluent Spanish – more to the six-year-old Hispanic girl next to her in the emergency room than to me. Which was fine with me: I was tired and deeply angry and my stomach felt like an acid factory under aerial bombardment. As we drove home I was well on my way to nodding off when Karita abruptly broke the heavy silence that had settled firmly between us. "You know, unless it was just coincidence that Summer was there – "

I snorted my derision, too tired to elaborate.

"I'm not saying it was," Karita said somewhat petulantly; "in fact it probably wasn't; she's never been interested in spoken word and never goes to straight bars." She paused and I could feel her gather herself, and when she spoke her voice was as matter-of-fact as I'd ever heard it. "But I was going to say that no matter why she was there I think the best thing to do at this point is nothing."

I turned my head slowly toward her, looking at her face outlined in the dashlight glow and the confused wash of head- and

tailights surging around us.  Her hair caught familiar highlights and her
soft features were compelling in the dim contouring light but there was
something unfamiliar about her, something suggesting a person I'd
never known, never met.  Behind her, across four lanes of traffic
heading west, vague alternating masses of light and tree and building
slipped past, flowing smoothly and endlessly away behind us into the
vast anonymous LA night, and looking at this, at her face, at the titanic
indifference that lay around us for miles in every direction, I forgot
what she had said, forgot that I should answer.

"I'm serious," she said after a moment, startling me.  "Trying to
talk to Summer now would aggravate everything, spook her into doing
I don't know what."  She turned to me for a brief moment, surveying
my silence.  "And of course saying anything to the police would be
pointless."

"I'm sure it would," I said carelessly, too tired and drunk and
queasy to give much of a damn about anything other than sleep right
now.  I felt as though my concerns were getting no traction, and it
struck me, finally, that Karita was going to protect Summer well
beyond any bounds I would regard as reasonable.  On some level I
could understand this, but I also felt, again, a vague insinuation of
distance between Karita and myself, a deep disagreement about
something fundamental, something whose boundaries ventured near
the irrevocable.  Some bridge had been crossed, a link which had now
disappeared into the abyss of Summer's obsessive hatred.  Or love of
Karita – I didn't know which and I'm not sure Karita did either.  Not
that it mattered.  There was a sick strangeness afoot here and it was a
stench in my nostrils, and, to mix my metaphors even further, it was
completing the circle of isolation that had been gathering and
coalescing around me ever since I rolled into this odd and blighted
place.  I shook my head at the realization, felt even more tired now.
Wished I was home, wherever that was.

"I give up," I said softly, not entirely sure what I meant.

"You're just tired," Karita said sympathetically, laying a warm
hand on my thigh.

"Yeah," I said, unconvinced and unconvincing.  "And on the
wrong fucking planet."

"No," she said.  "Just inbetween, like I said before.  Taking a
detour on a move halfway across the country, beginning another life
phase, a step further into independence – you'd be going through a lot

even without . . . everything that's happening here. And being here is still the right thing for you."

I thought of Hayden watching his lover die in Atlanta, and though I felt like I knew him less now than I did before I came here his sorrow weighed on me. "Those cornfields are lookin' better all the time, I think. I could use a big dose of nothing. And some sleep."

"You'll make it," she said.

I didn't quite know what she was referring to.


I woke the next morning to a half-familiar sense of panic and confusion, unable to recognize my surroundings. I'd whipped off the covers and was half out of bed before I recognized Karita's bedroom. With my heart still pounding and the first press of a blossoming headache starting to assert itself I lay back down, trying without success to recall our arrival home last night. Shit, I thought, I'm absolutely fucking losing it.

Karita was in the bed next to me, partly awakened by my movement, and she slid closer to me, pressing the length of her body against mine. She was naked, and in a moment I was too, and we made what I later realized was surprisingly conventional love: no paraphernalia, no Wiccan incantations, no weird foreplay. It felt very good, not just physically of course but mentally and emotionally as well. Something straightforward for a change. I was just a little too out of it to realize this normalcy should have seemed quite strange.


Hayden was in Atlanta again over the weekend, which passed uneventfully. On Monday morning I called the police – although I wasn't sure why I bothered; annoyance or anger, probably – to see if anything had turned up. It was Wednesday afternoon and three more phone calls before my suspicions were confirmed: nothing. No trace of Summer, no further developments. At least the detective I finally talked to didn't try to make it sound as though they were actually interested in the case. As if the boredom in his voice weren't signal enough, his terse explanation that they didn't have the resources to devote to such a low-priority incident made it redundantly clear.

I realized, over the course of the next few days and weeks, that for the first time in recent memory I had a lot of spare time on my hands but didn't have the wherewithal to do much with it. My money was perilously low, and even though Hayden was leaving much more cash for groceries and beer than was necessary I began to wonder if I was going to make it the rest of the summer without asking my folks for money – something I dreaded, given how generous they'd already been – or dipping into the few hundred dollars I'd set aside to cover my relocation to Iowa. With the books I'd brought with me destroyed I had no reading material at the house, and without much cash my mobility was seriously curtailed. I did make a couple of visits to the beach but never back to those barren, spiritless mountains, and I splurged as well on pilgrimages to the Norton Simon and J. Paul Getty museums. I even began spending a lot of time in the local library, since I couldn't get a card, reading for hours at a stretch. But I still found myself spending a lot of time in an overly large and overly empty house. Hayden, when he was around, was either morose or asleep, and Karita managed to spend an unbelievable amount of time away from home, to the point where I began to suspect she was avoiding me. I made a catty mental note to ask her about all that 'psychic togetherness' stuff she'd spouted when we first met, but I never got the chance.

I began swimming regularly, constantly ratcheting up the number of laps I'd make myself do. I began performing my *kata* at least twice a day, sometimes as many as twelve times, and in general began to feel like some kind of martial-arts monk. But no Zen-like *satori* or Taoist harmony of mindfulness was anywhere on my metaphysical horizon. I was keeping busy – and avoiding writing anything – out of a sense of deep disquiet and dislocation, a vaguely threatening sense of hollowness, and I began to feel haunted by an increasingly pressing sense that I needed to be somewhere else. I attributed it to this crazy business with Summer and my impending move, but I was never fully convinced there wasn't more.

And still I never recognized a true sense of foreboding.

My sense of instability was further heightened a couple of days after the police detective brushed me off. The real estate agent had called the night before, explaining that the offer/counter-offer ballet had been completed and a contract had been signed. There were the usual contingency clauses, including a house inspection in a couple of days. I of course told her I'd disappear, but to my surprise she said no, that her client had specifically asked that one of the housesitters be there and go on the inspection with us.  Sure, I said, thinking to myself that at least it would be a respite from boredom.

They arrived about eleven on Friday morning: real estate agent, inspector, prospective buyer.  I admit I was mildly curious about who would be buying such a house, although I figured it would be yet another rich old white guy, overweight, peremptory, authoritarian, large expensive watch on a thick forearm and a manner brusque enough to insult half the world – the usual successful corporate executive type.

Guess again nature boy, as Hayden might've said.

When I first saw him get out of the real estate agent's car I thought she must've made a mistake, for climbing out of her car was a Hispanic guy who looked maybe 25 years old and who, it quickly became apparent, was in no danger of being mistaken for any habitué of the corporate boardroom.  His scraggly goatee and the tattooed letters on the back of his fingers were my first clues, along with clothes that appeared to have come from a low-rent thriftshop; his heavily accented English quickly confirmed my suspicions.  'How the fuck can you afford this place?' I wondered.  Some kind of Latino rocker maybe?

Claro – that was his name – turned out to be one of the nicest people I've ever met, and he seemed to take me into his confidence almost instantly.  And without my asking he answered my question: he won the lottery.  Eighteen million dollar jackpot, and his the only winning ticket.  He found that terribly amusing.

I happened just at that instant to catch the real estate agent's eye, and she nodded once slightly, one eyebrow discreetly arched.  I sighed inwardly.  The fucking lottery.

Claro seemed more interested in telling me about the phenomenal wedding he was going to give his sister next month than in the house inspection, and I was glad for the distraction: watching an ex-contractor check plumbing fixtures and electrical outlets gets old very quickly, especially when he's dogged by a voluble and highly-strung real estate agent.  It took him over two hours to fully inspect the interior.

Claro pulled me aside as the others stepped out onto the patio.

"You smoke, man?" he asked slyly, reaching into his shirt pocket and pulling out a joint.

"Ah, not much any more, you know?  Especially not this early.  Thanks though."  I couldn't believe this.  I wondered if he knew Max.

He nodded, lit the joint and took a long deep drag. "Good shit, man, really clean." He held out the joint. "You sure?"

I shook my head. "*No, no gracias.*"

"Ah, *tu hablas español*, eh?"

"Just a little – *un poco*, um, *hace mucho anos que . . .*" I stopped, unable to remember the word for "studied."

Claro grinned, took another long drag. "Guess we better stick to English, eh? since my English don't suck as bad as your Spanish." He laughed. "I want to ask you, man, since you been livin' here, this house, it's alright?"

"Alright? Yeah, I guess so. I've only been here a couple months, but yeah, I haven't seen anything wrong. No leaks or stuff like that. It's a nice house."

Claro nodded thoughtfully, his eyes focused on the thin wisp of smoke rising from his reefer. "Yeah, but that's not really what I mean, man. That's what I got this dude for," he said, a jerk of his thumb over his shoulder indicating the inspector outside. He suddenly shifted his gaze directly to me. "What I mean is like this. When I was a little boy my *abuela* came to live with us in Monterey Park – you know '*abuela*?'"

"Yeah, uh, grandmother."

He nodded. "She was from Oaxaca, born and raised in the mountains there, spent her whole fucking life in a little two-room *casita* outside a little nowhere village that ain't even really a village. I been there couple times when I was little, and it was like maybe twelve people lived there, you know? And she lived outside that village most a her life, mostly by herself. An' you know why?"

I shook my head, wondering what the hell his point was.

Claro looked around melodramatically, his eyes already glassy from the pot. "She was a *bruja*, man. A witch. People there didn't like her, thought she killed her *esposo* – and before that a lover – with her *brujeria*, her magic, so people left her alone. She wouldn't leave, though, not until she got really sick and she came to live with us. Everyone thought she was gonna die, like the doctors said, but she lived for three more years, man." He paused for another toke. "She told me a lot a shit in those three years, you know? Nobody else in my family liked it when she talked that stuff, 'cause they're very religious an' they all thought she was a little crazy anyway, but I liked to listen to her stories." He shook his head, smiling at some memory. "The crazy shit she told me, man, you wouldn't believe it."

I was having trouble with belief, to be sure, but only because it was beginning to appear to me that there were witches coming out of the damn woodwork here in LA, even from other countries. It suddenly struck me that this was starting to feel like some sort of "Twilight Zone" episode, an "Invasion of the Body Snatchers" sort of deal.

"You ever read *Don Juan?*" Claro asked me. "You know, Castaneda?"

The surprise I felt must have been glaringly obvious, for Claro laughed again. "You prob'ly thought I couldn't read that good, eh? Shit." He shook his head, took another toke. "Actually you ain't too wrong, cause I don't read English much, but when I heard a teacher in high school talkin' about Castaneda I had to check it out 'cause it sounded like a lot a the stories *mi abuela* told me. And they kinda were, at least a little bit. Anyway, when she came to live with us she was really unhappy; at first I thought it was just 'cause she was sick and she had to leave her home to come to *el Norte* an' all that shit, but she told me it was more than that. She always had like plants and rocks and little statues and things in the house, especially in the room she slept in with my sisters, and she said it was 'cause a house is like a, like part of your soul that's like . . . shit, I don't think I can explain it too good in English – like something outside you but still you, you know . . .?"

"A projection?" I offered.

"Yeah, I guess, something like – like you feel at home in a place 'cause, well, she once said it was like looking in a mirror that took on the shape of your face."

I nodded, intrigued as I remembered Karita saying something very much like this, and in almost exactly the same spot in the house.

"She made us move twice because she could never get used to the houses we lived in. Said they was too unfriendly, too Anglo. No offense, man."

"None taken. I think I agree with your *abuela*."

Claro took another toke before carefully extinguishing the roach between two moistened fingers and returning it to his shirt pocket. "I don't buy all that *brujeria* stuff, man, but I been thinkin' about all that shit *mi abuela* told me and I wanna make sure I buy a house that's not unfriendly, you know? I mean, I know it's gonna be mainstream, you know, at least to start out with, but that's ok. So anyway, that's why I'm askin' you if the house is alright." He looked at me hopefully.

My first thought was to try to explain to him Karita's response to the house, which I think he might have taken favorably, but then I realized I'd have to explain Karita, and that I wasn't at all sure I could do.

"I think I know what you mean," was what I finally said, "and I'd say this is a friendly house. Yeah. Lots of parties I'm told, and good energies. No bad vibes, as they used to say. In fact, when my cousin first moved in here – he's the main housesitter, I'm just helping him out for a while – he said the only thing he found that the owners accidentally left behind was a shot glass, sitting in the dishwasher like it was waiting for him. I think that's a pretty good omen."

Claro looked like he was about to say something when the real estate agent stuck her head in the door and told us we were needed outside, the unmistakable edge in her voice clearly signaling a development she was not happy with. I followed a discreet distance behind Claro.

The inspector stood at the side of the pool farthest from the house, where the hillside dropped abruptly down to the canyon below. "I've looked over the entire house, Mr. Perez, and don't really see anything that's a serious problem." He consulted his clipboard. "Roof's gonna need a few tiles replaced, you need some regrouting in the master bath, termite inspection still of course, bit of corrosion on some pipe near the water heater, HVAC system's getting near the end of its life but you got a couple years, and there was a sloppy glass replacement job recently on one of the sunroom sliders. But that's about it for the house itself; previous owners took pretty good care of her. But here," he said, pointing with his pen to the textured concrete at our feet, "I see some things that concern me a little. Some of these cracks here are a little larger than I'd like to see, displacement really; there's definitely some settling goin' on here. Concrete always cracks, of course, but given where these cracks are in relation to the pool and the hill here, and the vertical displacement I'm seeing, in good faith I just can't tell you these are nothing to worry about." Out of the corner of my eye I could see the real estate agent visibly tense. "What I'd recommend," he continued, "is you bring in an engineer to take a look at this. Might be nothing, but you can see the previous owners did nothing to reinforce this hillside here when the pool was built, and I think it'd be worth the cost to find out just what's happening."

"Could just be nothing," the real estate agent chirped. "I have cracks in my driveway larger than this."

The inspector nodded. "Could be, but it could also be that you got some movement on this hillside, some settling or slippage maybe caused or accelerated by the weight of all this water, and if it were me I'd want to know what's happening before I made an investment like this."

Claro looked surprisingly calm through this; I wondered if through the buzz he was fully grasping the situation. He just nodded amiably. "OK, man, let's check it out."

"I can recommend a couple of firms," the inspector said. He turned his attention to his clipboard. "I'll write all this up, of course, and" – with a glance at the agent – "you can go back to the seller for an extension on the approval contingency."

The agent caught Claro's bemused expression. "Yes," she said, clearly unhappy, "when we get your report we'll contact the seller and change the offer to include approval of an engineer's inspection. Should be no problem."

And with that they took their leave. I remained outside for a while, staring down the hill. Immediately below the pool and for about fifteen or twenty feet it had been planted with something Hayden had called iceplant, saying it provided a kind of living firebreak and didn't need much water. Apparently fire had been much on the Parkinson's minds when they built here, for the house not only had a sprinkler system and multiple smoke detectors, but they had installed rainbirds, some of them mounted six or seven feet above ground, along all the sides of their yard that bordered on the chaparral that was native to these hills. "This stuff's *supposed* to burn," I said aloud, and was suddenly answered by the muted chatter of a grey squirrel in a sycamore at the far corner of the yard. "You tell 'em, Nutkin," I laughed; "tell 'em how fires clear out the underbrush and enable seeds to germinate and control pests." But the squirrel had fallen silent. I stared down the hill into the canyon, the air rippling slightly already with rising waves of heat. "Yeah," I said, suddenly glum, "it's come to this, talking to squirrels in a house that's sliding down a hillside. I live with a depressed HIV-positive gay guy, am captivated – I think – by a witch, and I'm being stalked by a wacko artist. This sounds like a fucking soap opera or second-rate novel, and I need to start thinking about getting the hell out of here. And about not talking to myself."

I'm being absurd, I thought – or at the very least pathetic, and decided to get a beer. As I turned to the poolhouse I noticed – I couldn't believe I'd missed it before – that someone from one of the houses across the canyon had a kite up in the steady breeze, a huge delta-conyne, completely black, that must have been at least eight feet across. Its grim angularity showed sternly against the smog-dimmed sky, and from the line just below the kite hung a long windsock, also entirely black, a fragment of funereal nightmare snagged in midflight. I shivered in the warm breeze and remembered the way the ancient Romans could read dismal auguries in the flights of bird. Shit, I thought, I don't fucking believe this. Trying not to think about omens or the English paper I'd once written on omens in literature I scurried quickly to the poolhouse refrigerator, grabbed a couple of beers, and ducked into the house, keeping my eyes firmly on the ground.

I still somehow missed it at the time, but that was a moment of pure foreboding.


The heat had been so bad the past few days I'd taken to doing my kata indoors in the empty dining room; about halfway through my routine this morning the doorbell rang. I was expecting no one.

When I opened the door I thought for a startled instant my old high school chemistry teacher had followed me to LA, for the man on the porch could have been his double: short and stocky, atop his blocky face a flat-top greying at the temples. In his brown polyester slacks and short-sleeved white dress shirt he looked exactly the way old Mr. Hicks looked, like one of those NASA engineering geeks you see in film clips from early 1960s space flights.

"We're burnin' daylight, son, so say hello so we can get down to business," he said amiably, startling me out of my reverie.

"Sorry," I stammered; "you reminded me of someone, a teacher I once had."

He nodded. "Lotsa people tell me that; don't know why."

"Well, uh, hello. What can I do for you?"

"Howdy." His grip was like the press of a boulder. "Name's Dwight, Ed Dwight. From GeoTech. This here," he said, jerking a thumb at the thin man standing morosely behind him, "is Aldo, my assistant. Understand you maybe got a pool headin' downhill." He chuckled.

"Well, yeah, um, but I was told you weren't coming until next Wednesday. Not that that's a problem; just wasn't expecting you. Come on in."

"Glad it's no problem, son, 'cause I'm here now. Plans have changed; whole crew and I are off next week to Qrain or Bahrain or one a them overgrown Arab oil wells they call countries, so it's today or sometime next year. Course normally I woulda called it off 'cause we can't do a full stability assessment in one day, but I know what your problem is so I just came by to refresh my memory. Don't need to come inside, though, since we're inspecting a hillside and I doubt you got one in there." He chuckled again. "Pool's this way as I recall." And he stepped poolward.

"You know what the problem is? How so?" And how, I wondered, do you know which way the pool is?

He chuckled. "Sure do, son. You ever meet doc next door?"

"No, he's out of town for a while but I met his daughter."

"Ol' Doc's a fine man, built himself quite a place there. We did the engineering for him on his basement. Took some cores, even ran sonar. Put a fair amount of structural steel in that basement; can't truly trust the top three or four meters of soil up here if you're serious about riding out the big one." He gave me a steady look. "Can never be too prepared, son."

I nodded. Earthquakes, California's great underlying instability. The Ur-rootlessness, the geologic version of that atomic particle uncertainty stuff Hayden understands so much better than I do. But forget Heisenberg here in the foothills; it's the West Coast Uncertainty Principle, where everything is slippery and nothing is quite as it appears. Maybe it *could* explain some things, I thought, smiling to myself. No shortage of things needing explaining around here.

The engineer was still talking away in his flat Midwestern drawl. "One a my crew also found the start of a small mineshaft down the hill aways on the other side, though that didn't affect anything; only went about twenty foot in."

"Mine shaft? I didn't know there was mining around here. What were they looking for?"

"Gold, most likely. There's some in this part of the state, though nothin' like up north. Best bet in this area was to sluice, though, an' at higher elevations, which was popular for a while; diggin' a mine in these foothills is a pure waste a time. But that didn't stop 'em from trying; no accountin' for folks when greed's in the air. Nothin' to worry about here, though. Not like where I come from: deep Southern Illinois, place is riddled with coal holes."

"A mine in this hill." I shook my head. "You sure there's no gold?" By this time we'd reached the far edge of the pool and the engineer's gaze was firmly on the cracked concrete. But he chuckled at my question. "No gold worth the getting. Granite, mostly, least right here, and reasonably solid once you're down a few meters. Problem is everything except ol' Doc's basement is perched on top, and even then you're OK, at least till the big one, as long as you aren't too close to the side of the hill with a lot of weight. Which is exactly the situation you got here. Knew it when we were doin' Doc's basement. Figured back then it was only a matter a time."

"And that's what these cracks are, then? Not just routine settling? But if the pool's moving wouldn't there be cracks in the pool itself?"

He gave me a quick glance. "Son, that pool's been pebble-coated recently; even I can tell that. Surprised they didn't re-do the deck while they were at it." He shook his head. "If there were cracks in the pool, they're patched. An' if it were leaking, you'd know – be fillin' it regular. You have to fill it much?"

"No. At least, I don't think so," I added, not really sure what "much" was in this case.

He nodded. "Well, sounds like your plumbing's OK then, and it's not likely a gunite pool wouldn't be havin' problems, since this concrete issue ain't that bad yet. But you never know. Anyway," he continued, "I got a lot of the data I need already, 'cept some measurements. Me and Aldo'll take care a that right now." I watched for a few minutes as the two men went about their arcane business with tape measure, transept, and laptop, then disappeared into the house to escape the heat. Some forty minutes later I stepped back outside just as they were finishing.

"Well," he said as he entered the last of the measurements into his laptop, "I'll write this up and get it in next week 'fore we leave." He glanced down the hill again briefly, shaking his head. "Were up to me, I'd fill it in and plant roses. Course I'm mighty fond of roses, grow 'em myself for competition. And I don't care much for water, so that's easy for me to say."

"Fill it in? Is it that bad?"

He shrugged.  "Depends on the size of your wallet and your fondness for swimming, I guess."

"What exactly needs to be done?  A retaining wall?"

"That's what we're talking about, son, but not somethin' flimsy with landscape timbers or Keystone.  Do this right you gotta get down to some solid rock to anchor a wall for at least thirty, thirty-five feet here, so we're talking some serious drilling, some steel, lot of concrete – a big bushel a money."

"Shit."

"Yeah, that's about the size of it.  Me, I'm mighty fond of roses."

"Is this something that *needs* to done, to sell the house?  Bring it up to earthquake code or something?"

Ed Dwight shook his head.  "I think as long as it's on the disclosure nothing needs to be done if the buyer don't care, but I'm not a real estate agent or a lawyer.  I only know that with the soil conditions and the possibility of seismic activity you're looking at a limited lifetime for this pool unless you get more downslope stability.  Course, could be years, maybe even a lot, but I gotta recommend my wall."  Abruptly he thrust a beefy hand toward me.  "Well, listen, son, gotta run.  Thanks for your help."

And with that he and his silent associate were gone, and I was left to wonder about earthquakes and bedrock and the pervasive illusion of stability here in a land built on its opposite.

I related all this later that day to Hayden, who for some reason I couldn't determine found it quite amusing.  His reaction puzzled me but it'd been so long since I'd seen him in a good mood I just let him have his laugh.  He'd need it: when he'd returned Sunday night he told me, with a weariness that made my own heart ache, that Joshua's T-cell count had fallen almost to nothing; the drugs weren't working and the cancer had metastasized and affected his kidneys and liver; the doctors were giving him a couple more weeks at most.  But tonight Hayden found the story of the pool amusing, so I played it up for all it was worth.  At least I could give him that.

Only a few weeks ago I would have sworn to a deep fondness for solitude, but on Friday I found myself facing with a colorless and enveloping dread the prospect of another too-quiet weekend; Hayden was driving directly from work to the airport and Karita had flown to Denver for some sort of weekend art dealers convention. She said she'd wanted to take me along – at her expense, of course – but it was strictly business and I would have found it dull. Yeah right, I thought. What happened to all that mystical union stuff? This whole fucking crazy quilt is unraveling rapidly.

And then it unraveled a bit further.

No: a lot further.

Kyoko on the phone. I'd given up on her, I realized with surprise, and for a brief moment was half-tempted to be angry or at least indignant that she'd waited so long to call me, until I realized I'd not thought of calling her. How the hell did that happen?

Her call was to invite me to her apartment to watch her favorite movie on PBS, something called *Mr. Blandings Builds His Dream House*. Sammi's parents, she explained, were in town for a visit, and Sammi'd be out with them tonight, so why didn't I come by? I'd never heard of the movie but agreed.

A few hours later the phone rang again: a distraught Kyoko this time, explaining that Sammi had just had a blowup with her parents – apparently they'd been ignoring all her hints about her sexuality and when they pushed the "get married and have grandkids" button too hard tonight things went very south. Now Sammi wanted to stay out of their apartment for a while so her parents couldn't get come by or get hold of her. Kyoko begged out of our movie, but the thought of spending the evening alone, now that I'd been anticipating company, was too depressing to bear. I told her to bring Sammi and watch it here; with Hayden out of town there'd be no problem.

And half an hour later they arrived. When I saw Kyoko I felt again the same libidinal tug I'd been unable to resist that night in the mountains, but Sammi – shit, she was a large splash of ice water. Maybe it was the fight she'd just had with her parents, maybe just her personality, but she radiated a razor tension so trenchant I could taste it before she got fully through the door. Her features were sharp and chiseled, buzz-cut black hair accentuating the overall impression of prickly severity. She was tall and lithe, almost angular, and her movements, though spare, bespoke the high degree of physical conditioning of the martial arts instructor she was. She said little on our tour of the house and yard, and when the movie began sat impassively in front of the TV, refusing the popcorn and wine that

Kyoko and I both consumed eagerly. Twenty minutes into the movie Sammi complained of a headache and asked if she could lie down somewhere; I showed her to one of the still-furnished bedrooms and returned to the TV room with a second bottle of cheap chablis.

By the time the movie was over – what little I remember of it makes me wonder to this day why it was Kyoko's favorite – Kyoko and I had gotten thoroughly drunk. At some point Kyoko decided she needed to go home; moving rather unsteadily she went off in search of Sammi, but came back alone, reporting that Sammi had fallen asleep and she didn't have the heart to wake her after the day she'd had. So we kept drinking and talking and drinking, sometimes watching the TV and then ignoring it for half an hour at a stretch, and the next thing I knew I was coming groggily awake, still on the couch, Kyoko slumped against me deeply asleep. I couldn't see a clock but could sense we were well into the wee hours. Sammi must still be sleeping, I realized after a foggy minute, and it looked like I had the choice of waking Kyoko or remaining right where I was. The slight throbbing in my head, which I knew would get much worse by morning, told me moving would not be particularly pleasant, so I decided to remain put, at least until I needed to piss, which I was sure would be soon. Shifting to make myself a little less uncomfortable I caused Kyoko to stir. She murmured something unintelligible, and when she stopped moving her face was only inches from mine. In the vague glow I could make out the curve of her lips and the softly rounded arc of her nose, and I stared as though I'd never seen her before. And I felt again that libidinal tug and wondered what it was about her that did this to me.

And then I did one of the stupidest and most repulsive things I've ever done in my life.

To this day I can't explain why. I was still drunk, of course, quite drunk, but that's only a small part of the explanation. I think I need to confess, to my everlasting shame, my revulsion even, that there's simply a part of me – my "Bluebeard closet," to steal a great phrase from an old Bernard Capes ghost story – I had never really known until this shitty summer in LA, a bent and repressed part of me that when it opened up was, or at least now in retrospect is, nothing less than repugnant. I know this sounds like some calculate evasion, and I grant that it may well be that, but I swear that there was or is something about SoCal, a something perhaps intensified by that particular house and/or the head-shaking strangeness of my experiences that summer, that brings out the worst in me. Or maybe not the worst – or, well, yeah, maybe that *is* a fair term for what I did. Shit, I don't know. Except for one thing: I know my personal confusion, my failure of self-knowledge, reached an all-time high sometime during this twisted summer, and its rise dampened some of the things I've always most valued in myself. And I still wonder how much of them I'll recover.

I looked at the soft contours of Kyoko's pale face, gentle in the dim light and the heavy peace of drunken sleep; I listened to her soft and slightly irregular breathing in the stillness of the canyon's night air and after a long moment I reached carefully around and unbuttoned the top button of her blouse. I watched my hand, that hand, with a strange sense of detachment, as though it were someone else's, an agent of some stranger's foul volition. Or maybe I just tell myself that now, trying to interpose some sense of distance, hoping somehow to diminish my sense of guilt and shame and self-loathing. I don't know; I *was* quite drunk. But not drunk enough to have lost all hand-eye coordination, for the button surrendered easily. As did the next, and the next, and the one after that, leaving her blouse open almost to the waist. Kyoko hadn't moved and I lay still for a moment, staring intently at her bra. At the same moment that I realized I had an erection I noticed that her bra hooked in front. And with a care and caution that even then reminded me of the protagonist of Poe's "The Tell-Tale Heart" planning the murder of a helpless old man I moved with profound care and concentration and with only the slightest fumbling unhooked her bra. She stirred but did not awaken, and her movement was to my advantage, for it caused part of her left breast to show beyond the edge of the bra cup. With what felt like a fierce pounding in my crotch and fire in my eyes I pushed her bra back far enough to reveal her nipple, large and dark and, I saw with delighted surprise, pierced with a thin gold ring. I stared, fascinated, never having seen a pierced nipple before; how the hell have I missed that I wondered with what now seems embarrassing arrogance. I thought about trying to expose her other breast but her position on the couch made it seem that would be impossible without waking her. I watched with dark delight as her nipple gently moved with her breathing, a faint pin-point glimmer of light moving almost imperceptibly back and forth along the arc of the gold ring as her breast rose and fell.

I watched for what must have been five minutes before a

libidinal surge washed away what few shreds of self-control remained to me; by shifting my position and craning my neck I was just able to gently caressed her ringed nipple with my tongue. She stirred but still remained more or less asleep, and somehow emboldened by that I placed my mouth over her nipple and sucked gently, tonguing the ring as I did so.

I'm tempted to say at this point that I don't know what I was thinking, but since I know I wasn't thinking in any kind of rational sense of the word at all during this episode I'll just finish the story. Kyoko came groggily awake with a soft sound of protest. It wasn't loud, and it struck me, at least in my drunken self-absorption, as not entirely sincere, for when she pushed me back and looked at me I could see not only confusion in her eyes but desire. She looked at me in silence for a long moment, her mouth open as though about to speak or suck, and I could swear she was about to move toward me in an embrace or kiss, but just then the light clicked on.

Sammi.

I'd forgotten about her entirely but something, perhaps Kyoko's noise, had awoken her and now she stood there glaring at me with an almost feral intensity. No, "glaring" is too soft a term. Even as groggy as I was and half-blinded by the sudden brightness I could see the chilly hate-backed anger in her eyes and face as her gaze flicked from me to Kyoko, lingering on the blouse Kyoko was trying to fasten, then back to me. She took a step toward me and something in my increasingly useless brain told me to stand up for defense, but I was slow and I think she might have done me serious harm if Kyoko hadn't somehow scrambled to her feet and interposed herself between us.

"No, Sammi, it's not – it's OK," she cried, and for a very long moment it looked to me like Sammi was going to push Kyoko aside and come at me. I'd gotten to my feet by this time but knew that even sober I wouldn't have a chance against someone of Sammi's skill and now, with my dumbfounded drunkenness and her pressure-cooker hatred, she could easily have killed me. Sammi stopped short, her eyes locked on mine and lit by the fires of hell. I don't know if it was the alcohol or the growing realization of my vulnerability but my knees started to tremble violently, and I needed desperately to sit down. Sammi held my gaze for a moment longer and I could see some measure of self-control assert itself within her; slowly and with a perilous grace she raised her right arm, extended and with her clenched fist, knuckles foremost, pointed straight at my throat. A trachea blow. She held that pose for a very long moment, saying nothing – needing to say nothing; fear and failure must have been resplendently obvious on my face. And in an instant Sammi had spun on her heel and taking Kyoko almost fiercely by the arm strode off in the direction of the front door. Kyoko looked back at me once, briefly, her eyes filled with a mixture of emotion that I simply could not read, and I opened my mouth to say something but my mind refused to cooperate. Just as well. As I sagged wearily back to the couch the door slammed, and I never saw nor heard from Kyoko again. And I never found the courage to call and apologize.

As I sat helplessly on the couch, close to tears and aware of a rising wave of nausea, Hayden's long-ago words about life-lessons rose again, tauntingly it seemed, in my mind. I was learning a valuable life lesson alright, but the extent to which I could disgust and disappoint myself wasn't exactly what I'd had in mind when I'd accepted Hayden's offer. It wasn't until well after sunrise, and after throwing up for what seemed like hours, that I calmed down enough to sleep, and my sleep was restless and disturbed for days afterwards.


Saturday's mail brought a check from my parents, and while both a genuine surprise and a touching act of generosity typical of my parents it bothered me as well, for there was something about my very need for money that brought with it a growing nimbus of failure. It was through no fault of my own that my summer job had turned out to be more temporary than planned, but the fact remained that my source of income, as meagre as it was, had disappeared abruptly and I had no alternative plan. Of course replacing a windshield hadn't been included in the budget – and there again I was confronted with my failure to plan, to expect the unexpected, to be able to cope with anything other than what I had anticipated, as though my paltry mental sketch of what would be was all that could be, all that fell within the realm of existential possibility. What troubled me most, I quickly realized, was not just a brush with cashlessness that I knew would only be temporary but how this was all a part of a larger sense of, well, the word "insufficiency" comes to mind. I've always thought – with a naiveté so egregious it is grotesque, I now realize – that I was fairly independent and moderately resourceful, but the cumulative effect of the past couple of months, added to my exploration of the depths of stupidity last night, had me gravely doubting the wisdom of that self-assessment, any self-assessment. Maybe I needed to abandon whatever sense of myself I'd constructed in my life, I thought in my anger and self-loathing. I was sure of nothing that day, other than the fact there are few worse feelings in the painfully smoggy glare of a hangover morning than a sense of one's total inadequacy in the face of life.

And at the moment there was, as far as I could determine, nothing I could do about it.

The rest of the weekend passed uneventfully. I did everything in my power to keep as low a profile as possible, avoiding even the grocery store or a simple pointless drive. I watched television and did my *kata* and swam and tried to write and read and waited. For what, I have no idea, but something just below the level of consciousness was letting me know, in some vague way, that the shit had not yet stopped hitting the fan. This, I suppose, was as close as I ever got to foreboding during this entire foul and dangerous season. I found myself thinking repeatedly of James' "The Beast in the Jungle," which I'd read earlier in the year, and wondered some more: the idea of nothing ever happening sounded real good to me right about now. It began to seem as though the scheduled day of my departure would never arrive.

Hayden arrived home late Sunday night looking worse than I'd ever seen him: eyes red, face strained, uncomfortable energies of despair and tension radiating from him like a siren's blare at midnight. The repeated trips to Atlanta were catching up to him; he was jet-lagged and weary and constantly irritable – not that I saw him that much, which both relieved and troubled me. We had talked little in the past few weeks; he clearly wanted distance and I was happy to give it to him. Tonight, though, he seemed to want to talk, for instead of retreating into his room as he so often did these days he came into the TV room where I was watching a *Bladerunner* and dropped wearily into a chair, a large can of Ensure in his bony hand. He'd taken to drinking two or three cans of the stuff a day, relying on it for the bulk of his caloric intake as far as I could tell. I thought, not for the first time, of asking him why, with HIV, he didn't do more for himself nutritionally, but I couldn't bring myself to do it. Would probably never be able to, now.

Hayden sat in silence for some minutes before I finally

remarked on his evident weariness.

He nodded. "As my old college roommate used to say, glad you noticed; I'd hate to feel this bad and have it be my little secret." His smile was wan and half-hearted. "Truth be told, I'm feeling pretty damn weary. In a lot of ways."

"I know what you mean," I said, eager to empathize, to fling some kind of bridge across the distance that had, inexplicably and inexorably, grown almost daily since my arrival. "I'm pretty wiped myself. Had a very weird and crazy weekend." Of course I hadn't told him about Kyoko.

Hayden's laugh was short and sharp, a bark of derision. "With all due respect, little cuz, I doubt you do know what I mean. For you, being weary is just that, and it'll pass. When you live with HIV, 'feeling weary' can mean just that – " he paused dramatically, and I could see what was coming – "or it could mean you've just been handed a death sentence. Try living with that kind of fear on a daily basis and then you'll know what I mean." And he lapsed into silence, leaving me to feel both sympathetic and insulted. It's not like I wasn't trying, after all.

Hayden cleared his throat. "Sorry. Didn't mean to snap at you, cuz; nerves are a bit frayed these days."

"Forget it," I said with as much warmth as I could muster; "you've been going through a lot, all that travelling – the jet lag alone would be driving me up the wall, and probably a padded one at that."

"Lot of airport and air time," Hayden said faintly, nodding. "Gives me a lot of time to think, and that's the worst part. I'm busy when I'm here and I'm very busy when I'm with Joshua, but on the flights I can't work, can't really even read. So I spend most of that time thinking, and it's usually death on my mind these days, no surprise."

"How's Joshua doing? I mean, given that... you know, his cancer..."

"As well as can be expected. His doctor's generous with meds now so there's not much pain, for him at least, but watching him turn into a living skeleton is the hardest thing –" his voice caught – "the worst thing I've ever had to do in my life." The emotion choked him off for a moment, and I thought he was about to cry. He stared hard at the can of Ensure in his hand and I reached for the remote to cut the volume on the TV.

"You ever lose anyone close?" he asked after a moment. The question caught me by surprise – which, now that I think about it, it shouldn't have; how could I not be thinking about this while living with someone going through what Hayden was going through? – because it occurred to me that no one had ever asked me this before and Hayden had already become to me among the last people I was expecting to share deep feelings with. When I told him "No, I haven't, really" it occurred to me that I *had* lived a sheltered life. "Closest would be Uncle Bob, my dad's older brother. Heart attack. But they lived in Tacoma and I only saw him like five or six times that I can remember. Even all my grandparents are still alive."

He nodded abstractly. "Nothing like AIDS to give a gay man a densely populated memory. But even though many of those were dear friends, nothing can prepare you for a loss like this. I've never cared for anyone the way I care for Joshua – never loved anyone, really, before him, and though I've seen people die of Kaposi's before it never really prepared me for this." His gaze drifted up, out the window across from the couch where he sat and into the dark canyon night, and I knew I could never see what he was looking at. I was glad to recognize his revelations were not making me uncomfortable, which is certainly the reaction I would have predicted. Maybe there's hope for real connection yet, I thought. "Watching someone so vibrant, so alive – his two great passions were opera and the company softball team – slowly lose himself, bit by bit, like watching a person bleed to death – it's a very long and very painful good-bye." And the tears that welled in his eyes reflected a blurred glow of the TV and all I could do was say "I'm sorry" and it came out in a half-whisper that somehow seemed appropriate. A faint attempt at his patented lopsided grin was his acknowledgement.

Hayden stood, weariness evident in every movement. "Just so you're prepared, it's only going to be a matter of days now, so don't be surprised when you get a call from me saying I'll be staying in Atlanta for a while. After the funeral I'll need to take care of some things – I'm Joshua's executor – and I pretty much have carte blanche on taking leave from work, so I don't know that I'll be in a great hurry to get back."

Hayden was right, for he called me Wednesday from work,

catching me as I was just about to break my self-imposed isolation and go to a movie simply to get out of the house and away from my grim monotony. Joshua's doctor had called, saying Joshua had just been admitted for kidney failure and that he expected the end in a couple of days at most. Hayden would be catching a 5.30 flight to Atlanta and figured he'd be gone at least a week to ten days. "OK," I said lamely, "hang in there, man. Stay steady."

If only I could have done the same.

I returned from the movie to find Karita walking down our driveway, having come in search of me. I'd tried to reach her since Sunday night but to no avail; she explained she'd stayed on a few days in Colorado to do a little extra buying. "But now," she said, "I've come in search of my poor northern child –" the phrase which before had always struck me as endearing if a bit silly now sounded odd and dissonant, although I said nothing – "for tonight is a special night, and especially propitious for Aries this year."

"In what way?"

"Many ways," she said airily, "and it begins with me treating you to dinner. To make up for Wormwood's."

We went to an outstanding vegetarian place in some little college town called Claremont and had a long and pleasant dinner, talking as we hadn't talked in quite a while. This struck me as odd, of course, given that our relationship, if that was ever a fair term for it, seemed to be getting a bit ragged lately, unravelling around the edges and possibly at the center as well. For all of our talk, Summer's name never came up.

As we walked to her car she suggested a drive in the mountains but I tried to beg off, explaining how I'd found the San Gabriels here drained and dispiriting, bereft of their natural energies by the overwhelming press of humanity.

She nodded and said nothing yet pointed her Beemer toward the greybrown foothills to our north. We sped past the customary stucco sprawl of identical subdivisions and soon were beginning the climb up Mt. Baldy Road. I tried to protest but she laughed me off, said to wait and see if there wasn't still something in these mountains for me to discover after all. I slumped in my seat and stared rather glumly out the window, watching the last dim glow of daylight illumine the thunderheads that gathered around the peak. Thinking of Hayden's metaphor, I found my mood slowly slip into a darker register.

Lost in my own thoughts I paid little attention to the darkening scene beyond the car window, barely noticing as the chaparral slowly gave way to scraggly pine. I really wasn't interested; I'd given up on these dry hills. Nor did I notice where Karita had turned, but came alert when I realized we had left the main road and were easing our way slowly up a narrow undulating strip of asphalt, the crowding pines making the gathering darkness all the denser, creating an almost claustrophobic sense that I'd never experienced in mountains before. Must be the car, I thought, too close to the trees. We passed what appeared to be a few cabins, set back from the road and evident only by lampglow through their windows, small geometries of light that lent depth to the darkness and suggested into being a vague sense of the mystery of the forest's dark expansiveness, and for the first time in my experience the mountains of Southern California seemed to possess some glimmer of energy, some half-guessed-at trace of the numinous potency that was a palpable and ready presence in the deep redwood forests of my native Humboldt. I smiled into the darkness, half at the pleasure of the discovery, half at the irony that it was a discovery made possible by human artifact, by the lights of people going about their lives, seen from a car.

Another abrupt turn and we were bumping slowly down a dirt road now, not much more than a wide path, bordered closely with rock and pine and brush as the Beemer's headlights picked out a narrow channel through the mountain night. I couldn't believe Karita was taking such an expensive car down such a road and was about to make a joke about four-wheel drive when suddenly the road ended in a small clearing where several vehicles were parked. As the dust drifted past us in the headlights' glow I could see a chain link fence, gated and very tall and disappearing into the woods and up the hillsides that sloped sharply away from the narrow valley floor.

I glanced at Karita, who was looking at me steadily, a slight smile evident in the headlight's glow. "You are going to explain this, aren't you?" I asked.

She smiled, then plunged the clearing into darkness by flicking off the headlights. "Come," she said, lost in the darkness beside me, "one of the last presents I can give you." Before I could ask for explanation – not that I thought one would have been forthcoming – she slipped out of the car and started toward the fence.

At the locked gate she produced a key and in a moment we

were on the other side.  As she locked the gate behind us I asked, my voice unwittingly hushed in the stillness of the mountain evening, just where the hell we were and what's with all the mystery and security.

She laughed softly.  "Mystery's very becoming, remember?" and as she moved forward without further explanation I indeed remembered: an earlier conversation with Karita, what felt like months ago, half a lifetime ago, and since that conversation there had been so much strangeness, so pervasive a sense of existential dissonance and a loss of mental traction that I wasn't at all sure I wanted anything to do with mystery of any sort ever again.  I also figured there was no point in trying to get any explanation of what were doing so I followed in resigned silence as with an almost uncanny effortlessness Karita followed the dusty path, dusky-pale in the tree-filled darkness, further up and into the woods.

We walked for what must have fifteen minutes as the path rose slowly through the scruffy pine forest.  I was concentrating so hard on the trail, little more now than a dim suggestion in the valley darkness even as my eyes adapted, that I bumped into Karita when she came without warning to a complete stop.  We were at the edge of a small clearing, a hollow that swaled below us and then rose abruptly at the three low hills that ringed the hollow's floor.  A small stream gurgled through the hollow, bisecting it north to south as it wove between boulders and a few stunted oaks.  I was surprised to find any water here at all at this point in the summer.

I could see all this by the light of the bonfire that burned near the center of the hollow.  I turned to Karita and paused a moment, taken by surprise at the almost rapt expression on her face, a look of focused concentration suffused with a gathering joy and she looked suddenly younger, and yet more a stranger, than I'd ever seen before.  Another of her many subtle transformations, I thought, though from what into what I had no idea.

She looked at me expectantly, as though already anticipating the question uppermost in my mind.  "Lammas," she said softly.  "Lughnasadh.  The beginning of the harvest festival, a Celtic harvest festival that celebrates the bounty and abundance of the Goddess as summer ends and fall begins."

"But summer doesn't end for another, what, seven weeks."

Karita shook her head.  "Oh, poor northern child.  The scientific Western calendar is as out of synch with nature as the civilization it serves.  But the ancients knew that summer would crest, not begin, on the longest day of the year, and they knew that fall begins when the fruits and grains begin to grow ready, well before late September.  Wicca follows the wisdom of the old ways; this is our first fall festival, celebrated with wine and bread and thanks to the Goddess for the bounty of the world and the life she gives us."  She paused, gestured at the fire below.  "It's also the feast of Lugnasadh, the Celtic god of light, commemorating the death of his mother, but this coven doesn't put much emphasis on Celtic roots; they're eclectic, mostly nature-focused.  But tonight they're going to do a Catherine wheel, which they haven't done for a couple of years.  I thought you might like that."  She grinned widely, tapped me on the arm as though sharing a joke.  "Last time they did one they almost started a forest fire.  But they say they're better prepared this year.  At least it'll be the first Sabbat I've ever witnessed which had fire extinguishers ready."

"Wait – a what wheel?"

"Catherine wheel.  Named after St. Catherine – mythical, like most of them – whose feast the Roman Church tried to impose on Lammas the way they tried to co-opt most of our special days and rituals.  But the origin's pagan: they cover a large wooden wheel or disk with pitch, set it on fire, then roll it downhill.  A symbol of the sun god's decline as the nights start to lengthen and autumn comes on."

This struck me as sophomorically silly, to say nothing of dangerous and surely illegal since we were after all in the Angeles National Forest, but I said nothing.

"It's not my style," Karita said, but by now her apparent ability to read my thoughts surprised me not at all, "but this coven has a flair for the dramatic.  One of the members does production design for movies, and another works for a talent agency, so it's to be expected, I suppose."

"But how the hell can they do that here without starting a forest fire?  That's crazy."

Karita smiled, a quick Cheshire flash in the unfolding darkness.  "They almost did, the first time, but they told me now they have some kind of wire thing rigged up.  The wheel's suspended, just glides down the wire above the ground so it goes right where it's supposed to, and they use some kind of high-tech flammable material that doesn't drop off, some movie special-effects stuff.  Plus doing it over a cleared dry gulch should make it pretty safe."

Wicca meets Hollywood.  I shook my head.

A slight shift of the breeze brought the bonfire's smoke directly toward us, and beneath the creosote and pine tar I could smell something pungent, herbal.  But another question loomed larger for me.

"I remember reading that Lammas is important for Wicca, so why aren't you involved?  Why are you hanging out with a confused secular humanist like me?"

She smiled at me but I could see her eyes cloud slightly and the skin around them draw slightly tighter.  "I'm currently a Solitary, and I've been sticking to that even on the Greater Sabbats."  Her smile turned rueful.  "It's not easy.  I've been in covens since I was eleven, so you can imagine how much I want to be down there, although this isn't a coven I would join.  But still, the Craft is who I am, and I always do something special  to celebrate the Sabbats.  Like tonight.  This is very special, although in a different way."

I smiled back at her, wondering ever more insistently just what was really going on here, in this place, in her head, in the whole crazy web in which I seem to have become entangled.  "Can I ask why you're a, whatever that term was – not in a coven, or is that too personal?"

"A Solitary: someone in the Craft who for whatever reason is not or chooses not to be in a coven.  Not too many witches I know have ever tried it, but, like I said, I've been in covens since puberty and I was priestess of my own for nine years, and – "

"You had your own coven?"

"Why does that surprise you?  Yes, the Golden Oak Gathering.  But come two years ago at the winter solstice we disbanded.  I, well, let's just say I needed some space to further explore who I was, examine more closely my personal relationship to the Goddess and the Craft.  It's been a very good growth experience for me, a necessary one even, although I think it won't be too much longer before the Gathering is an active coven again."

"OK, but why did you bring me here?  And why aren't we down there with them, whoever they are?"

"They're the Coven of the Ravenheart Dream.  I've known the priestess, Ravenheart, for years, and her husband Astral is high priest.  Two of their members were in the Golden Oak, and several of the others I know to some extent.  We aren't down there because you can't be; you're outside the way of the Craft.  Even if covens allowed outsiders to participate, which they don't, you couldn't. You couldn't give yourself fully to the spirit of the Goddess, of the Way; you're too lost to self-consciousness. You insist too firmly on the current structures of your Self." She looked at me, her smile sad now in the fireglow. "Yet you also understand that. That's why you're so close, and why we came together in LA and why we're here on this hill tonight, but being close isn't enough to allow you to cross the Circle."

"But," I protested, "you let me into that session at your house that one night."

"Yes," she said slowly, "but that wasn't even an Esbat, a monthly circle, let alone a Greater Sabbat such as this. And you saw how well that worked out; some of the others took such offense that we had to break the Circle."

"But these folks here" – I tossed my head in the direction of the fire below – "they know we're here, don't they?"

"Of course," she said; "they're my friends and they trust me, although even then it took some persuasion on my part to get them to agree. And we can stay for only a small part of the ceremony; when I tell you we need to leave, we need to leave."

I nodded my understanding. "But you still haven't explained why you brought me here."

She turned to me, holding my gaze for a long moment as I tried but failed to read her expression by the flickering light of the distant bonfire. "Last present I can give you, like I said." She looked back at the fire but even in the uncertain light I could see her gaze was focused on something much farther away, something not on the earth I walked. "You've been so troubled by what's happened lately, with Summer and all, that it's come between us, interfered seriously with what was growing." Her eyes flicked back to mine. "You don't fully trust me now," she said flatly, and in the shock of her truth I looked quickly away to the hollow below. A figure approached the bonfire and added more wood and a few handfuls of something from a large pouch, then retreated back into the shadows at the hollow's edge. "It's OK," she said, her voice softened; "there's no reason I should always get my way. I hoped there would have been much more between us, but with Summer, well, who can foresee things like that? And I understand how it can be upsetting, distracting, how such inner turmoil can send any of us off whatever path we're on."

She paused, and in the stillness the fire popped, flinging sparks into the darkness like fervent hopes rushing heavenward. Following their ascent with my eyes I felt, suddenly and awkwardly, like Young Goodman Brown.

Karita laughed softly. "English major that you are, you've probably been thinking of that story by Hawthorne, one of his witch-hating ones, what's it called?"

I stared at her wide-eyed, for a moment my old surprise returning; my mind flashed for an instant to that day in the driveway when she'd correctly identified my sign. "'Young Goodman Brown,'" I said, recovering. "Yeah, I admit I was thinking of that story."

She laughed again. "Of course you were; you're an English major. Much of your perception of the world, even of your participation in it, is drawn from a vast web of allusion and metaphor based in the fictive, the unreal. And in the remote, in stories and poems about people and experiences that aren't you, aren't yours. And only very rarely are the actual people you meet in the world."

I had no idea how to confront that and was desperately certain now was not the time. "But it wasn't a witch-hating story," I said to cover my confusion. "It's about the loss of faith, the loss of certainty, moral self-doubt, stuff like that."

She shook her head. "Against a backdrop of stereotypes and slanders that perpetuate all the evil and the hatred that Christians are supposed to be against. And he wrote other things, too, like that; most Wiccans don't like him, you know." I was about to protest, mount some sort of defense of Hawthorne but she held up a hand. "Now's not the time, professor. Look, they're about to start."

The sound of a drum, some kind of Irish or Celtic drum, I think now, rhythmic and lilting in the darkness, came to me with a warm aural rush. A flash of light, and another, then another, appeared in the hollow below, and a small procession of dark robed figures, indistinct in the firelight, moved to the center of the hollow and formed a loose half-circle around the fire. It occurred to me to count them: twelve. It felt more Gothic or medieval than Wiccan.

Then a belltone, dark and rich and startlingly solitary in the night, and one more figure emerged from the trees edging the hollow, saying something in a soft female voice. None of her words reached me distinctly but in the intervals of her pauses the others ringing the fire responded one by one. I caught something about the bounty of the Mother from one, something about blessing and harvest from another, from the last to speak came some mention of the great wheel of the seasons.

That was the cue, for just then a bright spark flared on the hillside across from us, above our heads, and in an instant a flare of light illuminated rock and brush as the Catherine Wheel came alight. To my relief it appeared smaller than I had anticipated, perhaps two feet in diameter , and was flaming brightly but without sparks, without dropping the thick gouts of flame I feared might turn the Angeles National Forest into a wasteland of cinder and charcoal. The wheel burned, hanging stationary for a moment, then slowly began to slide downhill, picking up only a little speed, and, oddly, not turning. Its motion was uncannily, almost supernaturally smooth as it slid until it came to a stop just above the bonfire burning on the floor of the hollow. Success, I thought; no forests were harmed in the making of this sabbat.

And then out of some dark internal nowhere I suddenly felt a staggering wave of doubt wash over me. This was bullshit, I suddenly thought, surprising even myself. Not some spirit-driven engagement with the primal mother forces of Nature but pathetic theatricality, a frantic longing for meaningfulness pursued with posturing and puppets, straw men. We are the hollow men, we form the empty circle. A sad joke. And me the clueless spectator, probably more lost than any of the robed figures below me in the darkness at their stagey spectacle.

With a start I realized Karita was looking intently at me, the pale features of her face only a touch less dim than the surrounding gloom that now seemed mockingly empty despite the sound and movement in the hollow below us. "Time to leave," she whispered, turning quickly from me to lead me back through the overhanging oak forest, back to her car and to the long, winding ride back down Mt. Baldy, under thunderheads that, sometime during the night, dissipated without rain.


The off-axis darkness that had been gathering across the unfamiliar psychic terrain that surrounded me edged much closer two nights later, and it's exceptionally hard for me to talk about because not all of this summer's darkness, it turned out, was in Summer's black heart of hatred. But I can't hide this, can't pretend it didn't happen. It can't be purged if it isn't confronted, and if it isn't purged it will corrupt and corrode.

I hadn't heard from Hayden since his call Wednesday telling me of his immediate departure for Atlanta; I assumed Joshua was in desperately bad shape, if he was even still alive. I felt bad for Hayden in an abstract kind of way but I wasn't thinking of him much these past few days, although I realize now I should have been. I hadn't even tried to contact Karita since our trip to the Lammas sabbat a couple of nights ago. I was too busy, I think, feeling sorry for myself, and feeling lost.

I spent the night quietly, drinking too much of Hayden's beer and trying to watch TV without much success, for I couldn't sit comfortably in the TV room without thinking of Kyoko and Sammi and that caustically ugly scene last week. So I swam a bit, watched the few visible stars for a long while, wondering about much and reciting random snatches of poetry aloud. I tried to write but could find no words, kept drinking. I finally poured myself into bed around eleven.

Something very wrong woke me at 2:47. I remember the time exactly, the green LED readout of the bedside clock burning in the darkness of my bedroom as I listened, groggy and a little dizzy but coming awake quickly, for a repetition of the sound I knew had awoken me.

It came, a quick muffled thud followed by a scratching. An odd sound, something about it prompting me to get out of bed. Racoon maybe? Moving with as much care as I could muster I stepped into the gallery, pausing to gain more balance and listening for something that would provide me a direction. In a moment it came again from somewhere in the direction of the master bedroom and but it was much louder and different, too metallic and too sharp to be some sniffing animal. Someone breaking in, I suddenly suspected, and I hesitated, thinking I should call 911 as the adrenaline rush began to bring me reasonably close to awake, though my eyes stung a bit and my mental processes clearly remained in low gear. And then the scratching again, and I thought shit, it is only a raccoon you idiot; bring the police up the canyon for that and you're really gonna look like a drunken moron.

The master bedroom had its own spacious bathroom, as I've mentioned, in which was what the real estate agent called a garden shower, a large tiled stall one wall of which was glass, opening onto a small fenced fern garden. Most of the glass was a fixed pane, but at about shoulder height was a glider window, for extra ventilation I suppose. It was really quite a beautiful space, completely private and genuinely serene; I'd showered there a couple of times even though it meant extra clean-up work just to experience the effect. As I slipped into the master bedroom and the scratching was repeated I knew this was where the noise was coming from.

Before it occurred to me to wonder why a raccoon or perhaps possum would be so persistently interested in a shower window I peeked carefully into the bathroom, not wanting to startle the creature away until I got a good luck – and felt my heart pause painfully for a long moment before it slammed back into action. No fucking raccoon: there was somebody in the garden area, a small dark silhouette, trying to get the window open. 'Shit,' I thought, but before I could back away and get to a phone something caught my attention. Something about the shadowy shape trying to jimmy a window almost over its head.

"Shit!" I almost shouted as I realized it was Summer, and I did clamp my hand, like some comic-book character, over my mouth in that instant to ensure my silence. Or maybe it was in anger. I watched, waiting to be absolutely sure, and a moment later, when the figure outside dropped something into the soft dirt and stooped to retrieve it, I knew I was right. Summer, that fucking little piece of shit.

And then I made a profoundly stupid decision – what is it with these stupid decisions I keep making, drunk in the LA night? clearly an evil habit by now and too well established – so perhaps what came after was appropriate punishment. I should have called 911, let the cops grab her, take satisfaction from her arrest. That would have been the intelligent and reasonable thing to do. But intelligent and reasonable had been scarce ever since I arrived in LA and they were nowhere to be found now. Even as I watched, the shadowy figure at the window uttered a muffled curse and turned to the fence, reaching for the gate, and I knew she'd given up and would be long gone by the time the police arrived. And my anger, my weeks of accumulated rage, couldn't accept that.

Moving with quiet speed I slipped through the bedroom's French doors, out through the private sitting room and around the back of the house toward the enclosed fern garden. Crouching low, my heart pounding and my brain still fogged by the alcohol although I didn't realize it through the false clarity of the adrenaline, I crept to the corner of the house just a few feet from the privacy fence. Peering carefully around the corner I could just see, in the distant dim glow of the streetlight, Summer edging through the gate. She stepped clear, turned her back to me in order to fasten the latch silently, and I was on her in an instant, grabbing one of her upraised arms and pinning it behind her back as I shouted "Freeze, you fucking little bitch!" Not exactly appropriate or original, but the best I could come up with at the moment.

Careless of me, to grab the wrong arm, for it was the other which held whatever small tool she'd been using to try to jimmy the window and though I had her pinned tightly against the fence she managed to swing her other arm down and jab her tool – a small screwdriver, I think – into my left leg. It dug a gash rather than penetrating directly, but pain flared and took me thoroughly off guard. I stepped back, releasing her arm in order to clamp both hands to my thigh, and before I could recover she'd pushed me over backwards. But she had to step over me to get to the front yard and as she stepped I reflexively kicked at her, knocking her into the privacy fence so hard she stumbled and fell, sprawling headlong just a foot or two away and dropping the screwdriver. I reached for her as she scrambled to her feet and just managed to get a fistful of T-shirt and as I pulled her back to the ground I could hear the taut sigh of fabric tearing. But it held enough – too much, for I pulled her into me and we both went down again, tangled.

From what seemed like a mile away I could hear her swearing, feel her hands clawing and pushing ineffectually at me, but with just a slight shift I had her pinned to the ground. And I suddenly realized, with an odd visceral shock, that I had torn her shirt almost completely away and now one of her breasts was close to my face, the dark nipple distinct against the sickly paleness of her skin. She squirmed again and her tiny breast heaved up within inches of my me and before I knew what I was doing – and I swear to whatever gods there might be that it was without intention or thought; some dark animal part of me, some monstrous surge from the brainstem or something – I clamped my mouth on her breast, taking her nipple and virtually all of her breast in my mouth and sucking hard, quickly. In the same instant that I realized what I was doing I also realized she had hunched her shoulders forward, an automatic response not of struggle but pleasure – that much I was sure of, would swear to in a court of law. (At least, I would tell the smirking attorney and the dour judge, I was sure of it at the moment. As though it excused anything.) But that was only an instant and was followed by her conscious response: a sharp blow to my ear that, while it moved my head enough that I released her nipple, didn't really hurt. It did, however, piss me off even further. I caught her wrist as she tried to deliver another blow and pinned it to the ground beside her, an action which brought my head back over her exposed breast. Again I took it in my mouth. This time some part of me knew what I was doing, and even recognized at least dimly that it was some libidinal brew of anger and lust – some primal macho shit that should have been so repulsive this moment never would have happened – that drove me. Yet I sucked fiercely and held her wrists pinned to the ground as I lay atop her. We were locked in physical struggle, with all of the hormonal and chemical turbulence struggle always involves; I was deeply pissed at this psycho bitch – someone I found physically unattractive and socially repellant – who'd been stalking and threatening me for weeks, yet here I was wearing only running shorts, my mouth on her tit, sucking hard and loving it and acutely aware of an erection so stiff it hurt and wanting to shove myself into her and knowing that if I did I'd come with a rush, an ecstasy, I'd never felt before. And then, from some part of my mind that's probably as close to holy as I will ever get, something else came to me, a remembrance half-formed of what Karita had told me of Summer being raped, and instantly an acid wave of self-loathing began to rise up in me and I threw myself off her, half rising and stumbling backward against the garden's privacy fence. Without a sound Summer was up and off, running for the street, and I staggered into the house, fumbled my way to my bathroom. In the mirror I caught a glimpse of myself, haggard, half drunk, the pain in my bleeding thigh reasserting itself, and I threw up, the bitter taste of my vomit erasing the taste of Summer's skin but not the confused and wrenching memory of what had happened, what I'd done and what I'd felt. After bandaging my thigh – I should probably get stitches for the jagged cut but couldn't bear the thought of facing the questions, the possibility of the police becoming involved, and besides, it didn't look that bad, not too deep – I opened a beer but could not bear the taste.

I awoke the next morning in the atrium, my back stiff from having fallen asleep in a wicker chair, my leg and head throbbing and my heart sickest of all. I stumbled around the house aimlessly that day, unable to focus, almost unable to face myself in a mirror; the rhythms of my *kata* would not come and the water of the pool felt clammy and alien on my skin, and my leg throbbed despite the pain relievers. I more than half-expected the police to arrive, arrest me for assault and attempted rape. I thought about calling Karita, even twice picked up the phone to do so, but realized I could never tell her what I'd done last night but neither could I bring myself to tell her only part of the story. Maybe Summer would tell her, and if that happened I knew I'd never see Karita again, but I wasn't going to – I simply couldn't – precipitate that falling out myself. Despite the distance that had developed between us, despite my not really knowing her as well as I once imagined I did, I now realized with a mixture of rue and resignation I didn't want to cut off whatever there was of that relationship. Not now. She wasn't objective about Summer anyway, I reasoned, so I'd just keep my ugly story to myself.

Stuck then with my thoughts, I relived the repellent events of last night over and over, dozens of times, maybe hundreds, only to feel myself sinking further into what I recognize now was some form of despair. Worst of all was the discovery that thinking about my mouth on Summer's tit, my momentary desire to fuck her, kept giving me an erection.

No, that wasn't the worst. That came a little later in the day. I finally succumbed to the building sense of sexual frustration by masturbating, and I did so while fantasizing about Summer, recalling the feel of her breast in my mouth last night and elaborately imagining that I had indeed fucked her, harshly and with fierce ecstatic abandon.

Raped her, I reminded myself immediately afterward, in a rush of shame and self-loathing that brought me to the edge of tears. No other word for it. Rape. And I have never in my life felt worse about myself than I did at that moment.

And I knew that I had to get out of LA soon, very soon now, and I spent the remainder of the afternoon and evening drinking Hayden's beer and thinking about what I would say to Hayden, and when I would say it. I had no idea when he'd return, and I couldn't very well leave the house unattended while he was in Atlanta with a dying, or perhaps dead now, lover. Yeah, that'd be the crowning glory of your stay here, I told myself. Skip out on your promise to your cousin while he's away at his lover's funeral.

Shit.

I didn't realize how deeply I'd slipped into the swamp of my own despair until the ringing of the phone a few days later caused me to jump to my feet and rush to answer like some teenager waiting for a date. I'm not sure who I was expecting or hoping for more, Karita or Hayden, but my dismay was a heavy cloud sinking down to smother me when I hear the chipper voice of the real estate agent, never sounding more loathsomely cheerful than now. And her news was worse: Claro had agreed to buy the house despite the engineer's analysis – what's another bucket of money to someone who's won the lottery? I thought bitchily – and she anticipated closing in about four to five weeks.

Three or four weeks ago this would have been unwelcome news, rushing me out of LA before I was ready, but now – hell, I could be on my way to Iowa in fifteen minutes and without regret, if also perhaps without a sense of closure.

Closure, I thought, smiling bitterly to myself as I wandered the house, letting the details of the rooms sink in one more time should I ever find use or need for them. How pre-postmodern can you get? How can that matter now? How even be possible?

When in answer to the chimes of the doorbell, annoying me as they never had before, I yanked the door open to find Karita, my sense of relief was a warm embrace wrapped inside an explosive release of unsuspected pressure – until I moved as though to embrace her. Seeing her hesitate slightly, almost lean back, I stopped, welcomed her in with a sweeping gesture to disguise the fact my chest suddenly felt tight and that sense of relief dissipated almost instantly in the face of this reminder of the distance between us. I noticed without comment that Karita was wearing – whether by accident or intention I never learned – the same outfit she had worn when she first came into the house to cancel that lunch date. It felt like a hundred years ago, another lifetime.

This time she'd brought a thermos of herbal tea – another trade secret, she said – and we sat again by the pool, she on the diving board, me on the edge with my feet in the water, its rippled surface reflecting a fractured pointillist blur under the fading earth-tone smears of sunset. And somehow I relaxed, whether because of the tea or some calming energy she brought with her, or both, and felt if not comfortable then less outside of myself, less alien to myself, than I had in a while. It never occurred to me at the time that Karita might have somehow sensed I needed whatever was in that tea.

So much did it relax me that I did not visibly start at the mention of Summer's name, and Karita's lament that Summer remained incommunicado eased me back toward a sense of composure, now that it seemed likely I wasn't going to be arrested, that fully caught me up and so approximated a feeling of calm – what the hell was in that tea? – that only the sound of Karita's voice some moments later reminded me she was still there.

"I'm worried most," she was saying, her voice soft, riding just above the trill and buzz of insect noise from the canyon below, "because she can't have much money left unless she found a job somewhere. She hadn't had a regular job since early last year – just some occasional work, enough to supplement what she was making from her art. She was starting to sell some pieces, too. Not enough to live on, by a long shot, but a good start."

"Hard to imagine," I said, speaking from anger and apparently having forgotten my admiration for the work of hers I'd seen in The Golden Oak.

Karita seemed not to hear me. "But now, she's not completed anything since . . . since she was attacked" – I flinched involuntarily – "so she's got to be out of money soon, if she isn't already." A long pause, awkward for me. "Remember that piece you saw the first day you came to the Oak, the one you tried to complement Summer on?" I nodded, remembering it clearly now. "That piece – she first called it "Labial Balance" but after the incident changed the name to "Spare D, Opening Gambit," whatever that means – that piece meant more to her than any other she's ever created. The complexity of it, the way it brought together disparate elements and materials into a kind of tangle that resolves in harmony, a confluence of turbulent energies and clashing forms that ultimately unifies, you could say, that resolve themselves, find an interplay, an interdependence that transcended the origins and nature of the individual elements to achieve – I really think 'peace' is the best word. Or something very near, anyway. I was saddened when she changed the name." She paused, smiled. "Sound like an art dealer, don't I?"

I laughed. "Yeah, or like those wall placards at museums. But you have an excuse; art history will do that to a person."

She nodded. "Do you remember that piece?" she asked, looking at me directly for the first time in what seemed like hours.

"Yeah, and as much as I hate to admit it, I like it."

"You know, when she finished it she was reluctant to talk about putting it in the Oak, or any other gallery. Then, after the rape, she said she'd never sell it; I think it had something to do with the fact it was the last piece she created before the attack, the last work she created when she had some measure of peace, of balance within herself. The fact she put it on sale – just a couple of days before you first saw it, in fact – testifies to her sense of desperation, I think. Maybe her anger, too, at my changing the nature of our relationship." She paused, looked into the distance for a moment, then turned to look at me again. "And you know what? It sold, just last week. Over fifteen hundred net for her, and now I can't even find her to give her the money when she needs it most."

"Think she'd even take it? Given everything that's going on and all the associations that piece must have for her, maybe it's best you can't find her right now."

"Perhaps," she said slowly. "But I wish I could. I'm sure she needs the money. And a friend."

I said nothing, drained the last of my tea, then stood, thinking for a foolish moment that I might persuade her to come inside with me. Then wondered, even in the mild mood that the tea had given me, if that was what I really wanted, or what I could handle right now. I sat back down on the diving board, not really disappointed, I was surprised to discover. The distance between us lingered on the margin of consciousness now like a pathetic but troubling ghost and I felt a dim but palpable sense of relief when Karita left a short while later. Apparently I'd become resigned, or maybe numb, to the fact everything had pretty much crumbled around me.

I'd spent a few of the dollars my parents had sent me the other day at a used bookstore in the village, among my finds a slim volume of poetry my thesis director used to rave about, John Durbin's *Melatonin Dreams*. I'd just begun the first piece when the insistent tones of the doorbell chimed hollowly in the house followed immediately by a rapid knocking. Before I'd reached the door the knocking was repeated, this time with more than a hint of the frantic lurking in its tempo.

A glance through the peephole and I froze: Karita, but her face so taut and pale I barely recognized her. An alarming rush of anxious energy hit me and I fumbled clumsily with the deadbolt, flinging open the door and blurting "What?" as she half-lunged, half-fell on me, her arms draped around my neck.

"What?" I repeated, frightened now at seeing a behavior I would never have expected from someone as self-possessed as she had always been. Her body pulsed with a couple of repressed sobs before she made an effort, palpably physical in its intensity, to collect herself. Not until she stepped back and wiped the tears from her face did I notice she was holding a small box of cheap cardboard.

"Summer. . ." she said, her voice tremulous as she sought for control.

Instantly I felt a familiar anger course through me, just behind the shock of hearing that loathsome name yet again. "What?" I said again. "She hurt you? What the hell's she done now? I – "

Karita shook her head and held the box toward me. "She – oh, Goddess, I can't believe she did this."

With a very bad feeling in my gut I lifted the lid off the battered box, noticing as I did so the mailing label, the shaky scrawl of Karita's name and address in thick red letters. There was no return address.

I noticed first the thin scrap of cotton lining the bottom, daubed all over with what was unmistakably dried blood, dark now and crusted. On the cotton lay what even in its dried and wrinkled condition was recognizable as a human ear, the lobe still adorned with an earring, a golden ankh half-obscured by clots of dried blood. I suddenly felt cold and could feel acid splash in my stomach and I wanted very much to sit down.

"What the fuck is going on?" I said to Karita, this time my voice a strained whisper as with shaking hand I struggled to replace the box lid. "Is this some sick fucking joke? It's not even original." As though that somehow mattered.

She shook her head, again brushing away tears. "It's Summer's. That earring – I gave her those. Before I knew she hated the ankh; she never wore them." I offered her the box, not wanting it or knowing what else to do, but Karita seemed not to see it. "She put that on just so she could send it to me like this." I walked toward the kitchen, eager to get the box out of my hand, and Karita followed. "I can't believe it," she said again as if still struggling to convince herself, "and I can't believe I misread her anger. It's my fault, it's all my fault."

"No, come on," I said, finally hugging her. "She's responsible for her actions, as you kept telling me the other day. She's an adult, and if she's going to do some wacked-out Van Gogh trip you can't blame yourself." I shook my head. "I just don't understand what she was trying to prove, to do. Hurt you? I can sort of understand why she's after me, but this – shit, this is brutally weird." I paused. "Maybe she's trying to send a signal, some token of the pain she feels and she wants to make sure you know. A *cri de coeur* sort of thing."

Karita stepped back and through reddened eyes gave me cold stare that brought me up short. "Does anything ever happen to you that doesn't call for some kind of allusion? By the Goddess you are such a fucking English major sometimes."

"Sorry," I said sharply, feeling genuinely wounded because I thought my response was perfectly legitimate. I'd never seen Karita lose her composure before and her angry response took me by surprise. She turned away from me, walked quickly into the family room. I followed, standing behind her as she stared out toward the pool and the dusky canyon beyond.

"Do you remember," Karita asked hesitantly, and only after a long pause, "the day you met Summer, when I was first telling you about her?"

I nodded, remembering that conversation through a mist of memory so dense it should have accumulated only after years, not weeks.

"I asked you if you'd heard of that group, the Lesbian Avengers, how Summer made them look like the Young Republicans or something?"

"Yeah. You were right."

Karita sighed, clearly willing herself to go on. "More than you know," she said quietly. "And maybe I should have told you sooner, I don't know; I didn't think it made any difference. Guess I was wrong."

"Told me what?"

"Summer helped start the local chapter of the Lesbian Avengers, but after just a short while they asked her to leave. They're nonviolent, you know, and Summer, well, she became . . . unhappy with some of their policies. They said she was too disruptive at their protests, was risking their message and their action. So they asked her to stay away."

"And she did?"

Karita nodded. "Because she found something else. I thought it was a passing thing, since I'd talked to her about it a lot and well before you arrived she'd seemed to give up all contact with them, but now, this" – she looked with a frail shudder at the box on the table, grew visibly paler – "I wonder if she's gotten involved with them again, or at least is willing to return to their methods, to their....." She shook her head, brushing away tears.

"Their what? Whose methods? What are you talking about?"

"Circe's Daughters."

I shook my head. "Never heard of them."

"No reason you should have; I think there are maybe half a dozen of them at most, and only here in LA as far as I know. It's not like a legit group; they're beyond fringe. They're dangerous people, or at least act that way."

"Sounds like Summer's in the right place then. What, are they like psycho lesbians with knives?"

She looked at me, hopelessness welling in her eyes behind the tears. "That's just about exactly what they are, or at least imagine themselves to be. I think it's mostly posturing, really, but...." She shook her head. "Gender terrorists, they call themselves. They claim they're acting in defense of lesbians and other oppressed women, that their violence is a legitimate response to the physical and emotional violence perpetrated on women every day – you know the sort of rhetoric. When Summer was hanging out with them she talked a lot about their plans to castrate rapists and things like that, but it was just talk. I never heard that they actually did anything."

I almost laughed despite myself. "Sounds pretty sophomoric to me. Why do you think she's back with these people? 'Cause she cut off her ear?"

"I don't know she's with them again, like I said, or even if they're still any sort of group, but the fact she would do something so horrible to herself tells me she's very far out of herself at the moment, and the fact she associated with them before shows she's susceptible to the seductions of violence." She shook her head fiercely, and I could see the glint of tears again. "This is worse than I thought."

I didn't know what to say, and finally, in what is apparently my characteristically clumsy way, tried to fill the strained silence with yet another misguided attempt at diversion. "Circe's Daughters, huh? Guess I'm not the only one fond of allusion. From *The Odyssey*, where the men get turned into pigs by the goddess Circe and Odysseus uses some herb to evade her spell and overcomes her by threatening her with his sword and having sex with her, which gets all his men turned back into humans." I nodded. "A sexually-fraught episode – I can see why they use the name."

Karita looked at me as though I was indeed a foolish child being particularly annoying, and I felt something between stupid and angry.

"So do we call the police?" I asked, eager to get away from that look. "I know you didn't want to before, but – " and I broke off as I suddenly realized how complicated, how deeply complicated, things would get if Summer were found. She'd talk about the other night, make me out to be a rapist. And no matter what I felt inside that night, I wasn't a rapist, I wouldn't be. I didn't rape her, after all. But, shit, my mouth on her breast – that's sexual assault. Shit. I didn't know what to say, what to think.

"Absolutely," said Karita. "You're right, I didn't want to before, though I think I should have, and I can't make that mistake again. Summer's in serious trouble. She needs help. She must have gone to a hospital, maybe they can track her that way." The tension in her face, so uncharacteristic, was painfully evident as she struggled to pull her thoughts together. "I'll call them, now, but from my house. Could you wrap that" – she glanced quickly in the direction of the cardboard box nearby on a counter – "in a towel? I'll need to take it but can't bear to touch it."

"I'll take it. I'll come with you," I offered half-heartedly. "I'm involved once you start explaining to the cops why Summer did this, so what the hell."

"Thank you," Karita said softly with a brief touch to my shoulder.

We spent nearly two hours with the police once they finally arrived, with Poe's "The Tell-Tale Heart" running through my mind the entire time. But no terrible secrets were divulged, no wrenching confessions extracted though Karita's revelation that she and Summer had been lovers certainly caught the officer's attention. But they stayed fully professional to my great relief. Their caution about remaining available for further questioning was disconcerting though hardly unexpected.  Their departure came none too soon.


    More than a week later Hayden finally returned, late, from Atlanta and Joshua's funeral, a ghost of himself in many ways.  I'd wager he was down to 1% body fat and looked as though he hadn't slept in days.   He seemed quietly relieved when I brought him up to speed on the sale of the house but said little, and was in bed less than an hour after getting home.

    From somewhere deep in REM sleep I must have heard the sepulchral chimes of the doorbell, sonorous and thick in the night air, for the consuming dream I was having – not a shred of which I remember except for this last detail – had something to do with a Gothic cathedral, a dusty shattered mass of dank grey stone looming above me with an impression of immanent collapse yet with its bells impossibly chiming with a weighty solemnity that seemed to shake the ground.  I was slow to awaken; as the chimes rang a second time I was still groggy, still not awake enough to realize it was our doorbell reverberating through the echoing darkness of the house.  Something, though, some thin and unfamiliar yet readily recognizable voice of urgency was telling me to wake up, to move, but I struggled to do so, stretching hard and rubbing my eyes.  Only when I heard Hayden muttering as he shuffled groggily down the hall could I finally force myself to get up, to see what was happening, and I struggled to a sitting position at the side of the waterbed which sloshed noisily beneath me. I was reflexively looking about for a t-shirt – I was, as usual, wearing only running shorts – when I heard the deadbolt click back and the door open, and with a wire-taut sense of abrupt unease that cut through the clinging remnants of sleep I guessed that Hayden, probably more than half-asleep himself, had made no effort to first find out who was at the door.  I lurched to my feet, suddenly anxious, alert, aware somehow that something was very out of joint.  As close as I've ever come to foreboding.

    And then thunder exploded in my head.

    The blast echoed along the gallery and was followed instantly by a dull thud; I jumped, my heart slamming so hard in my chest I thought I might choke.  With a shout of "What the fuck!" and a panicked rushing flood of adrenalin unlike anything I'd ever felt I rushed to the door of my room and out into the gallery where in a bent rectangle of yellowish streetlight spilling through the open door I saw Hayden lying on the floor, slumped against the wall.  In one terrifying, knee-weakening instant I realized the sound I'd heard was a gunshot and that the dark spreading stain on Hayden's white t-shirt was blood.

Reflexively and despite a numbing sense of disbelief I moved toward my cousin but was brought up short by an outraged screech of "Shit!" as a shadow in the doorway moved and a figure stepped into the hallway: Summer.  For an instant I froze in absolute confusion, not knowing whether to flee, help Hayden, or launch myself at her.  She looked panicked, wide-eyed, both hands clenched around a small pistol and a large white pad taped to the side of her head where her left ear had once been.  My thoughts were confused – not even thoughts, really; I was panicked and frightened and angry and reacting like I don't know what.  I thought of the phone and 911 and half turned to the kitchen when Summer finally saw me in the shadows and screamed "It's you I want dead, you fucking prick."  I know now of course that I should have fled, but hearing her strangled-chicken screech I felt an anger well up in me like nothing I had ever known and I was out of myself, screaming something incoherent as I lunged for her, thinking only of strangling her, shooting her, killing her any way I could.  But she was nearly thirty feet away and I'd only taken a couple of steps when she raised the gun and with a look in her eye that will burn in my mind until I go to my grave she fired again.  There was a small flash and another deafening explosion and I felt a monstrously hard tug at my right shoulder, and I thought, weirdly, that someone was behind me, trying to restrain me.  But a fire came alive in my shoulder and I realized I'd been shot and then a wave of pain so surprising in its intensity I staggered and fell to my knees, clasping my left hand to my shoulder and instantly feeling the warmth of blood flowing through my fingers.  I knew I had to do something, keep moving or I was going to be killed, and somehow I was up and rushing at Summer again.  But the recoil from the first shot had caused her to move back a few steps and the extra distance gave her time to fire again.  I flinched in preparation for the pain but her aim was off.  She stepped quickly backward and fired again.  This time I had enough of my wits about me to dive, just before she fired, into the wide archway of the dining room.  But even though I had possession enough not to try a shoulder roll the impact of landing flat even on carpet caused another wave of pain to course through me, and it was all I could do to roll over, looking for a place to hide or a way to get out of the house.

Just as I looked up she appeared in the archway, shaking her left hand furiously, the barrel of the gun clutched awkwardly in her right. She clumsily transferred the gun to her left hand so she could fire again, but though I willed myself to move, to lunge at her or run or something, with one hand pressed to my bleeding, fiery shoulder I was unbalanced and I faltered as I tried to get up. And she smiled there in the half darkness, a smile as sickening as the look in her eyes. She screeched "you fucking prick" and raised the gun again but I somehow found the energy to duck and roll to the side. Again the wave of pain in my shoulder as the gun exploded harmlessly behind me. But I had trouble getting my legs under me; the roll had been too much for my shoulder and the pain made it hard for me to leverage myself up using my right arm. I wanted to scramble into the solarium but she had already turned the gun on me again. And I felt myself tremble as I realized I was about to die.

She took a step toward me, still screeching invective and, I swear, gloating, and I stopped scrambling when I suddenly realized through the panic I might have an opportunity to stop her if she moved close enough before firing. She was saying something about shooting my prick off as she stepped toward me and I knew she might kill me if she fired but just another step or two and I could bring her down with a leg sweep and –

"SUMMER!"

She turned in the direction of the shout, lowering the gun slightly, and as the shadow in the doorway stepped forward and I saw Karita backlit by the streetlamp, her hair wild and one hand out in a gesture of restraint or pleading. I drew my energy to myself and lurched to my feet. Summer whirled to look at me, raising the gun, and again Karita shouted and pleaded and said all kinds of things, her voice a thread of hope for me and a confusion for Summer, who looked from me to Karita and back again, over and over until she screeched "NO! You bitch you abandoned me and it's your fucking prick fault" as she whirled to face me and pulled the trigger. And I think I would have died because when the trigger clicked the barrel was pointed at my heart. But nothing happened. I took one large quick step across the distance between us and whipped out a snap kick that caught Summer square in the chest and knocked her hard against the wall of the dining room. She slumped to the floor, apparently dazed, the gun loose in her left hand. I rushed to her, thinking only to get the gun out of her reach, but as I knelt down her eyes snapped open and she moved with a whip-like speed; even as the gun slammed into my bleeding shoulder I knew I'd been decoyed. The surge of pain stunned me for a moment and I fell sideways; in that instant Karita rushed in, edging between me and Summer and pleading for Summer to give her the gun. Summer tried to rise and Karita put her hands on her shoulders, trying to keep her on the floor, and having lurched unsteadily to my knees I was about to grab for the gun again when with an incoherent shout Summer pushed Karita hard, directly into me, and we both went down. I scrambled away from Karita and got to my knees just in time to see Summer point the gun at me and again pull the trigger. Again nothing. Screaming like a madwoman now Summer pounded the gun with the heel of her right hand, futilely clicking the trigger. She began cursing incoherently, slamming the gun over and over and even in the half-light gloom I could see tears streaking her face. I paused for a moment, baffled by the surreal weirdness of the scene but recovering quickly was about to grab for the gun when she suddenly shifted it, looking down the barrel as though she could see what was wrong, continuing to pound the gun and swearing even as her left hand remained clasped firmly around it.

And then it went off.

Maybe a bullet was stuck in the clip somehow; I don't know. I've never cared or known anything about guns, and have even less interest in them now. I later overheard one of the cops – the same one who took my statement when Summer trashed my clothes – say something about "a cheap-shit Chinese peashooter." Whatever happened, the bullet took a part of Summer's left cheek off on its way through the back of her skull. The explosion startled both me and Karita into immobility and for a very long moment we stared dumbly at Summer. Then Karita moved toward Summer, slumped against the blood-spattered wall and her face a bloody mass of tissue and tooth and bone that turned my stomach even in the half-darkness. Karita held together just long enough to utter some kind of invocation or spell, speaking so softly I couldn't make out the words and touching Summer gently on the crown of her head. Then Karita lost control, tears turning to sobs that wracked her entire body. I put my good arm around her shoulder but she never seemed to notice I was there, and after a moment I stood, shakily, and went to where Hayden lay in the gallery. The pool of blood around him was huge, larger than I could ever have anticipated – do we have that much blood in our bodies? I wondered disinterestedly – but I could see even as I knelt gingerly beside him that he wasn't breathing, and seeing the blood I remembered a distraught Hayden cutting himself on a beer bottle cap, warning me about the blood, his HIV, and I remembered too his comment about "death lessons," and that to me seemed more important now than any concern about my safety. Yet still I stood up without having touched him and walked slowly to the kitchen and dialed 911. But the police were already on their way, arriving in a matter of minutes. Then lights came on and an ambulance arrived and there were questions and bandages and more questions and a ride to the hospital and finally, thankfully, a dreamless sleep.

I couldn't stand being back in that house, its empty spaces now feeling as though they could swallow me, subsume me into some vast nebulous fog of nothingness in an easy, languid, and yet somehow thoroughly horrible way. But I had nowhere else to go, and while I avoided the house as best I could I still found myself there more than I wished, and uncomfortable, unsettled, every restless moment I was there. Everything had, with a haste that was both surprising and somehow unseemly, been expertly cleaned and patched – within a week there was absolutely no indication that anything untoward had ever happened there, which itself I found disturbing and almost uncanny – but it was a sick and troubled place for me now and I didn't even like to touch the furniture, the walls, anything. Yet I stayed, and I think, now, that I did so as a means of punishing myself, forcing myself to suffer for my part in Hayden's death. I've relived the events of this accursed season a thousand times and have yet to figure out what I should or could have done differently, given what I knew at any given moment, given who I was at the time. Despite that I blame myself, to this day, for what happened, and staying in that cursed house for the days remaining seemed an apt gesture of thoroughly merited self-flagellation.

Hayden's funeral is so difficult for me to think about I have trouble recalling it in much detail. While there, I felt sure every glance in my direction was a dart of hatred, everyone thinking "He's the one, he's why Hayden is dead." And they're right; Hayden would be alive if it weren't for me. I could barely speak to his parents, and felt the worse for that. My parents came down for the funeral too, of course, and tried to persuade me to return to their house until it was time for me to leave for Iowa, but I couldn't accept their offer. That would have felt like running away, like losing ground in some vague way I couldn't quite understand.

The night of Hayden's funeral, for the first time since his death, I dreamt. But it was not of Hayden. It was Karita, just her face, motionless and pained, looking at me from across some vast distance, across a remote landscape I'd never so much as glimpsed before. And she was a complete stranger whose gaze I could not bear, and yet I could not look away.

I knew, of course, that our relationship, our lives, everything had changed. Changed not by any act of will or recognized desire; just changed, altered in some obscure and ineffable way by these acts over which we seemed to have no control, in which we had what felt, probably incorrectly, like no shaping participation whatsoever.

Yes, I know she'd disagree with that. She'd say our very presence here, my coming to LA, our meeting, our mutual inhabiting of the same space and all the emanations from that, created the circumstances – no, these things *were* the circumstances – that made possible the bizarre events of the past weeks. Especially Summer's rage, Summer's hatred of me that still leaves me feeling strangely violated, targeted in the crosshairs of some fast-moving malevolent glacier's gunsights, if that's not too tangled a metaphor. Or even if it is.

Fuck it. I'm too tired to care, too empty to have anything left to invest, emotionally or psychologically or in any other which way, in pretty much anything. Summer, Hayden, Karita, Kyoko – even the ones still alive feel like ghosts, vague outlines of a receding tragedy which leaves in the end only cold traces, half-remembered, half-felt, on those places in my heart where such things register. I think about my next step, my move to Iowa for doctoral studies, and it feels as remote and as irrelevant as if it were happening to someone else.

Which maybe it is.


A couple of weeks later, after too many hours spent talking to attorneys and detectives and family and after formally vowing I'd return for any further depositions or testimony if need be, and – a strangely pleasant surprise – after Claro stopped by briefly one evening to offer condolences (and a joint, which I accepted but never smoked) and tell me he'd retracted his offer on the house, earnest money be damned, I took my leave of Karita.

In truth it would be more accurate to say she took her leave of me: the doorbell rang at midnight, and I awoke, momentarily panicked and with my heart pounding, from a dreamless sleep to stumble to the door. She looked tired, changed somehow, but maybe that was me, or just the late hour. I found it hard to look at her. She stood silently on the porch until I gestured for her to come in. Without a word she stepped past me and walked slowly down the gallery, heading not toward the main part of the house but toward the wing containing the empty bedrooms. I followed her, not much caring what she was going to do, down the darkened hallway, past the haunted image of the faux El Greco St. Francis, past the black hollows of the bedroom doors and into the empty master suite. In the center of the room she stood to face me then without a word dropped, with what I always thought of as her elegant awkwardness, to a cross-legged position on the floor. I sat facing her, still silent; to my left the French doors led to the sitting room and beyond that the small patch of lawn and the hot tub, none of it visible on this moonless night.

I felt more than saw Karita extend her hands to me, and with no act of volition I can remember I reached forward and took her hands, strangely warm, in my own. Her fingers pressed firmly into the backs of my hands; I could feel with an almost hallucinatory clarity every piece of jewelry on her fingers, felt as much as heard her soft breathing in the expectant stillness of the room.

After a long moment she spoke, her voice a whisper that slipped like gentle imagined fire through the space between us. "The web of the world parts for us here," she said slowly, "and our paths lead to the people we're becoming. I treasure what we've had, very much, and treasure you. But now our paths diverge. In sadness and in hope." I could see her pause, see her wan smile, somehow, in the darkness. "So mote it be," she said very softly, just above a whisper. A fragment variant of the Wiccan Rede, I knew. So must it be indeed. I just nodded.

"Poor northern child. I hope you find your way to the edge of the cliff, and the will to step off." She paused, a catch in her voice.

"Think of me sometimes when you see the moon rise above the Iowa corn."

I nodded again, but with so little sense of conviction I hoped she couldn't see me. My heart, like the Mariner's, felt as dry as dust. I wished I could feel something, anything.

And that was all.


The next morning I loaded the last of my possessions in the back of my truck and drove as quickly as I could to the I-10, trying with great success to think not at all about the places that passed by outside my windows, the streets I had driven, the endlessly repeated stores and strip malls, the infinite glinting river of vehicles. None of it touched me now, and when I found myself accelerating up the onramp a flash of surprise coursed pleasantly through me: I was out of here; I was on the freeway leaving this damned insanitarium forever behind. Don't think, I told myself; keep your eyes on the road and get out. Focus on what lies ahead, what matters for me, to me, or at least what is supposed to matter, what once did and may perhaps again. Who knows? Eyes ahead.

But as I sped east out of LA on that smoggy morning I could not help but turn my eyes to the north for one parting glimpse of the San Gabriel mountains. And saw, for the last time, thunderheads over Baldy.

www.ingramcontent.com/pod-product-compliance
Lightning Source LLC
Chambersburg PA
CBHW071251130626
46556CB00003B/1257